Falls the Shadow

Falls the Shadow

Regina Ross

DELACORTE PRESS / NEW YORK

Library of Congress Cataloging in Publication Data

Ross, Regina.
    Falls the shadow.

    I. Title.
PZ4·R8253Fal   [PS3568·0844]   813'·5'4
                                        73–13966

0-440-02642-3

For

ELLIS AMBURN,
*kindest and most
encouraging of mentors*

Author's Note

I GRATEFULLY acknowledge my indebtedness to Mr. Nicolas Adam, whose article "Who Holds the Crown?" (*Observer Colour Magazine*, May 11, 1972) inspired the present story. Colonel Arpad Taldy, Ferenc Szalasi, Stephen, first Christian king of Hungary, Pope Pius XII, Pope Paul VI, Cardinal Mindszenty, American Ambassador Selden Chapin, Archbishop Rohrach, Cardinal Innitzer, Cardinal von Faulhaber, Cardinal Spellman, Lieutenant Commander Thomas Howe and, of course, the Holy Crown of Saint Stephen did or do exist. The parts these personages played in the history of the crown are matters of historical fact. Any similarity or apparent connection between the other characters in this story and actual persons, living or dead, is purely coincidental.

Prologue

NICOLA BEAUFORT sat in the lotus position on the rim of the indoor pool at Hurst Grange Beauty Farm. She was midway through her hour's yoga exercises. That was Dr. Lew's idea and not a regular Hurst Grange practice. But, then, hers was not a regular Hurst Grange problem.

A fat woman in a pink terrycloth robe waddled carefully over the tiles, giving the girl an inquisitive look. She had an impression of a tall, marble-white figure topped by a mass of coppery hair above a young, tragic face. For a moment she felt the quick, automatic stab of envy for youth, but, when she saw the empty eyes, the envy faded.

She went hopefully toward the Salad Bowl which undoubtedly held the elixir of youth, Hurst Grange-style, in the shape of a glass of carrot juice, *sans* salt, *sans* everything. There would be a pink glow in the pretty, informal dining room which would make the three prunes look plumper and juicier and, mysteriously, make the women look prettier and thinner. In the rosy, cozy atmosphere, she could forget the sad girl in the mock-jungle garden room.

Everything about the Beauty Farm was planned to cushion the guests against reality, to make them believe that within its luxurious walls lay the answers to all their problems. They came hopefully and trustfully, armed with their checkbooks—those who were drowning in their own martinis, those who were encased in their own fat, those bowed down with their years, withered by time, deseeded by nature, robbed somehow, somewhere, by someone, of their looks, their figures, their potency, their health. The pink robes, coral nylon uniforms of the staff, magnolia walls of the rooms, made rose-colored glasses superfluous. They came willingly to lay their money at the feet of the proprietor, the dispenser of dreams.

All except Nicola Beaufort.

She had been brought there during a stormy, windswept night when the guests were asleep and did not hear the keening, mad sound of a voice that could have been the wind, shouting in fury.

That had been twenty-four days ago. Nobody had seen her until this morning, when she had stalked through the languid warmth of the garden room like a displaced princess.

Something about her eyes and the proud walk was intimidating, so nobody spoke to her as she moved purposefully along the corridors and down the wide oak stairway to the hall. She turned sharply to her left to reach the garden room at the end of the short passage. In spite of the vagueness in the eyes, she walked as if she knew the way.

"I heard," one woman whispered to her companion, "that she swims during the *night*, when nobody is around! Do you think she's *neurotic?*"

Two puzzled pairs of eyes followed the girl's progress.

They were drinking their mid-morning glass of lemon juice when a car arrived at the entrance. The girl, beautifully dressed in a violet linen suit, came out from the Grange, stood for a moment with her hand on the car handle, then got quickly into the car.

"I thought she was going to change her mind, didn't you?" said one of the slimmers.

The other looked uneasy. "I thought she looked afraid." She was a compassionate woman. Her eyes followed the car anxiously until it was lost among the trees.

Falls the Shadow

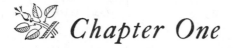 *Chapter One*

THE hissing of the shower water almost obliterated the ringing of the telephone. He paused in the act of hanging the rope-threaded oval of soap on the hook, switched off the jets of water and listened. The ringing went on and on.

He frowned. It was probably the girl who had presented him with the leather-edged cinnamon towel which he fastened round his waist as he stepped out of the shower stall. He wondered briefly what kind of madness had possessed him when he had allowed her to tart up his bathroom with the monk's-hooded matching bathrobe and the thick, fluffy brown towels. Dammit! he could hardly remember her name. He was used to taking, but not exactly like that. He felt oddly on the defensive.

As always, he lifted the receiver and waited, saying nothing.

"Forsyth? Neville speaking. Hope I didn't get you out of bed. I'm at home."

He could picture Henry Neville two floors below, gazing vaguely out over St. James's Park while that devious mind wove the intricate patterns that spelled life, death or suffering for some individual.

Charles Forsyth's lips tightened in involuntary distaste. He respected Henry Neville, acknowledged the value of his work and even its necessity, but there was a barely concealed mutual dislike. While both could kill and maim without remorse, Forsyth could be upset by the death of a colleague. Neville never was. The hard core of steel in the older man excited in Forsyth both admiration and contempt. It worried him when Brett, Neville's secretary and man Friday, told him that he was getting more and more like the boss each year. It was then that he decided to get out.

He rested a hip on the edge of the table and reached for a cigarette, taking a small, sour pleasure in keeping Neville waiting. "Just getting dressed," he said pleasantly. "Don't tell me you need to borrow a cup of sugar." He grinned at a grimy London pigeon strutting on the windowsill.

"*Au contraire.* I hoped you'd join me for breakfast. Shall we say half an hour?" The phone went down with a sharp click.

An order, bigod! Forsyth winked at the pigeon. As good a time as any, he decided, for telling the old boy to go sell his papers somewhere else.

He took particular pains to choose the clothes that he knew annoyed Neville, who always looked like a rain-soaked Sussex farmer and hated anything that smacked of the dandy.

From the mirror his face looked back at him with its habitual expression of good-humored disdain. The wintry blue eyes were bright with speculation and the big lean frame with the surprisingly powerful legs was tilted so that the thin sunlight slanted along the rocky outline of the jaw. He was thirty, but looked almost a decade older. Already the thick, dark hair was streaked with gray, and experience had drawn deep furrows down each cheek from nose to chin. It was a look that had served him well.

He whistled expertly, moving, without being conscious of the change, from the latest hit tune to the sleepy bird songs heard at dawn on his father's estate.

His mind explored the possible reasons, not for the summons, but for the totally unexpected invitation to Neville's flat. Until now, that had been sacrosanct. He knew that the layout was a carbon copy of his own, but no more than that. Characteristically, he had no curiosity about Neville's private life, though he had no doubts that the head of the Department had already made a thorough examination of his flat. That he accepted without rancor, even with relish for the puritanical disapproval that the older man must have felt on occasions.

In spite of himself, as he waited for the opening of Neville's door, he had the slight feeling of euphoria that always preceded the start of an operation. He had to remind himself that there would be no new assignment.

He had not expected to see Brett there. He was a thin, stooped man with a weary, gray face that looked as if it had never been young. Forsyth had seen him only in the Eton Avenue house at Swiss Cottage, moving like a shadow between Neville's desk and the wall of filing cabinets. He could not recall ever having seen a flicker of expression on his face.

"Good morning, Mr. Forsyth. Mr. Neville would like you to join him in the kitchen." The flat accents made that sound a normal procedure.

The big sunny room beyond the narrow hall was exactly what he had expected and the furnishings were near enough to his own to bring a wry twist to his mouth. It was certainly time to get out. A quick glance took in the deep, leather club chairs, the Russell Flint prints, the book-lined wall, the workmanlike leather-topped desk. In the moment it took to cross to the open door of the kitchen, Forsyth had time to assess the peace in the atmosphere. He knew then with absolute certainty that the flat had never had a going over. His respect for Neville increased.

He paused in the doorway and sniffed appreciatively. Neville was flicking hot fat over eggs in a pan. A mound of curling bacon stood ready on the top of the oven. On the blue counter top a coffeepot gurgled throatily. Neville's back exuded a vast contentment.

"Make the toast," he commanded, with a jerk of his head toward the breakfast nook where the table was already set for two. It would simply not have occurred to him to repeat his "good morning" greeting.

Since Forsyth also hated to waste words, he merely said, "How many?"

"Three slices for me."

They ate silently, completely at ease with each other.

When Forsyth quirked an eyebrow in the direction of the sitting room, Neville said testily, "Brett never eats breakfast. He has an ulcer. The damn fool won't accept that the best thing is to feed it regularly." He shrugged philosophically. "He took a bad beating there once . . . the Societé des Mains Rouges. Naturally, he hates the bastards. Useful." The hooded eyes flew upward.

Forsyth saw the questioning malice in the bright blue gaze. He stiffened. "Bonneaud's lot? I didn't know that." He stretched his legs comfortably under the table. There was the roar of a vacuum cleaner from the adjoining room. "When you're making out your Christmas list, just remember that I'd like Bonneaud's guts for garters. No Rolls Royce . . . no gold cigarette case . . ." he said dreamily, "just that bastard's guts separated from his body. Yes, indeedy . . . Mama, buy me that.".

"You're in the wrong department, sonny. This is self-service. You know . . . where you help yourself."

"Not this time." Forsyth shook his head slowly. "Not any more. I've practically lived in Hardy's for the past week. There's a stretch of river with my name on it— Charles Isaak Walton Forsyth."

"The fish can wait. This job won't." He put his fork down carefully. "I know you want out. The Prague assignment was tough, but that was three months ago. If it's any consolation, Bonneaud took a bigger hiding than you did, but he's back on the job now."

The younger man smiled. "No dice. So Bonneaud is a great big, strong boy and I'm a crybaby?" He shook his head slowly. "The fish won't care. Let someone else make the Frenchman cry uncle. I've already written out my resignation. I have it upstairs."

"I know." His voice was indifferent. "I read it last night."

Forsyth laughed.

Neville heaped marmalade on a piece of toast and eyed it stolidly. He put it down untasted. "I came into the Service when I was twenty-five," he said quietly. "They took us in younger then. I've been in it for almost forty years and, in two respects at least, I imagine I'm unique. In the first place, I've survived. Sometimes I feel like the last dinosaur on earth. It's a lonely feeling."

" 'A thousand, thousand slimy things lived on and so did I,' " Forsyth quoted flippantly. Neville wasn't going to get him this way.

That drew a bleak smile. "Don't worry. I have no intention of appealing to your pity. No. It will be much simpler." He had to raise his voice to be heard above the whine of the cleaner. "In all those years, I gave orders. Never once did I ask a man for a favor. I'm asking one now, Charles. Take this assignment." The crispness and precision of the military man was in the clipped accent and in the neat sweeping away of the plates between them, as if he had an urgent need for clarity and simplicity.

Somehow Forsyth sensed that it was important that his decision should come quickly, that something valuable between them would be lost if he hesitated.

"When do I start?" he asked evenly.

Neville looked at him.

Almost simultaneously, they got to their feet and moved out of the sunny peace of the kitchen.

Brett was winding up the cord of the vacuum cleaner. He took the machine into the kitchen and shortly returned carrying a tray with a pot of coffee and three cups. He scarcely glanced at Forsyth as he handed him the coffee, but the younger man felt intuitively that Brett had known all along exactly what would happen. He felt no resentment.

Neville took his chair behind the desk, which was set diagonally so that he could see both the door and the windows. The two men settled themselves in the leather chairs on the other side.

Brett's face looked grayer than ever. With a sigh, Forsyth got to his feet, lifted Brett's cup and went back into the kitchen. When he put the glass of milk on the table at Brett's elbow, he thought he saw a flicker of warmth in the man's faded eyes.

Neville ignored the incident. He spoke very fast in Rumanian, firing routine questions at Forsyth, obviously less in order to get information than to satisfy himself that Forsyth still had perfect command of the language. It was a favorite trick when briefing a man for an assignment and was usually the first indication to the operator as to where the job lay.

Forsyth thought nostalgically of the golden girls he had known in the discreet little house on the Kiseleff Chaussée in Bucharest. Maybe it wouldn't be too bad. He settled himself deeper into the chair. Momentarily, he saw his father's disappointed face and remembered with a kind of anguish the Hardy's catalogue open on his desk upstairs.

It was very cold in the cellar. Tony estimated that it was the morning of the third day. The men had brought two lamps which they had fastened with short lengths of rope to iron rings high up on opposite walls of the windowless room.

They had scarcely needed light for their task, which was one they had done often before. But the light was strong enough to let the Englishman see the pools of blood beneath each of his feet. They felt as if they had been sprayed by a blowtorch. The second beating was always the worst. It had been bad, but they had a long way to go with him. He had relieved his feelings with elaborate, meaningless curses.

Deliberately, he allowed his thoughts to become a little maudlin. The blood suggested the slogans heard in far-off days in Sunday school . . . washed in the Blood of the Lamb. He sang raucously:

> *"Wash me in the water*
> *That you washed your dirty daughter*
> *And I shall be whiter*
> *Than the whitewash on the wall."*

As the sound of the parody died away, he allowed his head to droop until the golden beard lay on his chest. It was, after all, only the third day. He was almost ashamed to use the trick, but it was time to faint. He held his breath and presently the roaring in his ears began. . . .

Neville glanced at his watch. "We have an hour," he said briskly.

"An *hour!*" Forsyth's head came forward belligerently. "What the devil do you mean?"

"You leave for Brussels. There you'll catch a Tarom BAC-111, Flight number RO 205 for Constanza. You should be in the Hotel Modern in Mamaia soon after midnight." He touched a bundle of papers on his desk lightly with his fingers. "Everything is here—passport, visa, air tickets, money, maps and a few new toys that Brett will tell you about. These glasses, for instance." His forefinger touched a spectacle case. A ghost of a smile flickered at the corners of his mouth. Forsyth followed his eyes to the valise standing near the door. "Brett packed your kit while we were eating. He selected your stuff yesterday."

Deliberately, Forsyth controlled his anger. *You should choose your neighbors more carefully,* he told himself savagely. At least, the Department's efficiency was reassuring. He schooled himself to speak without emotion. "When and how do I report?"

"You don't—not unless you get into serious trouble." Neville smiled frostily. "Come—you know better than that, Charles. You've never yelled for help yet. I see no reason why you should do so now. Don't drink too much *ţuica*; leave the women alone and get back here within a week." He paused. "Bring Tony Rothman with you."

"So that's the assignment?" For the first time, he felt the stirrings of doubt. He knew Rothman well, a big, likable chap whose mop of blond hair and beard gave him the look of a swashbuckling Viking. He packed a formidable punch, as Forsyth had found in bouts at the gym, but behind the engaging smile and the look of wide-eyed innocence was a razor-sharp intelligence. Brett had once remarked, "He could play tag all day in a cage of monkeys and not be It."

If he was in trouble, it was big trouble. Suddenly the sense of euphoria was back. He eyed Neville steadily, remembering the throwaway reference to Bonneaud. Neville was never casual. No doubt it was all in the notes which, as usual, he would read in the plane and then destroy.

"I have to know why you want Rothman brought out."

Brett got up and went into the kitchen, closing the door behind him. So it was personal.

The light from the window showed up the scragginess of Neville's neck and the way in which age had lapped the bony cheeks. For the first time, Forsyth noticed the liver spots on the folded hands.

Neville's voice had its usual dry precision. "My wife died

nine years ago. We had been married for twenty years. It was a happy marriage, though we had no children. Five years ago, I married her cousin—Amy Beaufort, who had a daughter, Nicola. Amy often jokes that I married her just to get Nicola. She is twenty-two now and a damned attractive girl. It was a shock when I discovered that somehow she had met Rothman. She fancies she's in love with him. It will break the girl's heart if anything happens to him." His voice hardened. He breathed deeply once, then said harshly, "Get him out, Charles."

"Why the panic?"

"Two days ago, a waiter in Mamaia, Jan Balanescu, passed the word that Rothman had been picked up. The descriptions fit two of Bonneaud's men. As you know, they play for keeps."

"Why was Rothman in Rumania?"

"Have you heard of the Holy Crown of Saint Stephen?"

He didn't bother to answer that. A few months previously, one of the Sunday magazines had printed a fairly detailed article on its history. He remembered the assertions made in the article, but it had been the speculations that had intrigued him.

"Surely we are not all *that* hard up for regalia? As I recollect," he said lazily, "it isn't even in good condition. Didn't some nursemaid sit on it and bend the cross at the top?"

Neville looked sour at the flippancy. "You'll get the details in the file. Brett can tell you more about it than I can. It was his show. That's when he had the run-in with Bonneaud."

As if on cue, the kitchen door opened and Brett returned to take his place quietly opposite Forsyth. He was wearing his overcoat and carried a bag which he placed carefully at his feet. When he saw Forsyth's eyes on the bag, he said, "I'm going with you as far as Brussels. I can brief you while you are waiting for your plane in Brussels. We'd like to get our hands on the crown. It would give us a terrific bargaining power, but we are almost equally anxious that those bloody-minded communists in the smr shouldn't get it. That wouldn't do at all. It looks as if Rothman has tracked it down." He glanced at his watch. "They seem to have had him now for almost two and a half days. You had better get him out soon. Shall we go?"

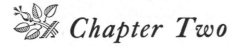 *Chapter Two*

IT was a sunny, blowing morning with scuds of white clouds in a swept sky. London sparkled in the clear air, so that Forsyth felt a pang of regret as he stepped from the car at Heathrow.

He left Brett looking hungrily at the array of whiskies in the Duty Free Shop while he went downstairs.

The girl cannoned into him as he emerged from the men's room. Automatically, he put his training into operation, bringing his arms round to protect his body, tensing his forearms to steel bands, then gave the quick forward jerk that hurled her to the ground. She lay in a sprawl of violet linen skirt and white underwear, her face concealed by a soft mass of coppery hair. He picked up her handbag and felt the gun at the bottom.

She recovered quickly. When the screen of hair had been brushed aside, tilted amber eyes looked up at him, the expression as disgusted as if she had stepped on a cockroach. Her mouth looked distraught but she controlled the trembling of her lips. He made no move to help her, but she came up like a cat, smoothing her skirt, pulling down her jacket, tossing back her hair as if she had merely taken a tumble on the tennis court. She put out a hand for the bag. The half-smile on her lips said that she knew how to be a good sport.

He was totally unprepared for the stinging blow that rocked his head sideways.

Behind her, a portly man in heavy tweeds laughed appreciatively.

She moved swiftly and elegantly into the crowd, a tall figure, slim hips swaying with angry provocativeness. Forsyth's eyes followed the splash of violet color, their expression grim as he touched the tender spot on his jaw.

He said nothing about the incident to Brett.

When they had been airborne for half an hour, he went to look for her, moving casually down the aisle with the air of a man who intended to stroll to Brussels. He found her toward the back of the plane, asleep in a window seat, her head lolling against the porthole and her face paper-white with exhaustion. The strong light had exaggerated the blue undertone of her lipstick, so that she looked vaguely ill.

He studied her impersonally, noting that the long lashes were her own and that her hair had the unmatchable fire of the autumn leaves in the woods of his home. No rings. Delicate, well-manicured hands. Fine bones. A face that was pretty now, but would be beautiful someday. Expensive brown calf shoes. The bag had felt as soft as glove leather. He reached forward and lifted it gently from between her feet. A Gucci label inside. No passport or papers. He did not recognize the gun. He slid it into the left-hand pocket of his jacket.

He took the empty seat beside her and waited.

The rattle of the drink cart wakened her. She stretched delicately, arching her body while her eyes remained shut. Her jacket slid open showing the soft leather belt around her waist with the attached pouch like a golfer's money belt.

"That was a mistake," he said rebukingly. Her eyes flew open. "Your belt is too slack. I could have slid it around easily and taken your papers. That is careless." She looked very young. About twenty, he estimated.

His hand went out casually, but her reflexes were good. She probably *had* played a lot of tennis. She chopped swiftly at his wrist with the side of her hand. It was like being struck by a steel plate. The pain shot up his arm to the elbow. The hand would be useless for at least ten minutes. *She could,* he reflected wryly, *have broken my wrist.*

He smiled stiffly. "I think I'll marry you," he said. "We would have no disciplinary problems with our children. But, if you keep this up, you'll have a very battered bridegroom."

He was surprised at the strength of his anger. At least Brett knew nothing about this hellcat. He could imagine Neville's amusement.

She was clutching her handbag, her eyes very wide and her face whiter than ever.

"Give me back the gun," she commanded. "If you don't, I'll create a scene—swear that you threatened me with it."

Silently he handed it over.

Still with those strange eyes fixed on him, she dropped it into her bag, snapped the clasp shut and stretched upward to press the bell for the stewardess. The red light blinked above them like an inflamed eye.

While they waited, she said with strained fury, "I want you to know something. You are the most detestable man I have ever met. You are arrogant and cruel and a boor. You have all the marks of a cheap hood. You have the manners of an ape and just about as much finesse. I'm warning you. Keep out of my way or you'll get hurt."

Forsyth looked at her impassively.

Above him, the stewardess said, "Can I bring you something?"

"Yes," he said evenly, "a glass of strychnine for the lady and a large whisky for me."

The stewardess smiled uncertainly, scenting a lovers'

quarrel. So he was not surprised when the pretty young girl got to her feet and said breathlessly, "I'd like to change my seat, please."

She noticed that the man did not move his legs to let his friend pass and that his mouth looked suddenly very cruel. *Not my type,* she thought uneasily, ushering the girl down the aisle, well away from him. She hesitated about going back and having a word with him, but decided against it. After all, in fifteen minutes they would be in Brussels. It was no use looking for trouble.

Forsyth lit a cigarette and flexed his fingers gingerly. His wrist would ache for a long time. Already the thin red line was darkening. He looked at it steadily and with a reluctant admiration. Her perfume, he decided suddenly, was Joy. He knew because he had presented that to the donor of the bathroom towels. He found the thought disturbing.

After a minute, he extinguished the cigarette and went back down the aisle toward his seat.

The blur of violet caught his eye. She was staring blankly at a copy of *Vogue.* He bent over her and whispered, "If you ever dare to try any of those tricks on me again, I promise you that I'll turn you up and spank you. Remember—I'm that boor with no manners, so don't risk it."

The shock in her face satisfied some sadistic streak in him.

Close up, her eyes had little green flecks. He had found and treasured semiprecious stones like that in Highland brooks. Usually after the brooks had been in flood, he remembered.

The eyes widened. Her voice was a contemptuous whisper. "Get back to your cave!"

The woman beside her gave him a fatuous, understanding smile. He raised the injured hand in a courteous salute and went forward to sit beside Brett.

Almost immediately the stewardess brought him the

whisky. He tossed it off and handed her the glass, knowing, but not caring, that Brett would wonder when he had ordered it and where he had been. It required an effort of the will to control his ill humor. At least nothing of it would show in his face.

The flat Belgian landscape slid under them like a green sampler latticed with brown stitching. He looked at it with acute dislike and thought longingly of the silver splash of the River Losk and the way the fat carp dreamed in the shadowy pools under the willows.

"What are you frowning over?" Brett asked.

"I was just deciding that I'm all in favor of burning witches."

"Forget about your women." Brett's voice was unusually sharp. "When I was young, we used to sing something about a sweetheart, a streetcar . . . there would soon be another one along. Hang on to that thought and forget them. You'll need your wits about you for this job. Rumania is a big country. Rothman could be anywhere and you have to move fast. You know that eventually he'll tell them what they want and then they'll kill him."

"What about the crown?"

Brett shrugged. "Rothman gets first priority." He riffled through the papers in his briefcase and gave Forsyth the severe look of a disappointed schoolmaster. "Here—take this." He handed him a double page of typewritten notes. "That explains about the special eyeglasses. You've got night binoculars and a box of hypodermics. If the Customs people get inquisitive, tell them that you are a diabetic. The ampoules are labeled insulin. You'll find the instructions behind the top labels. At the bottom of your valise is a dartboard." The gray face became censorious. "I believe you have had plenty of practice in pubs. They tell me you can throw a double six every time?"

Forsyth grunted.

"I advise you to keep in practice. The darts with the

white flights are normal. Don't prick a finger on those with the green flights, unless you plan a sudden meeting with Saint Peter. Any questions?"

"When do I get the lowdown on Stephen's bauble?"

Brett glanced at his watch. "We are early. We will take the fast train into Brussels. We can do it in sixteen minutes. We'll lunch in La Grande Place and I'll give you the outline then."

"Do you go back at once to London?"

Brett gave him a cold look and tightened his lips, then decided to be more explicit. "No. I'll be on the Continent for several days. But don't look to me for any help."

"I won't." Forsyth's tone was humorous. His bad temper had completely evaporated. He had had the feeling as he had walked away that, in spite of her brave words, the girl had been crying quietly. He wrote her off.

He would have liked his errand to have been less run of the mill, with some element of strangeness in it. Perhaps Hungary's Crown of Saint Stephen would provide that. He looked hopefully down at the terminal buildings rushing to meet them. There might be time to send Neville a crude statue of the Mannikin Pis. The thought of his disapproving face cheered him enormously.

 *Chapter Three*

BRETT spoke rapidly and intimately without looking at Forsyth. He walked through the golden radiance of La Grande Place as if he were in a desert.

Forsyth's irritation erupted. He flapped his right hand, cutting across Brett's flow of words. "Doesn't this mean anything to you at all?" He sounded personally affronted.

Brett's mild gaze took in the Gothic splendor of the soaring buildings, the lacy spires, the rosy flush of stone, the staring gargoyles. "I've seen it before," he stated flatly.

Forsyth laughed with real enjoyment, his good humor restored. "I had forgotten that you live in a world of fantasy. A stone version must be a little heavy for your palate."

He put an arm round the older man's shoulders as they crossed to the Coq d'Or, carefully guiding him around the groups of tourists. Above the door of the restaurant, two birds flew up with a papery flutter of wings. Both men followed their flight toward the cap of blue above the square. Surprisingly, both thought fleetingly of Rothman.

Inside, the dining room was as exclusively quiet as Forsyth remembered. Without consulting him, he ordered for Brett a creamy soup, an egg custard and a glass of milk. He raised his eyes from the menu to find the washed-out gaze of the older man fixed on him strangely. For himself, he chose fish poached in champagne and a bottle of Alsace

wine, a Gewuerztraminer, Grand Reserve, Chateau de Mit-
telwihr 1967, a big round wine, medium dry, with a full,
fruity bouquet.

"Rumanian wines," he said disdainfully, "are better than
their water, but that's all you can say about them. But any
nation that drinks *ţuica* can't expect to have a palate. *The
things I have done for England! . . .*"

"Just remember your reservations about their plum
brandy." Brett spoke drily. "A careful drinker like Bonneaud needs only that little edge on you and—pffft!" His
hands flew upward in an expressive gesture.

"What makes you so sure that he is involved?" Forsyth
speared a morsel of fish and examined it delicately.

"His mother's name was Taldy."

Forsyth's eyebrows climbed. "Hungarian?"

"Yes. Take your mind back to World War II. In 1945,
when the Russians were sweeping toward the capital, the
war criminals and the looters were scampering for safety.
The pro-Nazi Hungarian security chief, Colonel Arpad
Taldy, was right in the van of that mob. He accompanied
Ferenz Szalasi when practically the whole of the contents
of the Hungarian National Bank was hustled into a train at
Budapest. That train was bound for the Austrian border
and a destination which has remained a mystery for almost
thirty years. We know for a fact that there was gold, silver,
bonds, foreign currency, rare manuscripts—dozens of
chests of treasure. We also know for a fact that at the last
minute a large black trunk was rammed into the train." He
paused impressively. "That held a scepter, sword and orb
and, the supreme treasure of the Hungarian nation, the
one thousand-year-old Crown of Saint Stephen.

"Bonneaud's branch of the family was only distantly
related to Arpad Taldy, but it was the wealthy branch of
the family. Indeed, it was immensely wealthy and influential. They had estates in Austria, Czechoslovakia and, of
course, in Hungary."

"I suppose all that went up in smoke?"

"Yes. Bonneaud will barely remember the good times. He didn't enjoy them for very long. He was born on his mother's family estate about ninety miles from Schwarzach. Do you remember your war history? It was at Schwarzach that the Hungarian crown jewels disappeared. You'll find a fairly full account of the affair among your papers." He looked oddly furtive. "Read them on the plane and destroy them before you get to Constanza.

"There are conflicting stories about what happened. An American, Lieutenant Commander Thomas Howe, who was an officer in the MFAA, the Organization for Restitution of Monuments, Fine Arts and Archives, claimed in print in 1946 that in the previous year he took charge of the jewels at the official collecting point in Wiesbaden. He claimed also that American troops apprehended a Hungarian officer with a trunk. Up to here, we have been dealing with facts."

"Ye-e-s." Forsyth eyed him thoughtfully. "I haven't thought about this for a long time, but my recollection is, from all that I read, that here the waters become muddied. I seem to recall an apocryphal story that Colonel Pajtas formally handed over the scepter, sword and orb at some abbey near Salzburg. Wasn't it said that he held on to the crown because he felt that the Americans didn't appreciate its value and significance?"

"Correct! Some say that the Americans have the crown now in Fort Knox; others that it has been in the Vatican for the last twenty-seven years."

"Why?"

"Mindszenty is supposed to have been involved in plans for the restoration of the monarchy in Hungary."

"Aha! I'm beginning to get the picture. A *very* hot potato for both the White House and the Vatican . . . a *very* hot potato. Yes . . . didn't I read somewhere that, around 1965, there was a great brouhaha because of a theft from the Vatican?"

"Correct! There were a few crossed wires then. An Italian television newscast announced: 'Unknown thieves have stolen from the Vatican a number of extremely valuable historical relics, including the Holy Crown of Saint Stephen.' " Brett quoted precisely as if he were reading from a page of print. "There was a great fuss involving Interpol, and an announcement was made sometime later, stating that the relics had been recovered."

"Who stole them? What happened to the thieves?"

Brett gave him a sardonic look. "Nobody knows the answers to those questions—at least, no member of the public. *But,*" he paused, "the Vatican then claimed that the Crown of Saint Stephen referred to in the robbery was a copy and not the original. The entire business has been stirred up again because of Mindszenty's release from Hungary early in 1972. I don't need to tell you about his proposed Central European Catholic Monarchy. You can follow how essential the lost crown is as a symbol for that."

"Well . . . if he can't get it out of the pope, who can?"

"But does the pope have it? Certainly, in 1947, a formidable array of big nobs, including Mindszenty himself—Count Zoltan Csaky, Cardinal Innitzer of Vienna, Archbishop Rohrach of Salzburg, the American Cardinal Spellman, Cardinal von Faulhaber of Munich—urged the American ambassador, Selden Chapin, to remove the crown from the custody of the United States Army at Wiesbaden, transport it to Rome, and place it in the safe custody of His Apostolic Highness, Pope Pius XII. As to whether or not that was done, your guess is as good as mine." He glanced impatiently at his watch. "I don't have the time now for further details."

"But what are the Hungarians saying now?"

"Nothing."

"What has the Department got to do with a bashed

crown?" He watched the other man's eyes become icy points.

Brett shrugged. "Ours not to reason why."

"You might as well finish that quotation." Forsyth's tone was bitter. He carefully cut a Partagas cigar and puffed slowly. "Something about this assignment stinks. I don't like it. It's like running blind." He leaned forward and looked his companion straight in the eye. "Brett, I think you have deliberately gone out on a limb. I think that, for some reason which I haven't worked out yet, you have exceeded your orders." The pale eyes did not flicker or soften. "Neville never gives chapter and verse for an assignment—at least, not to me. He was unusually garrulous. His throwaway remark about the Crown of Saint Stephen was meant to be exactly that. I had the impression that compared to bringing Rothman back to the fold, the crown didn't rate. He was, in fact, saying to me then, 'If any reference to this crops up during the operation, disregard it—it isn't too important.' I got that message, loud and clear. You don't agree with it. Thanks."

He leaned back and watched a gray veil of smoke float lazily towards the heavily embossed ceiling. His voice was dreamily reflective. "Neville calls me The Shadow." He searched Brett's face, trying to find from its expression some knowledge of the nickname, but he simply looked back impassively. "Once I had dinner with him at the Carlton Club. We talked about T. S. Eliot. It seems that old Neville is stuck on "The Hollow Men." He quoted some lines from it, quite out of context, I suspect. I meant to look them up." The good-humored disdain was very evident. "There was something about between the thought and the deed or the action . . . *falls the Shadow*."

It was very quiet in the small dining room. Somewhere in the background a waiter rattled cutlery and breathed an apology.

Brett said briskly, "Don't get too fanciful. Just keep to the assignment. Bring Rothman out."

"Only that? Really only that? I don't have to stop something?" Forsyth laughed gently. "Why the cloak-and-dagger equipment? Don't you usually give that kind of thing to the hatchet men? My brain, my fists, my gun . . . up till now that has been my equipment. Is Neville becoming shaky in his old age? What makes this job special? His girl has her eye on Rothman? I don't buy that."

Brett got to his feet. "Time you were getting back to the airport. I'll leave you here." He put out a hand. In Forsyth's grasp, it felt thin and dry. His eyes had lost their freezing intensity and were again opaque gray pools. "Take care and—good luck." He left quickly.

At Brussels National Airport, Forsyth sauntered, looking for the girl. In the crush at the main newsstand, there was a flash of violet. Satisfied, he moved on.

In an age of violence girls skilled in karate were by no means rare. Any fat little schoolteacher could learn the art at night school. He massaged his wrist gently. In itself, her quick defense was meaningless. The collision at Heathrow could have been accidental.

But the gun worried him.

It was not by any means because he was unused to guns. They were, after all, the tools of his trade, at which he had served a fairly long and hard apprenticeship. But it was the first time that he had come across a gun that he had not recognized. That bothered him, but, he told himself, no more than an incomplete crossword puzzle would have done. Patience and perseverance . . . he would find out about it.

He halted under the announcements board, gazing unseeingly at the flashing red signs. His thoughts worried at the problem.

He was well aware that Neville regarded him as neatly and accurately pigeonholed—tough, durable, experienced

—but Forsyth was almost arrogantly conscious of possessing peculiarly sensitive antennae, which had earned him a reputation for smartness. The antennae were out now.

In the midst of his self-analysis he felt an obscure satisfaction that, in underrating this, Neville was as subtly wrong as he was in the rest of his estimate of him—solitary, self-contained, unemotional. The last category carried a sting. While both discounted the casual female contacts that starred his career, rightly dismissing them as meaningless, Forsyth felt himself capable of a depth of feeling that Neville would have denied him. The potentiality was enough for Forsyth; the lack of fulfillment did not trouble him. Perhaps someday . . .

He glanced at his watch. With luck, he might catch Valmy before the plane left.

The call to Marseilles went through quickly.

"René Valmy?" He could picture the small, anonymous room on the waterfront and Valmy's ferretlike nose twitching anxiously.

After a moment, there was a cautious assent. He could hear the wheezy rise and fall of the Frenchman's breath. "Morrison here . . . Robert Morrison."

Naturally, his own name was not known to the dealer. He was Morrison in France; Castle in Germany; Wild in Belgium; Arrow in Spain . . .

"Ah, Monsieur Morrison! A thousand pardons. I was wool-gathering. I hope that I see you soon. It has been too long." The relief in the unctuous voice was almost tangible.

Oily devil! thought Forsyth. "Maybe . . . maybe. I promised the boss to pass on a message to you." He laughed softly. "You'll owe me a drink. It was my suggestion. He wants a repeat of the little piece you made for him. *Tout de suite!* Can you do a really fast job? If things work out, maybe I'll collect it myself . . . let me see . . . say, three weeks from today?"

The silence stretched. Forsyth tensed.

"What piece, Monsieur Morrison? I do so many. Describe it." The voice was loaded with suspicion.

Forsyth forced impatience into his tone. "Don't waste time, Valmy. I've a plane to catch. You know the piece . . . the special small job, about four inches long . . . double barrel, twin triggers. Don't do a sloppy job on this one." He sounded convincingly angry. "The firing mechanism on the other was too stiff."

"You mean the barrel for the cyanide?" The Frenchman was furious. "That had to be. He understood that. I made it perfectly clear to him. Too easy and he might have killed himself accidentally. That's why the extra button is there. I shall complain." He was offended. "Besides, I thought it was supposed to be a special job?"

"Take it easy. Remember that I'm the one who will be using it. Bitter almonds is not my favorite perfume, but I have to act fast—very fast. The slightest stiffness could mean curtains for me."

"Well . . ." He was mollified and said with leaden humor, "Don't forget to use the amyl nitrite just as fast. Do you want a supply of that and of the thiosulphate tablets? You'll remember to take the thiosulphate as the *first* antidote? The other is the *second*."

"Sure. Don't worry. I'm not likely to forget. Thiosulphate before; amyl nitrite afterwards. Just see that you do a good job again. The bullet mechanism was perfect. If it's at all possible, I'll collect personally. Look out for a new bordello for me." There was a lecherous chuckle from the Frenchman. "*Au revoir!*"

Forsyth was smiling as he replaced the receiver.

In Marseilles, Valmy plucked at his lip. There had been no bullet mechanism. The second barrel had been for the paralyzing drug, the curare derivative. Slowly he dialed a number.

Whistling gently, Forsyth strolled toward the newsstand. The girl in violet had reached the front of the crowd. She was choosing a pile of magazines and, with some difficulty, was fitting them into a green rubber book-holder. Again Forsyth was struck by her youth.

He took his place beside her and studied the boxes piled with tubes of sweets and packets of chewing gum.

The stolid girl behind the counter had a round, pleasant face. She said, with monotonous patience, "What would monsieur like?"

"A packet of thiosulphate tablets, please."

Beside him, the hand holding the magazines tightened convulsively.

From behind the pile of newspapers and journals, the attendant looked at the tall, craggy man with puzzled displeasure. A tiny crease appeared between the kind eyes. "I am afraid that we do not stock those."

He reached for a tin of fruit pastilles. "These will do."

From his right came the quick tap of departing feet.

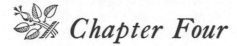 *Chapter Four*

F ORSYTH was wedged uncomfortably in a window seat. He had been doubly unfortunate in being assigned one of the three-in-a-row seats as well as in the fact that his companions were two garrulous English-women whose ample curves overflowed the boundaries of their own seats. He had dealt coldly and efficiently with the second disadvantage, so that he had quickly been left in peace to study the papers in his briefcase. There was little he could do about his cramped quarters.

He drew aside the window curtain on his left and looked down through the blackness to where a great Ferris wheel of light marked the position of Vienna. Obviously a nodal city, he reflected absently, marking the beautiful symmetry of the spokes of light radiating from the hub of the town.

It would not be too long until they were in Constanza.

He wondered anew what madness had brought him into the field of espionage. His end was predictable. He would die in some anonymous gutter with a bullet in his head and only his father would grieve and wonder.

A frisson of actual pain shot through his chest as he thought of his father's peaceful face, while he sipped his after-dinner port in the library and studied the latest issue of *Horse and Hounds*. His serenity and dignity in his lone-liness gave him a saintlike stature in his son's eyes.

Forsyth's fingers, tapping an impatient tattoo on the

leather case, told him why he repeatedly rejected the comforts of Stanmore Manor for the dangers and uncertainties of each operation. Now the story of the treasure hunt for the Hungarian crown burned in his brain. He itched to solve the problem. When he had destroyed Brett's closely annotated account of the mystery, his memory would retain every word.

Even as he opened the case, extracted the papers and put them neatly into a jacket pocket, his mind was busy on the possible connection between the story and Tony Rothman.

Again and again his thoughts went back to the fact that Neville had carefully omitted to tell him precisely what Rothman had been doing in Rumania. He had implied that any connection between the crown and Rothman was fortuitous.

In the flat overlooking St. James's Park, Forsyth had briefly considered probing, insisting on the facts, but had dismissed the thought almost at once. Neville would have lied. In this work, lies were taken for granted but normally were employed only in the big affairs when the boss considered that it would be dangerous for an operator to know too much.

Dangerous for the operation, not for the operator, Forsyth reflected cynically.

His mind scurried over the generalizations it had formed. Someone, probably Rothman, had got on to the whereabouts of the crown. That, he suspected, had been Rothman's mission. Rothman's cover had been blown, with the result that he was now somewhere in Rumania—why Rumania?—enjoying the hospitality, not, Forsyth was convinced, of the Rumanian Secret Police, but of the French communists, the Societé des Mains Rouge. The crown's monetary value to Bonneaud would be enormous, but its bargaining power? . . . Forsyth's pulse leaped at the possibilities. So . . . the affair was international.

But what was Britain's interest in the crown?

The elderly lady in the neighboring seat looked with alarm at his grim face. She whispered uneasily to her companion, who eased herself forward to study him surreptitiously. Forsyth became conscious of their interest and got abruptly to his feet.

In the tiny washroom, he shredded and burned Brett's notes and dropped the ashes into the toilet bowl. When they had gone, he peered into the mirror and raised both hands to smooth back the thick hair.

The hands froze in mid-air.

An item in the English edition of the *Brussels Gazette* seemed to leap out at him.

Hurriedly, he washed his hands, straightened his tie and went back down the aisle to his seat.

His nearest companion was reading his paper, churning it into a soggy mass of assaulted pages. When she saw him, a painful flush rose from the neck of her floral frock and suffused her face. In her nervousness, she bundled the paper into a ball, pressing it against her chest, while she squeezed herself against the back of her seat to let him pass. Finally, both women had to scramble into the passage before he could reach his seat, where the flustered woman had quickly dropped the wreck of his paper.

His face stiff with annoyance, Forsyth smoothed ineffectually at the pages while he searched for the item. He reread it slowly, pausing with a sinking heart to verify the date of the proposed World Peace Conference. In fifteen days, Britain, along with the other members of the European Common Market, the United States of America and Canada, would, if all went well, sign the first major world peace treaty with the Soviet Union and with China.

The USSR in particular had been behaving like a skittish dowager, simultaneously inviting and rejecting rapprochement. Britain's ancient cunning and diplomatic skill had brought the Russians coyly to the conference table.

The EEC and her allies were anxious for the treaty, not

only as an end in itself, but because it would open serious trade negotiations with the communist countries. It was important, too, that the latter should be involved with other members of the International Monetary Fund in devising a system of reforms for the world's monetary system.

Forsyth sweated gently as he considered what would happen if any of the Common Market countries could be proved, albeit falsely, to be actively promoting the restoration of the monarchy in communist Hungary.

Britain, wracked with internal political unrest and striving heroically to reestablish the stability of her ailing economy, had probably most to lose. Her old friend and ally, the United States, was equally vulnerable, though for different reasons.

His muttered curse pivoted the two female heads around as if they were on wires.

Obviously, Constanza could not come too soon for the three of them.

As Forsyth stood stretching his cramped legs at midnight on the tarmac of the Constanza airport, Rothman, every sense, he flattered himself, alert, came out of an uneasy sleep on the floor of the cellar. At once, he dismissed as unimportant an unfamiliar sense of physical numbness.

He had been lying on his side in an effort to prevent any pressure on the soles of his feet. Earlier, he had torn the sleeves of his shirt into strips and made rough pads in an attempt to ease the pain and staunch the flow of blood. The fetid atmosphere in the room stank of carbon dioxide, sweat, fear and dried blood.

The fear surprised him. It would be days before that was inevitable, but he knew that his instincts were to be trusted. The fear was real and it was his, an involuntary reaction to something unexpected.

Again he felt against his ankles the soft caress that had

awakened him. In the darkness, the red eyes of a rat glared obscenely.

Normally, Rothman would have gone back to sleep, completely indifferent to his roommate, but these rats would be cannibals. Within moments of scenting his blood, the others would be upon him.

Raising his blond head, he let out a blood-curdling yell that echoed round the room and sent the rat scampering into a corner. Faultlessly accurate, eerie, demonic, the wolf howls bounced off the sweating walls. He had last heard the sound in a snow-swept forest in Belorussia when he had been struggling for days to reach Baranovichi. It would be with him always.

Painfully, he drew his legs up under him, pausing momentarily in the menacing litany to groan once. There are some deaths from which the bravest of men shrink. He had a sickening picture of the rodents swarming over him like a dark tide, soft, tumbling, insatiable, fighting for his flesh. His mind raced.

On hands and knees, with his feet held rump-high, he scuttled in the direction of the door. In minutes, the shock of his cries would wear off. Hunger would overcome fear and the rats would creep closer. If his warders were on another floor, he was finished. He pounded frantically.

The thunder of the door banging against the wall and the swathe of lantern light entered the cell simultaneously.

"*Mon Dieu!* Rats—dozens of them!"

"Get the door closed!"

The two men began to back out. Rothman caught at a leg and hung on.

"If they kill me," he gritted in French, "Bonneaud will have you shot."

He tightened his hold. His feet had begun to bleed again. He could feel the warm moisture soaking the pads and cursed the weakness that was making his head swim. This time there would be no need to induce a faint.

Hands under his armpits dragged him roughly into the passage. As the door slammed shut, Rothman heard a crescendo of shrill squeaks and the thin scratching of dozens of tiny nails against stone. The sound seemed to be very close to his head.

He made a convulsive effort to push himself up from the floor.

The guards made no attempt to help him, but allowed him to sit up and rest his head on his knees.

From their position behind him, they did not see him clench his teeth, drag the pad from his left foot and toss it into the darkness of the passage beyond the door.

His teeth chattered and his eyes drooped shut.

The men argued about what to do with him, but he no longer heard them. He was far off in a special darkness where neither time nor place mattered.

"You're a genius," one of the men said furiously. "You keep telling me that all the time. Right! You decide what the boss would want us to do. We can't keep him here any longer. That cell was the only possible place here, but he has to stay alive until he talks. Those were the orders. Now, what?"

"No problem." The other's tone was contemptuous and superior. "The only difficulty, Jacques, is his size. If he looks like coming round, give him a crack on the head. We'll have him locked up good and tight within fifteen minutes. Then I'll phone."

"What about our stuff, Henri?"

"I'll get it into the truck. You keep your eye on Rothman. *Mére de Dieu!* Must I tell you every single thing?"

Practical considerations, not compassion, brought Henri Fossard back minutes later with a blanket. Together, he and Jacques Fouquet rolled the unconscious man onto it. They had to rest many times before they got him into the back of the truck.

Fossard hesitated before closing the truck door. He said slowly, "I think we had better pick Dr. Lupescu up. This fellow looks bad. I told you we should have fed him." He rounded furiously on the other. "*Salle cochon!* You were only interested in eating his share! If Rothman dies, Monsieur Bonneaud shall know of your stupidity." He failed to notice the sudden feral gleam in Fouquet's eyes. "Get in beside him. If he makes a sound, you know what to do, but don't use a sledgehammer to crack a nut."

He opened the door again and Fouquet climbed in, looking sullen and trying to conceal his fear. It would not be difficult to deal with Fossard, but Bonneaud was a different kettle of fish. He thought longingly of his village of Varennes and of the plump thighs of his Breton wife. He sighed in the darkness and wrinkled his nose in disgust as Rothman's odors filled the truck.

By the time Fossard had driven silently into the garden of Lupescu's house, Fouquet's head was whirling with half-formed plans. Minutes later, he shielded his eyes against the sudden brilliance of the doctor's flashlight.

The beam traveled slowly over the Englishman, lingering on the face and then on the feet.

"Tch! Tch! This won't do. Bonneaud is a fool not to have supervised this man's treatment. Bring him inside. Fortunately, I am alone in the house. My wife is on holiday at Sinaia."

The doctor's clever Jewish face looked thin and worried. He elbowed Fouquet aside when he made to grab Rothman roughly by the ankles. Holding his arms out, he showed the men how to make a basket of their hands, draped Rothman's flaccid arms round their necks and took up his position behind them to support Rothman's back.

"Isn't this dangerous?" Fossard whispered uneasily.

"Of course it is," the doctor replied testily. "You must take him away without fail tomorrow night. No member of the public goes to the cells after dark. Why Bonneaud sent him to a deserted house and not to the old Doftana Prison cells in the first place, I'll never understand."

So Rothman regained consciousness in a pleasant, pine-scented bedroom. He was wearing freshly laundered pajama trousers and his feet had been professionally bandaged. His body smelled clean.

He looked down incredulously at the spotless linen sheets beneath his hands and at the bright colors of the country patchwork quilt. The furniture was of polished pine, dark and simple, with good lines. Someone had draped a coarse white napkin over the bedside lamp, shading his eyes from the glare. Starched white dimity curtains fluttered in the breeze from the half-open window.

That and the feel of the goosefeather mattress beneath his body convinced him that he was somewhere in the country. Obviously, his hosts felt that he could yell his head off to no purpose. He decided not to put their belief to the test.

There was no pain in his feet. Probably he had been given a pain-killing drug. He had a terrific feeling of well-being and of confidence. He stretched his big body luxuriously and estimated that he could allow himself five minutes of comfort before dropping through the open window. He would, he decided, take the pillows with him and the dark woollen robe that hung from the back of the door.

Experimentally, he flexed one leg and was pulled up short. There was a subdued rattle from the foot of the bed. He threw the bed clothes back and gaped.

A leather dog collar circled each ankle. Fresh eyelets had been pierced in them to make them a snug fit. The collars were joined by a length of steel chain which emerged from padlocks on each round of leather to circle the bedposts and run loosely across the width of the bed, but it was impossible to step onto the floor.

Slowly Rothman pulled the bedclothes back into position and closed his eyes to consider the possibilities.

It was recognized psychological practice to confuse a prisoner with alternate harsh and kind treatment. Rothman thought of the neuroticism produced in rats by similar methods. His expression did not change, but he was smiling inwardly at the ludicrousness of the hope that such treatment might succeed with him. He would enjoy his new quarters; go to sleep; and build up fresh strength for what inevitably lay ahead.

His spirits rose. His chances of being rescued before he poured out his secrets had increased dramatically. Unless he had been under for longer than he thought, daylight would bring only the fourth day.

He was awakened by the crowing of a cock and the soft dawn noises of sleepy birds. Someone had been in the bedroom while he slept and had extinguished the bed lamp. Drowsy and content, he listened to the barking of a dog, hungry for breakfast. With growing alertness, he strained to catch the lowing of cattle, the clatter of horses' hooves or the heavy tramp of men attending to animals. No such sounds came. Only a dove cooed seductively and came to rest on his windowsill.

He was not on a farm, he decided. Probably he was in a fairly substantial country house. His mind pigeonholed the sounds and the direction from which the rosy morning light struck the window. The pattern of the green, hand-woven linen side curtains was indelibly stamped on his brain. Someday he would recognize them.

His automatic watch was still on his wrist. When the hour hand reached seven o'clock, the door opened.

Lupescu came in. He was dressed in a long white surgeon's gown, skull cap and mask. Only his eyes showed, wary and intelligent. He spoke French with the broad, uncultured accents of the north of France, but Rothman listened to the guttural inflection and guessed that it was not his native tongue.

The Englishman chanted, softly and mockingly, " '*She-mah Yisroel Udushaim Elohenu Udoshaim Achad.*' "

The eyes behind the mask smiled.

"There is no need to recite the Jewish prayer before death," Lupescu said. "I have no intention of joining my illustrious forefathers yet and that prayer would be singularly inappropriate in your case. No doubt there is a special formula for the depraved and the pagan, but I do not know it. My intention is to bring you your breakfast. No death potions yet, Mr. Rothman."

He looked steadily down at the man in the bed. "I would like to satisfy myself as to your physical condition. You would be exceedingly foolish to attempt to seize me, injure me or to try to tear off my mask—for three reasons. In the first place, my identity is unlikely to be of interest to you for very long. Second, I am the only person inclined to show you a spark of kindness. Third, at the first imprudent move, you would certainly be killed. I would strongly advise you to settle for bacon and eggs, English style, not Continental style. My religious convictions need not influence the eating habits of a guest."

His examination was prolonged and thorough. He spent a long time testing reflexes and examining Rothman's eyes. At the end, he grunted as if satisfied.

"You are a very strong young man with a magnificent body. It is a pity to see such things abused, but you have brought it upon yourself." He sighed, his physician's instincts obviously at war with the dictates of his second career. "There is no point in disturbing the bandages. My feeling is that you will heal quickly. I stitched the worst of your wounds, but you will have a fair amount of pain and discomfort for the next forty-eight hours." He placed a small bottle containing white tablets on the bedside table. "There is no point in enduring pain unnecessarily and much to be gained by avoiding it. Take one tablet every hour, no more."

Rothman wanted to laugh. It was like a visit from an old family doctor.

As Lupescu was leaving the room, he hesitated and looked back. "How did you know that I am Jewish?" he asked.

"You wear your surgeon's cap as a rabbi would. Besides," Rothman nodded toward a high chest of drawers, "you forgot to remove the menorah."

Lupescu looked at the miniature brass Jewish eight-branched candlestick which stood in the middle of the white linen runner. "One always makes the simple mistakes."

He brought back a loaded tray and left Rothman to enjoy the bacon and eggs, poppy-seed rolls and thick Turkish coffee. "No *mamaliga,* boiled maize flour," he said smiling. "I doubt if you will regret the omission."

At the end of the meal when he had removed the tray, he said thoughtfully, "A wise host would secure your hands, but I fail to see what mischief you can do, except to yourself. Perhaps I should ensure that you sleep peacefully for some hours, but soon you will be experiencing a very long sleep, so I am reluctant to deprive you now of what comfort the daylight may offer you. I will leave you with your thoughts."

Soon after the doctor had gone, Rothman became convinced that he was alone in the house. Inside, there was a deathly stillness as if the building held its breath.

He began to be angry that he could think of no way to free himself. It was ridiculous to be helpless simply because he was secured by the legs.

It was impossible to bounce the bed nearer to the open window. He tried that, but he might as well have tried to move Gibraltar. Fuming, he lay back and considered the position.

He had pulled himself high up on the pillows and, as he

gazed vaguely round the room, he made a discovery that jerked him into complete alertness.

Reflected in the mirror of the dressing table was part of the view which lay outside his range of vision through the open window. A green meadow dropped abruptly to what looked like the beginning of a narrow valley. He could distinguish the pink outline of a long, low building which, even at a distance, struck a chill into his heart. It looked bleak and vaguely menacing. He calculated that he could have walked to it in about five minutes. He strained his eyes, trying to distinguish details and gradually he was tantalized by a sense of familiarity.

Not a factory, he decided. There was no sign of life. An institution of some sort. He thought about the house he was in and the fact that there seemed to be no road separating it from the meadow where the long building stood.

"Got it!" he breathed suddenly. "This is a doctor's house attached to that building." Certainty grew in him. "I'm on the outskirts of the oil town of Cimpina. That's the old prison of Doftana, now preserved as a museum."

He recalled that the terrifying place had once been devoted to the punishment of communist prisoners. The irony of his situation struck him.

That was where Bonneaud would hold him.

He wondered how he could pass on the information, how to leave a trail that an intelligent operator could follow.

He swallowed one of the tablets and scrambled to the foot of the bed. Pulling the corner of the mattress well back, he seized the chain, searching till he found a sharp-edged link. Laboriously he scratched on the bedpost, well below the level of the clothes, his own initials, DOFTANA and the date. A person making the bed would not notice the scratches, but, he hoped, if his trail had been picked up, a thorough search of the room would reveal the message.

Satisfied, he neatened the clothes and lay back.

There had been no rain for a long time. He remembered that the grass reflected in the mirror had had a dry, brownish look. Shortly before eleven o'clock, he heard the shrill, excited laughter of children. He pulled himself high on the pillows to look, feeling, he told himself, like a bloody Lady of Shalott.

A stream of *paparude*, young gypsies, decked in leaves, danced through the meadow, leading one of their companions, a fair-haired girl of about ten years of age. She was dressed in a garment of leaves. There was a wreath of flowers in her hair and garlands of crimson poppies and delicate blue mayflowers hung round her neck. They were engaged in the ancient ritual of propitiating the gods and invoking rain. Their song floated into the sunny room.

> *"Papulunga!*
> *Go up to Heaven.*
> *Open its windows*
> *And let the rain down,*
> *That the corn and the wheat*
> *May grow well and ripen."*

For a moment, he thought of yelling, but it was unlikely that his shouts would be heard above the sound of the singing and the noise the children were making. They ran toward the cells and he thought sourly of the doctor's displeasure.

He remembered suddenly that most of the minority groups in Cimpina, as in Ploesti, were Jewish, so the doctor's presence here was not so very surprising after all.

As the long minutes ticked away, he began to feel uneasy, impatient of the softness of the bed and the comfort of the heaped pillows. On each hour, he swallowed a tablet, at the same time resenting the reinforcement of the role of pampered invalid. The dog collars, which could not be felt through the bandages, seemed unbearably constricting. He recognized that he was in a filthy temper.

As the uneasiness grew, the handsome face took on a look of brooding anger. He was totally unaware that the psychological blitzkreig was self-inspired and self-propelled. He had completely underrated the extent of the punishment he had received, so could not arrive logically at the conclusion that Lupescu's treatment of him sprang solely from a desire to protect a valuable but ultimately expendable property. Had he gone that night to Doftana, he would quickly have recovered his mental equilibrium, but that was not to happen.

While Rothman lay fuming in the airy bedroom, Lupescu drove slowly back from Cimpina to his villa. He had collected a pile of medical supplies from the main chemist. Among his purchases was the dye that would locate the aneurism, a supply of oxygen, the new Swiss anesthetic and a packet of surgeon's gloves. His hands on the wheel were not quite steady. He had not practiced medicine legitimately for five years and he had never carried out a major operation.

His garden was practically carpeted with petunias. They flowed under the chestnut trees and fell in a waterfall of color from the fretted balcony of the house. He looked at it with love.

He was opening the trunk of the car when he heard the deep, wavering voice behind him, singing the lovely *Amigdalea*, the almond-tree song:

> *"The slender almond tree with snow white hands*
> *she shook,*
> *And shoulders, arms and hair were strewn with*
> *blossoms fair . . ."*

The postman, a rare visitor, stood grinning at him amiably. He was an old man, employed on a temporary basis, solely for deliveries in the Doftana area. He did not wear the regulation uniform, but, like many old men in the district, he was faithful to the native costume—picturesque white felt trousers, calf-length leather boots, a long, loose, surplicelike white shirt and a black, gaily embroidered waistcoat. His wrinkled brown face looked out at Lupescu from a wide-brimmed black felt hat.

"*Bună dimineaţa, doctorul!*" he called cheerily. He held out a letter.

Lupescu could barely be civil. "Good morning," he returned, aware of the man's eyes fixed inquisitively on his purchases.

Disturbed, he let himself into the house.

Bonneaud, Fossard and Fouquet were already in the shadowy sitting room, drinking *ţuica* with bored absorption.

"Where have you been, Vasile?" Alan Bonneaud looked impatiently at the older man. His eyes went to the cylinder of oxygen standing in the hall. "What the hell is that?"

"A bad omen," Lupescu's tone was grim. He had no great liking for Bonneaud, so it gave him a small pleasure to see how the Frenchman's eyes dulled with alarm.

Alan Bonneaud looked exactly what he was—a slippery customer, whom men instinctively distrusted. Of less-than-average height, he had a curiously ageless face. The doctor knew him to be in the early thirties, but the smooth, brown features often reminded him of an Oriental carving of a mandarin. The restless brown eyes and the wide, too-ready smile were off-putting. Only a fool would have underrated the cleverness of the devious mind. Only an optimist would have expected him to show the slightest compassion. He was physically brave, extremely imaginative and resourceful and, above all, ambitious. He was an evil man.

Characteristically, he waited now. Fossard and Fouquet were silent, clutching their *ţuica* and gazing almost vacantly at Lupescu.

He sat heavily down in the nearest chair. "Have you seen Rothman?" he asked.

"No. I was waiting until I had seen you. What has gone wrong?"

Lupescu shrugged. "Judge for yourself." He glanced at the others. "You have probably been told how Rothman came to be here. A fortunate move, as it happens. I gave him a light anesthetic when I stitched his feet. While he was unconscious, he babbled a little. Nothing unusual in that, but I noticed a curious slurring in his speech."

"Get on with it, man!" Bonneaud barked.

Lupescu ignored that. "This morning I examined him thoroughly. Within the last few days, he has suffered a slight cerebral accident. The slurring of speech is still present, a residue of paralysis remains on the left side and his reflexes are poor."

"Well?"

"The indications of an imminent cerebral aneurism cannot be ignored. Let me put it this way to you—Rothman is living on the edge of a volcano. Even with the best of care, he could die at any moment. With your kind of treatment, his fate is inevitable." Lupescu sat back in his chair and looked steadily at Bonneaud.

A slow flush had covered the Frenchman's face while the doctor had been speaking. It died away, accentuating Bonneaud's sallow look. He recovered quickly.

"Well, what do we do? Can you keep him alive long enough for us to get him to tell us where the crown is? Is there some drug you could use?"

The doctor clicked his teeth in exasperation. "Do you mean the so-called truth drug? There is no such thing. Under pentathol, he would pour out such a stream of fact and fantasy that you could spend years trying to separate the one from the other. Forget about drugs. Rothman is a sick man. He needs at least a week to rest. A couple of hours lying on the floor in Doftana and, at the very least,

he will have a slight stroke, but probably worse." He
sighed. "I have taken certain precautions. Naturally, I will
do my best to keep him alive. If the worst comes to the
worst, I am prepared to perform an emergency operation."

Bonneaud's eyes gleamed. "So there is still a chance?"

"Certainly. I suggest I keep Rothman here tonight, but
he must be out of here by tomorrow night. That is essential. My wife returns from Sinaia on the following day.
Rothman does not need carpets or fancy furniture, but he
must have a comfortable bed, warmth and light, nourishing
food, if he is to survive. There is no reason why he should
not go to Doftana, provided Fossard and Fouquet can
make suitable arrangements. Rothman *must* be kept
warm." He looked with something akin to pity at Bonneaud. "Patience, my friend. All is not yet lost."

"No." The Frenchman leaned back in his chair and
closed his eyes. The other waited. "I will go back to Bucharest tonight and wait until I hear from you. What will
be, will be, but there is no harm in giving Fate a helping
hand." Suddenly, a thought struck him. "Has he any idea
of this?"

"No . . . very definitely not. I have rarely met a more
optimistic man. Inwardly, he is laughing at the idea that we
could really hurt him."

"He must not know. If he suspected for a moment that
he might die, nothing we could do would persuade him to
talk." He laughed. "A little tender, loving care will puzzle
him so much that—who knows?" He reached forward and
refilled the glasses. "Bring your glass, Vasile," he commanded. "I have a feeling that Fate may not have played
us such a dirty trick after all."

The doctor waved a hand impatiently. "This is no time
for drinking," he said irritably. "There is a great deal to be
done."

Bonneaud's face darkened. He had noticed in Lupescu at
times an undertone of authority which came oddly from a

Jew, even in the more tolerant atmosphere of Rumania. He eyed him thoughtfully. The doctor was examining his fingernails and frowning.

Lupescu continued in a milder tone. "It should not be beyond the ingenuity of our friends here to rig up a temporary supply of electricity. I must have good light. The adjoining cell must become a makeshift theater." He sighed. "You cannot imagine the difficulties. If I have to use that theatre . . ." He rolled his eyes expressively. "Some of the equipment is here, but some things must be brought from Ploesti. It would be unwise to excite curiosity in Cimpina." He thought for a moment. "Tomorrow morning, I will shave Rothman's head. He must be ready at all times."

The Frenchman's laugh was subdued, but joyous. "That will puzzle him." He got up from his chair and slapped Lupescu on the shoulder. "I could not have devised a better softening-up process myself."

When the three men had gone, Lupescu sat for a few minutes, motionless in his chair. As he reached for the telephone and dialed the Sinaia number, his face changed. The eyes were no longer remote. The thin features had sharpened until they looked cruel and purposeful. When he talked to his wife, the cultured, leisurely tone became brusque and implacable.

The flow of Rumanian was like an icy stream. There were no interruptions from Sinaia.

Finally, he said, "Speed is essential. Tell them that they must move fast. I can make no predictions about Rothman and none about Bonneaud. I will be forced to recall Bonneaud from Bucharest in two or three days. A longer interval would make him suspicious. Rothman must be got out before then."

Quietly he replaced the receiver.

His thoughts were busy with the problem of Rothman's physical condition. The weight of his personal responsibility seemed to press down like a burden on his neck. He lifted a hand as if he meant to rub the top of his spine, but dropped the hand nervelessly on the table.

Now, he told himself, with a surge of relief, it was the immediate responsibility of the Komitat Gosudarstvennoi Bezopastnosti. His telephone call had done no more than speed up the KGB plan.

 *Chapter Five*

CHARLES FORSYTH had gone to bed in
Mamaia as dawn was breaking grayly beyond the French
windows of his bedroom and had fallen at once into a
heavy sleep, groggily aware of the perfume of honeysuckle, the strange full-throated song of hundreds of frogs
and the honking calls of wild duck on Lake Siutghiol.

He wakened early, dressed and stood looking from his
windows over the flat roof of the dining room to the waters
of the Black Sea. They stretched like an enormous sapphire
pavement, edged by a long, curving line of bleached-white
sand.

Mamaia is unique. It stands on a sandy peninsula midway between the waters of the Black Sea and the fresh-
water Lake Siutghiol. One side of the peninsula is a sophis-
ticated amalgam of skyscraper hotels of startling brilliance
and avant-garde design. The other is like a Japanese print,
with limpid waters, gently tossing boats, a sun-bleached
wooden pier and anglers casting, like figures in a dream.

For at least a dozen years, the resort has been a meeting
place for practically all the nations of the world. Practically all are tourists, pure and simple, who come to enjoy
the ten-mile stretch of magnificent beach, the boating or
the fishing on the lake. Others come to whisper secretly
and make the covert plans that will affect the lives of

people in the USSR, the Netherlands, the United States or Britain. Forsyth had done his share of that.

He turned quickly as the bedroom door opened and a waiter came in.

Forsyth frowned. There had been no knock. The man was middle-aged, with the sagging figure and empty face of an overworked servant.

"*Scuzaţi-mă*," he apologized. "Perhaps I am in the wrong room? My colleague said 'Jan Balanescu, the gentleman in room forty-three is ringing for his breakfast.' Did I do right to come?"

"It is always right to feed a hungry man."

The formula having been followed, Balanescu sat down on the edge of the rumpled bed. He accepted a cigarette, drew in a deep lungful of smoke and began to talk easily and quickly. "Rothman came here—I mean, to the Hotel Modern—two weeks ago. I had no contact with him. Those were my orders. He had been in Salzburg before he came to Mamaia; left by car, alone; went to Bucharest, Ploesti, Cimpina, Sinaia and Brasov. He returned to this hotel exactly a week ago. As far as I know, in each place, he visited churches. He seemed to do no more than that. He had time to do no more. On his return here, he went twice to Constanza, by bus. On the first day, he went to Ovid's monument, was joined there by an unidentified man —a pretty man, I was told—and they talked for some time. On the second day, he went to the large bookshop in the main street. Fifteen minutes later, he staggered out, got into a car with two men and they drove off."

"Bonneaud's men?"

"Yes. He was last seen in the capital, very drunk, in the forest restaurant at Baneasa. That was four days ago. His things are still in his room here. Naturally, when he dropped out of sight, I went over his room. It had already been searched." He shrugged philosophically. "Impossible to tell if anything had been found."

"Did you find anything?"

Balanescu went into a pocket and produced a worn black leather wallet. He shrugged again. "I do not know. Apart from toilet things, there was only one personal object, maybe of no significance. It had fallen behind a curtain. Was he a religious man?"

Forsyth smiled. "Scarcely." He took the card that the waiter held out. On one side was a crude picture of Saint Jude. On the other, in French, a prayer to the saint. He could see nothing remarkable about the document. He put the card into his own wallet.

"Good," he said. "With luck, Rothman may still be in Bucharest. I'll take a look. Where can I get in touch with you?"

"Here, of course. What is more natural than to ask for the waiter who recommended a restaurant in Bucharest? You have forgotten its name. Now, I will bring your breakfast." He paused. "Occasionally, a waiter makes friends among the influential. The daily plane service to Bucharest is always heavily booked, but I have a friend who can arrange matters. Shall I get you a seat for tomorrow?"

"Please do!" He watched the door closing quietly behind him.

There was little to be gained by leaving that day for the capital. The plane would save him an eight-hour journey and allow him to make at least one inquiry in Constanza. In the town, he would hire a car and drive along the coast to the border where Rumania and Bulgaria met. He felt jubilant. It would be practically a holiday. Obscurely, he felt that in some way he had scored a point over Neville. It was quite pointless at this stage to worry about Rothman.

The road to Constanza was as white and dusty as ever. The small, wooden, cottage-type houses had a shabby, weathered pallor. Outside the barracklike building of Sco-ala No. 2, the pupils, dressed in the uniform of the Pioneers, cavorted like young puppies. They were out of school uniform. Probably going on an outing. In the bus, a young gypsy woman with bold dark eyes, sallow skin and vividly embroidered costume swayed heavily against him. Fastidiously, he recoiled from the odor of the sickly perfume from her hair and body.

It was a relief when the bus rattled into the streets of Constanza. He was struck anew by the pervasive spirit of the Orient in the dignified, sprawling old town. Women wearing *shalvari*, baggy Turkish trousers, with heavy swathings of dark cloth over their heads and faces, glided silently past him. Later, he knew, he would hear the long drawn-out cry of the muezzin—"*Allahu akbar! Lā ilāha illā 'illāh!*" An old man, grasping in his horny hands a short string of blue beads, the Moslem rosary or *tespyeh*, fiddled with the thirty-three beads and looked after him with childlike curiosity.

Forsyth went quickly down the dusty main street, making for the Central Square. He was easing himself into the feel of the place.

He was not a superstitious man but all at once he had a sense of urgency, as if something important waited for him somewhere ahead.

A stout, middle-aged woman, obviously a teacher, stood before the statue of the poet, haranguing four uninterested young boys. "Do you remember," she said in a clear English voice, "that in A.D. 9 Augustus suddenly exiled Ovid from Rome here to Tomi, as Constanza was then called?"

Forsyth could almost smell the chalky air of a Manchester classroom.

"We don't know why. Probably because of one of Ovid's poems, 'The Art of Love.'" She pursed her mouth primly, and added, "And because of an indiscretion."

They moved away, the boys scuffing their feet.

Forsyth looked at the Latin inscription: *I who lie here, Naso, the poet, dealt lightly with the tenderness of Love.*

My very skill was my undoing. Stay, passer-by, and if you too have been a lover, have the heart to pray that the bones of Naso may rest softly.

It told him nothing. *The art of love . . .* Something tugged at his memory, but refused to be identified.

On the steep slope behind the square, the biggest mosaic floor in the world was being uncovered. Buried from the second or third century, the colors glowed in the brilliant sunlight. He skirted the excavations, making for the water.

A series of palm-fringed terraces, ablaze with flowers, dropped to a promenade. At the end was the bronze bust of another poet, brooding over his muse—the handsome young Rumanian Mihail Eminesco. The promenade was deserted.

From his sense of disappointment, Forsyth knew that he had been looking for somebody.

He hesitated, willing the antennae to work. There was an ironical smile on his face as he crossed the road.

The entrance to the Aquarium was bowered in roses. He paid the few *lei* and went down into the surrealistic world of darkness, lit by the uncertain glow from the wall tanks.

She was there, looking lost and bored, gazing indifferently in turn at the striped-peppermint beauty of the darting angel fish and the sinuous horror of the monster eels.

Until that moment, he had not known that he had been looking for her.

Some sound made her turn her head curiously. At first his features did not register with her, but in seconds he saw the eyes darken with loathing. Her head jerked as if she were looking for an exit.

A flicker of muted dismay made him advance cautiously, as if toward a startled animal.

"Don't scare me to death," he said mockingly and knew that it was the wrong thing to say.

It bothered him that he could neither deal with her nor disarm her.

Close to, he saw how her hands tightened on her handbag and how a tiny pulse leaped at the base of her throat.
The light from the tank gave her skin a greenish pallor
which, with the strange yellow eyes and burnished hair,
lent her a luminous, erotic beauty.

Unexpectedly, desire leaped in him.

He said quickly, "This is not the best place for a talk,
Miss Beaufort. You didn't come to Rumania to examine
fish. Suppose we get back into the sunshine. It is chilly for
you here."

She was wearing a simple frock of jade silk, with white
openwork sandals on her bare feet. The air was dank, but
she made a small dismissive gesture with her head as if her
personal comfort were of no consequence.

"Father sent you after me," she said accusingly. "He
shouldn't have done that. We had an agreement . . ." Her
eyes spilled tears. She backed away from him.

"No." He put a hand tentatively on her shoulder, ab-
sorbing a tremor which she had suppressed from the moment she had recognized him. "Your father is a friend of
mine, but I give you my word that he gave me no hint that
you were coming here."

His hand tightened on her shoulder, urging her toward
the stairway. He wondered what he was letting himself in
for.

The strong sunlight struck them like a blow. She fumbled in her handbag for sunglasses and, when she had put
them on, Forsyth found that they were so dark that her
eyes were completely hidden.

That barrier seemed to give her new confidence. She
walked docilely beside him, but her head was up once more
and her lips were under control.

They sat on the terrace of the former Casino, long since
the Palace of Culture. He ordered beer for both of them,
but neither touched their drink. The laughter of the people

at the other tables seemed to accentuate the awkwardness between them.

In an attempt to ease the tension, Forsyth said teasingly, "You certainly know how to fight back. Please, miss, I'm on your side."

She did not return his smile, but said very seriously, "Father taught me. He taught both of us—Mother and me. We don't know much about his work, but he said it was only fair to tell us that some day people might want to hit back at him, through us. We had to be ready to defend ourselves."

"You're good." Forsyth was genuinely approving and that won a faint smile. "But General Neville gets no marks for giving you that gun. Far too dangerous."

"Oh, but he didn't," she said innocently. "I stole it from him. He'll be furious."

She stared at him hazily, wondering why she was on the verge of telling this stranger what she could not possibly have told the General. Besides, the thin sardonic face with the humorous mouth could scarcely have been more unlike Tony Rothman's blond good looks. Her heart seemed to twist painfully at that thought.

Forsyth saw that it was going to take too long. He did not have the time for a delicate probing of her intentions and purposes. She could be an awkward stumbling block, who might foul up the whole operation. He set himself out to get rid of her as diplomatically as possible. This was one time when Neville might approve of his knowledge of women. He called on all his reserves of charm.

Leaning across the table, very gently he removed her sunglasses. She blinked, and returned his gaze steadily, but the wary look was back in her eyes.

She thought suddenly, *He's very attractive and he knows it*. She hardened her heart. This new kindness and his friendship with the General simply was not enough. Nothing he said was going to make any difference.

"I'm going to make you a promise, Miss Beaufort, and your father will tell you that I always keep my word. I'll have Tony Rothman back in London by the middle of next week."

She simply stared at him.

He plowed on, wondering bitterly what had become of that famous ability to bowl women over. The fact that it was not working with a twenty-year-old humiliated him.

"Will you do something for me? Will you tell me how much you know about your father's job? That doesn't commit you to anything."

She considered for a moment. "I don't know very much. He made it clear that his work was highly confidential and he trusted me not to pry. I haven't pried, but you can't live close to somebody and not learn a good deal—even if you don't know that you are learning it, if you know what I mean. We live in the country but the General has a flat somewhere in London. Even Mummy doesn't know where. His work keeps him there a lot. He told us that only two of his colleagues know where it is—the only two he can really trust."

Did he, bigod? Forsyth thought, strangely happy about the compliment. "Did you ever meet any of his colleagues?"

"No . . . well, only one . . . Tony Rothman." Before his eyes, her face seemed to change, the young curves of the cheeks sharpening and the mouth hardening.

Forsyth decided that he did not like the change and felt less guilty about his halfhearted enthusiasm for the blond giant whose fists had more than once made his ears ring. He squashed the impulse to say irritably, *All right! Don't look so tragic. I'll get lover-boy back for you.*

"I overheard a telephone call about Tony." She looked very directly at Forsyth. "This is a personal matter . . . nothing to do with Father or you. For you are looking for

Tony . . . aren't you? You were before you talked to me."

"Yes. That's why you should go home and wait. I'll get him back to you."

Her mouth twisted suddenly and he thought she was going to weep, but she simply said with great finality, "No. This is something I have to do. You can't make me change my mind. I know it is dangerous, but I can look after myself." She even managed a watery smile. "Don't be afraid that I'll go all feminine on you and mess up your plans. I won't. I'm twenty-two and, since I was seventeen, I've managed not to let the General guess how much I know about his work. I'm not exactly a fool."

I'll bet you are not! he thought respectfully. Obviously there was a little more to her than her spectacular looks. Somewhere under the immaturity, he was convinced, there was sparkle and brilliance. His own prosaic outlook on life made him wonder how he could exploit it. Everything, his creed told him, was there to be used. If you can't beat them, join them was still a good maxim. He came to a decision.

"Look here, Miss Beaufort, I suggest we pool our resources. We both want the same thing, for different reasons. I have to warn you that, if our interests clash, you don't stand a chance with me. Because it is my job, I have to be quite ruthless. The fact that you are General Neville's daughter can't mean a thing to me. If you can help me, I'll use you. If you can't, I'll get rid of you. It's as simple as that. I would not be honest if I pretended otherwise. I'll expect you to tell me anything that may be useful. In return, I'll tell you what I think you should know. No more than that. I have a job to do. I'm not running a Lonely Hearts Club." He heard the brutality in his voice and hoped that he had not overdone the shock treatment.

The big amber eyes became bigger and even more

deeply amber. She leaned across the table, the eyes sparkling like a young girl's at a play. "You're not so tough," she said softly. "It's almost eleven o'clock. When do we start? Shouldn't you begin by telling me your name?"

It was practically eleven o'clock before Rothman wakened. He had a clear head and a vague feeling that he was better. Better from what?

Dr. Lupescu had injected him the night before, explaining in his precise fashion that he was giving him a sedative. Rothman had believed him. He had believed him also when Lupescu went on, "During the night, do not be alarmed if you feel me giving you another injection. With luck, you will not waken in the midst of it, but, if you do, try to remember that there is nothing sinister about it. It will be merely an analgesic, so that the pain from your feet may not keep you awake. By tomorrow, they will cease to be a problem."

He felt like laughing in his face. What did they hope to achieve by this wrap-him-in-cotton-wool attitude? Surely they realized that by giving him recovery time, they were increasing hourly his chances of escape? That suited him, but why it should suit them puzzled him. He decided to enjoy his false role of invalid, as he enjoyed the breakfast of shirred eggs, toast and coffee. It was, he decided cynically, almost as good as a first-class hotel and considerably cheaper.

Yet it was curious, he reflected later, that he could endure—and had endured—many days in the stark misery of a dark, cold cellar without worrying too much about the passage of time. Now, in this padded comfort, he was plagued by boredom. He was sick of that damned dove.

That feeling vanished abruptly.

The bedroom door opened.

The previous evening and again that morning, Dr. Lu-

pescu had abandoned his surgeon's outfit. Now he was
dressed in it as he entered the room, closely followed by
Fossard, who was pushing a medical cart. On it, Rothman
could see a steaming steel bowl, several pairs of scissors, an
aerosol tin and what looked like a pair of clippers. As the
cart was wheeled close to the bed, he saw that on the ledge
below were a couple of bath towels. In spite of himself, his
pulse quickened.

"I am a busy man, Mr. Rothman. I do not propose to
waste time arguing with you or in entering into explana-
tions. I intend to shave your head. Protests or struggles will
be quite unavailing, so I advise you to cooperate. You will
appreciate that, without your cooperation, it can and will
be done."

Rothman was a vain man. There was nothing the matter
with his nerves but the thought of a plucked-chicken head
in place of the luxuriant fair hair enraged him.

He roared like a maddened bull, straining at the dog
collars on his ankles. The foot of the bed shook. The look
of alarm that crossed Lupescu's face puzzled him. The
whole damn business puzzled him. Why did Lupescu no
longer bother to conceal his identity? Were they planning
to electrocute him? Whatever the hell it was, he was not
going to submit tamely.

He did not feel Fossard administering the prick on the
back of his hand.

"Let's talk about you, Nicola. For a young woman, you
are remarkably resourceful. That can be useful. To arrange
your trip to Rumania at such short notice is no mean feat.
To steal such a special gun from someone as experienced
as your father could earn you a place on his professional
books. By the way, do you know exactly what that gun
does?"

"Of course. I also took his supply of antidotes."

"Hmm! On the debit side—the gun gave you away. As soon as I verified that it belonged to General Neville, you were known. Careless!"

"I'll grant that one." Her voice sounded very feminine and uncertain. Her smile was melting, the eyes luminous. She was probing for some weakness in him.

"You'll disappoint me if you say that you simply headed for Rumania. After all, it's a fairly large country. You must have had some plan?"

She replaced the sunglasses, but he saw the sweep of warm color flooding neck and face. "I eavesdropped. The General told Mr. Brett that Tony was last seen in the bookshop in the main street here. I went into the Aquarium to work out what I would say in the bookshop."

He shook his head in exasperation. "What could the perfectly respectable manager tell you other than that an Englishman was taken suddenly ill, but fortunately was helped to a doctor by two obliging gentlemen? Come on! Our inquiries start somewhere else. We are going to number 12 Strada Elena Pavel."

He noted with approval that her long legs kept pace with his as they walked back toward the square. They passed the mixture of modern villas and Oriental houses, festooned with lacy, wrought-iron balconies. She asked no questions as they turned into the starkly modern building which housed the Dobruga Regional Museum.

When he had bought their entrance tickets, he said to the attendant, "I would like to see the Directrice. Can it be arranged?"

Minutes later, they were seated opposite Madame Florica Malineanu, who greeted Forsyth like an old friend, but whose quick eyes seemed to take in every detail of Nicola Beaufort's appearance in several unobtrusive glances.

"Ah! you are back to have another look at Grigorescu's work?"

"Not this time, madame. I was told that you have a fine study of Saint Jude. I must have missed that."

She shook her head regretfully. "I am afraid you are mistaken, Mr. East. We have nothing of Saint Jude." She spread her hands. "I do not like to boast, but I know the treasures of my country very well. You will not find it in Bucharest—not anywhere in Rumania. I am convinced of that. An unimportant painting or statue of that saint in some village church . . . that is a different matter. That I would not know."

"Thank you. You have saved me some trouble. Obviously I have been misinformed. My friend must have meant exactly what you say—a church painting or statue." He rolled his eyes comically. "But where do I begin to look?"

She studied him thoughtfully. "In Rumania, there are 181 towns, 4,290 communes and 15,133 villages. It would take a very long time to find the church you want. So—we must think. Isn't this Saint Jude a saint of the Roman Catholic Church?"

"Yes. He's the patron saint of hopeless cases. Just the lad for me."

She accepted the pleasantry with her warm smile. "Roman—that helps. The churches with anything worth preserving I know about. There are not many Roman Catholic village churches now. I would expect to find them in Transylvania—in that direction."

Forsyth waited. Nicola Beaufort watched them both curiously, feeling gauche and ill at ease.

"The telephone is a great convenience, Mr. East. My staff has increased since you were here last and I would like to help you. It is like a puzzle, is it not? Where are you staying?"

"The Hotel Modern."

"Tonight at seven o'clock I will telephone you. What is

your room number? Do not leave without showing your friend Grigorescu's *Profil de Fata*." She smiled charmingly. "Forgive me, madame, if I am too personal. You have that gentle, dovelike expression that the great painter caught so well."

Dovelike! Forsyth thought and rubbed his wrist.

In the street, as they were passing the old mosque, the girl said suddenly, "Your name isn't really East, is it?"

"My passport says that I am John East and you had better not forget that." He hesitated, some obscure instinct making him hesitate to begin their relationship under a false name. "When you grow up to be a big girl, you'll get to call me Charles Forsyth."

"Yes, Charles," she said meekly. "And now what?"

"Now we enjoy ourselves. First of all, I try to get you a seat on the plane to Bucharest. We leave tomorrow. If I fail, you travel by train or fly the next day. You will stay in the Inter-Continental."

"And you?"

"Don't ask questions. Next, I hire a car and take you for a drive along the coast. If you don't behave, I can always push you into Bulgaria." Her smile acknowledged the thaw in the atmosphere.

Afterward, they were to remember that drive with a kind of wonder. He was surprised at the pleasure it gave him to tell her about the area and to steal a look at her intent expression as she listened.

He found himself saying abruptly, "Give up that perfume. I'll buy you Diorama."

She smiled a small, wise smile at that and looked pleased.

He pointed out the Dobrujan steppe, aptly called the Golden Gulf. They passed groups of young girls working in the fields, their heads and faces protected against the fierce sun by white yashmaks stretched across their mouths and pinned tautly at the backs of their heads.

Close to Eforie, an incongruous note in the peaceful, dreaming landscape drew a gasp of pity from her. Squads of prisoners were working steadily under the cold gaze of guards carrying submachine guns. But she obviously delighted in the perfume that pervaded the countryside and in the swift, crimson flash of pantiled roofs, glimpsed through the haze of early afternoon in the heat-soaked land.

The coast rose steeply, so that they looked down from flower-encrusted promenades and stark white terraces to swirling, milky-jade seas and bone-white sands.

They lunched under the glancing shadows of the trees in a restaurant at Mangalia, which Forsyth assured the girl was the loveliest resort on the coast. They were so high above the beaches that the crowds seemed like performers in an ancient silent movie. From above, the harbor was serenely lovely—a protective, encircling white arm, enclosing a sapphire pool, but nosing silently across the water like a thin, gray bullet was a man-of-war.

Forsyth saw her shiver and said quickly, "Let's go back to Mamaia. After all, the next stop is in Bulgaria."

Before they left, he showed her the old Esmanah Sultan Mosque, and as they stepped back into the sunlight, he said abruptly, "I don't know much about any religion, but I believe Moslems keep the same wife through all eternity. When I meet the girl that I want forever, I'll know it's time to get married."

"That's a pretty severe test for any girl," she said quietly. "I hope she feels the same about you."

He left her at her hotel, the Doina. "Get a good rest," he advised. "Maybe we will have plenty to do in Bucharest. I hope so. I'll phone before I call for you tomorrow. I'll take charge of the gun."

"No. This may be a partnership. It certainly is not a master/slave agreement. I do my own thinking."

He watched until she had pushed the heavy glass doors and gone inside.

It was almost seven o'clock when he reached his room. Promptly on the hour the telephone rang.

As he listened, the lines in his face softened. He said warmly, "Do you wonder that I always come back to see you, Madame Malineanu? You are my favorite Rumanian. Sinaia is always worth another visit. Is the Palas Hotel as magnificent as ever? Good! My warmest thanks for your helpfulness and perseverance."

He went downstairs and out through the back of the hotel to the path leading to the lake. It was a night without stars, but he walked with a sure step to the wooden pier. The anglers had long since gone. He could barely make out the small boats tossing like sabots on the smooth blackness of the lake. But the feel of the wood, creaking gently under his feet, and the chuckling, sucking noises of the water swirling round the poles, calmed him.

Another man would have drunk a large whisky to mark the moment when he learned where the Crown of Hungary lay hidden. For Forsyth it was enough to stand quietly in the darkness, listening to the small secret noises of the fish rising for a late fly and to consider again the new rod that he had looked at in Hardy's.

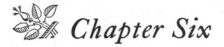

Chapter Six

THEY had lunch together in the Inter-Continental Bucaresti within an hour of their arrival in Bucharest. Forsyth liked the fastidious way she ate and watched the graceful movements of her hands with frowning attention.

When she raised her eyes inquiringly to him, he smiled. "It looks as though you would agree with what Maeterlinck maintains in *The Blue Bird*, that even bread and milk have a soul. You're poking at that *sarmale* as if it were alive. Eat up!"

She put her fork down. "I can't." She colored faintly. "I suppose I'm feeling guilty about sitting here, calmly eating lunch when Tony Rothman could be in terrible trouble."

"We can't help him by going hungry," Forsyth said practically.

"No-o-o. But I feel we should be doing something."

"What, for example?" He sipped his beer and tried not to show his irritation. No wonder Neville hated to use female operators. He was only slightly propitiated by her confusion. Neville had been right. She *was* a damned attractive girl, but she was also a nuisance. For a moment, he played with the idea of concocting some scheme that would take her out of harm's way, to the other end of the country. What Neville had said to her on the telephone would determine his course of action.

As if she had read his thoughts, she said hesitantly, "I've no intention of haring off to the Danube Delta or to some place like Arad. I'm not foolish enough to think that we are simply going to stumble across Tony. I know there has to be planning but . . ." She looked at him despairingly. "I simply don't know where we can begin."

"I do. We begin by getting you some new perfume. Finish your lunch and we'll take a stroll along the Bulevard Magheru. Our work doesn't start until this evening. For this afternoon, you have a choice—either the Cismigiu Gardens or we can take a taxi to Soseaua Kiseleff to what's called the Village Museum. It's a collection of folk architecture and folk art in the Baneasa Forest. Buildings have been dismantled in the villages of their origin and reerected to form genuine little villages with grass, lawns, flowers, trees, paths and lanes—the lot, exactly as they were in various parts of the country."

Her face lit up. "I'd like that."

"Besides," he added, "we can talk there, without having to keep looking over our shoulders."

He would tell her just enough to keep her quiet. No more than that. What had brought Rothman to Rumania was not her concern.

"What did your father say?"

Her eyes flickered. "Oh, he didn't tell me anything about Tony. He never does. Besides, he knows I have my own affairs to think about. We have a strict understanding—"

He interrupted the flow of words. "Never mind that." His voice was ominously quiet. "I'm referring to the phone call. You didn't make it, did you?" He waited, but she said nothing. "Let's go!"

She preceded him, like a child heading for punishment.

While they waited in her bedroom for the call to come through, he sat on the edge of her bed and examined her coldly. She was sitting very upright on a straight-backed chair beside the door. A shake of her head had sent the glowing hair tumbling about her face, half-concealing her expression. He remembered that, as they waited for the lift, she had gone very white and had put a hand to her mouth as if she feared that she was going to be sick. Now the pallor had quite gone. Her cheeks were burning and her eyes glittered as if she had a fever.

The phone rang sharply. There was a long silence in the Eton Avenue house while he explained the position.

"Send her home? Right. Do you want to talk to her?"

He replaced the receiver decisively and turned toward her.

His eyes widened with shock. Before her hand had reached the bottom of her handbag, he had launched himself across the narrow space between them. The chair tilted and went over. She gasped as his weight crashed down on her. Thrashing like an eel, somehow she wriggled free, scrabbling frantically toward the bag which had slid almost under the bed. Her skirts were round her waist, so that Forsyth had a view of curving hips and long, silk-covered legs. He opened a clenched fist and brought the open palm down with three tremendous slaps on the swell of her buttocks. As she screamed, he strained across her to reach the bag.

One hand tossed it onto the bed. With the other, he grasped her shoulder and pushed her around roughly to face him.

Her eyes had the insane glare of shock and hatred.

"I promised you that," he gritted. "Move just one finger and you'll not sit down for a week. You fool! What did you think you would gain by killing me? Do you think the chambermaid would have thrown the body out with the garbage and the Rumanian police would have let you wander about the country as if nothing had happened? You *fool!*"

He realized that his anger had a large element of fear in it, fear for her. The thiosulphate might not have worked.

She jerked away from him and was quietly sick.

Forsyth had rarely felt more at a loss. Compassion and anger struggled for supremacy. There was no rational explanation for her behavior. Nothing he had done, or omitted to do, could possibly have warranted her murderous attack. Surely the prospect of being sent home by him couldn't have triggered it off? Why, it was like the unpredictable behavior of a drug addict! His anger grew.

He went into the bathroom and brought back a towel and a soaking washcloth. The convulsive shuddering had stopped, but she lay, pressed against the carpet, as if she were dead.

She wouldn't be killing anybody for a long time, he reflected grimly.

Her shoes had fallen off in the struggle. He gathered them up and put them tidily under the curve of the dressing table. He hung her handbag on the handle of the door.

When he lifted her and laid her on the bed, she offered no resistance, but lay with her eyes closed and her lips pressed tightly together to suppress their trembling. In silence, he wiped and dried her face. When his hands went to the waistband of her skirt, she jerked convulsively and then was still. He slid the crushed garment over her knees, tossed it on a chair, then pulled the coverlet up to her chin.

"In a minute," he said quietly, "I'll get the chambermaid in to clear up here and to attend to you. Before I do, I've something to say. I've been trained to kill—to react practically instinctively to a dangerous move. You are very lucky that I didn't kill you just now. You deserved it, and believe me, I wouldn't have spent a sleepless night over it."

She lay as if carved in stone.

He went on inexorably. "It wasn't a sudden, uncontrollable impulse. You planned it before we even reached the elevator. That was when you took the first antidote for the cyanide. You play rough games, Nicola, but you are way out of your class. This isn't gentlemen versus the ladies, with the gentlemen gallantly conceding the game. There are no gentlemen in espionage—just cruel, cunning bastards who fight for keeps. Go home and wait for lover-boy. I promised I'd get him for you."

He hesitated, then rang for the maid.

Before he let himself out of the room, he took the tiny gun and the two vials of tablets, then hung her bag back on the door handle. There was no sound from the bed.

The smell of croissants and of freshly ground coffee triumphed over the heavy fumes of their cigarettes. It was almost lunch time, but the two Russians knew that they could afford to indulge themselves.

Following Madame Lupescu's call from Sinaia the night before, they had relaxed; had slept late; had told each other once again the latest scandals in Moscow; and now they were doing what they were very good at—simply waiting for the next couple of days to pass. They would move quickly enough when the Rumanian Jew gave the word. The car was ready, as always. Their permits for the hotel in Cimpina had likewise been arranged, but they did not expect to occupy the beds there.

Meanwhile, they were less conspicuous in Bucharest than they would have been in the vicinity of Doftana. All they had to do was to obey orders and everything would slot neatly into place. KGB operations always did.

Rothman's condition was a complication, but the USSR had the best medical services in the world. He would be flown to Moscow as planned. That was not something new or unexpected. He would certainly be given as much care as the crown would get on its trip to Britain. It was, both men felt, a pity that the two pawns in the game had to travel in opposite directions.

It was a matter of pride and genuine enjoyment to the two Russians that their superiors had devised such a simple, but effective scheme. When the crown had been safely planted in London and Rothman was reluctantly admitting in Moscow Britain's shameful involvement in the plot to restore the Hungarian monarchy, the whole world would see how hollow had been Britain's enthusiasm for the peace conference. Churchill's boast that England was good at games, especially cheating, was outdated.

Only one thought troubled the senior Russian in the room. Rothman was still the only one who knew the exact location of the crown. Getting the information from him would be a matter of minutes, once they got him away from the SMR, but there would not be a great deal of time to lose after that. After all, it could be anywhere in Rumania.

The parents of the younger man, Sergio Eliasberg, had been born in Riga. He had been fortunate to be accepted by the KGB, so he always felt that he had to convince his superiors of his zeal.

Now he drained his coffee and said anxiously, "What if Rothman decides to hang on to the crown for himself? After all, it is priceless."

His senior, Yuri Danilenko, did not trouble to turn away from the window. "He's threatened with an aneurism, not softening of the brain. He'll talk all right once we get him out of Doftana. *And* he'll sign the statement immediately —insurance, just in case he doesn't survive the journey. Everything's covered."

He yawned widely, pounded with his fists on the great barrel of his chest and wondered, irrelevantly, if his wife, Lora, and he would ever be awarded a holiday in Mangalia. He took out a toothpick and probed delicately at his perfect teeth.

"I like Rumania," he said suddenly. "I won't mind if we are sent back here again. Lora would like Bucharest, especially the shops." He began to button his jacket. "I think I'll get a breath of fresh air and buy my wife a present."

He laughed throatily. "Nothing much, or she will think that all our jobs outside the country are holidays." His voice hardened, so that Eliasberg stiffened automatically. "Don't leave the phone. I'll be back in a little over an hour. Then you can stretch your legs."

He paused in the entrance to the Ambassador Hotel to enjoy the warmth of the sun. Compared with Moscow, the place was nothing. He thought with nostalgia of the gilded onion domes of the Kremlin and the windy spaciousness of Red Square. It would be good to go home. Perhaps in three days . . .

Still, Bucharest had a dignity and some of the shops were good. On the previous day, the quick brown eyes had noticed one shop with the word *Cadouri* (Gifts) above the display window. He had to go only a few paces to get what he wanted, but there was no immediate hurry. Lora's present could wait until he was on his way back to the hotel.

Danilenko was a greedy man. By now, the croissants were no more than a pleasant memory. He hesitated, looking uncertainly along the street, wondering whether to go to a brasserie or to a restaurant. He had pleasant memories of the Athenée Palace Hotel, where he and Sergio had dined the night before. Rumanian food was not bad. He lengthened his stride and walked purposefully in the direction of the Strada Episcopiei.

When Forsyth left the Inter-Continental, he was so angry that he had to stand for a moment on the edge of the pavement to calm himself and consider what he wanted to do. After a minute, he strode into a men's clothing shop and bought a pair of bathing trunks, then went quickly to the Lido Hotel.

In his bedroom, he considered putting through a call to Neville, but decided against it. *Hell!* he told himself, *I'm not a nursemaid. As far as I'm concerned, I'm finished with Nicola Beaufort.*

He got into the briefs and a dressing gown and took the elevator down to the ground floor. People were already drinking tea in the lounge, as he went to the back of the hotel and out into the blinding sunshine of the garden. There was nobody in the water and he stood watching with pleasure the rush and curving symmetry of the artificial waves. Under his feet, the stone edge of the pool burned. The shade of the beech trees did not reach the pool.

Tension drained away as he dived again and again. He swam until the muscles in back and shoulders ached in protest. Time ceased to matter. He was floating on his back, half blinded by the spray of the waves when he was conscious of a shadow falling across his face. He opened his eyes and peered at a figure, aureoled in light.

Nicola Beaufort looked gravely down at him. She was stunningly beautiful. Only the bluish shadows under her eyes gave any hint that she had not spent the last hour in a beauty parlor. Analytically, his gaze took in the shining perfection of hair and skin. Either she had as much sensitivity as an armadillo, or she possessed impressive recovery power.

When she saw that his eyes were open, she smiled mischievously. She was dressed in a clinging white frock and held over her head a frilly white-lace parasol lined with pink chiffon. It cast a rosy glow over her features.

She ignored Forsyth's icy glare, twirled the parasol provocatively and said gaily, "Isn't it lovely? I found it in the wardrobe in my room. Somebody must be feeling shattered about leaving it. I've borrowed it."

"It looks stupid." He gave her a contemptuous look. "Get lost!" he said raspingly and jacknifed. He swam underwater and surfaced at the far end of the pool.

He had been wasting his sympathy, he decided, in imagining that she had been either ill or suffering a flashback from drugs. Probably she was simply a spoiled, neurotic young woman. He hardened his heart.

As he hung by his hands from the coping, her voice came clearly across the water. It could have been heard at the farthest end of the garden. "If you want me to shout, I am perfectly willing to do so, but I imagine you would prefer our talk to be private."

Two elderly ladies lowered themselves gingerly into the shallow end of the pool. They looked up, startled by her shout.

He climbed out of the water, picked up his dressing gown and went toward her.

He said evenly, "If you'll wait in the lounge, I'll join you in twenty minutes."

He deliberately kept her waiting while he showered and dressed. His dislike of her was like bile in his throat, but he reminded himself that all that really mattered was that she should not endanger the operation. He should have stopped her in Mamaia. It was not too late. Neville could go to hell.

He could not make himself smile as he went forward to join her in the lounge, but she ignored his grim face and chattered brightly about the hotel and particularly about the pool. Whatever she meant to say, he had no intention of making it easy for her.

When the tables in their immediate vicinity had emptied, she leaned forward and said almost pleadingly, "You are making it very difficult for me. Can't you try to understand? I've been almost out of my mind, for days . . . maybe you think I'm still out of my mind." She drew a deep, painful breath. "I'm sorry, really and truly sorry and deeply ashamed. I'm not going to ask you to forgive me. What I tried to do was unforgivable—"

He got to his feet. "We'll do without the histrionics. You would be good in vaudeville, but I'm not in the comic business this week. Good-bye, Miss Beaufort. I won't cry if we don't meet again."

"Wait!" She clutched at his leg as he moved past.

"Please, wait! If you won't listen to me and help me, I swear I'll go to the international press." He turned and looked down at her. "What you don't seem to accept is that I am determined to get to Tony Rothman. Whether I do it secretly with you or very publicly with a pack of journalists is a matter of indifference to me, but do it I will." She did not flinch from his flamethrower look. He went back to his seat. "I know what you are thinking, but before I left the Inter-Continental, I posted a letter to my lawyer. Maybe you wouldn't care if you were accused of my murder, but I suspect that you wouldn't want my father's name dragged in. It would finish you both with the Department."

"Your father seems to have trained you in more than karate. Cut the speechifying. What do you want from me?"

She hesitated.

He cut in savagely, "Shouldn't I be writing to my lawyer? Shouldn't I warn him that, before he buries the body, he should have it examined for a stab in the back?"

She blushed at that. "I suppose I deserve that. I give you my word now, on all that I hold sacred, that I will cooperate fully and honestly with you. I'll try to help, not to hinder. All I ask is that you let me go with you. I feel that you are the one who is going to find him."

He studied the lovely, flushed face. She might have been asking for a child's treat, but nothing about the pleading amber eyes or the tremulous, hopeful mouth moved him. It would be a bad risk to have her running loose in Rumania; a worse one to have her inviting the glare of publicity when so many delicate political and economic issues hung in the balance. Short of sleeping with her, he decided, he was prepared to do almost anything to keep her quiet, but when the exercise was over . . .

She shivered under the bleak look, but forced her lips to smile. "It's a bargain, then?"

"It's a bargain." He got abruptly to his feet. "I'll take you back to the Inter-Continental now and call for you at seven o'clock. We'll dine in the forest at Baneasa."

She went out, preceded by a cloud of Joy.

As they stood on the edge of the pavement, he said flatly, "Your perfume is beautiful, but it has associations for me. I would like you to change it. If we must be together, we might as well make the association as pleasant as possible."

Danilenko turned smartly into the gift shop and took his place quietly behind the good-looking couple at the counter. He ran a practiced eye appreciatively over the girl's slim figure. Quite ravishing, he decided . . . like a painting he had seen once in The Hermitage in Leningrad. A little on the thin side and, with those hips, producing children would not be easy. Too soft for his tastes . . .

The man's broad back obscured the objects on the counter. The cloth was English, faultlessly cut, but the style was decadent. Besides, the fellow was a hooligan—*ni-cultury*—he had pushed a bottle of perfume into the girl's hand without as much as a word.

Danilenko felt sorry for the tall young woman. For a moment, her lips had trembled, but she had smiled at the oaf brilliantly and said "Thank you" in a clear, well-bred voice.

When the man turned away abruptly from the counter, the Russian planted his stocky legs more firmly on the floor and remained motionless. There was a momentary hard impact of iron flesh meeting iron flesh. The Englishman muttered an apology and for a second their eyes met.

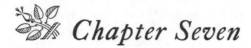 *Chapter Seven*

THERE was a soft wind blowing gently through the beech leaves, rustling them like a sibilant whisper repeated over and over again. Forsyth felt the uneasy stirrings of fear that all spies feel in an alien land. It was never the direct confrontation that gripped the gut or sent anxious tremors through the bowel. The gaze of a policeman that lingered the few seconds too long; the inquisitive look of an anonymous man on some street corner; the quick rattle of a foreign tongue falling uncomprehendingly on the ear—these could sometimes set up the waves of anxiety that might swell to a dangerous panic. But the true corroding fear came at unexpected moments from the strangeness of the country's sights, sounds and smells, as if the land itself rejected and threatened the intruder.

He stood in the deepening blue of the dusk and looked toward the old, secluded entrance to the Model Village, frowning as he considered the possibility that he had guessed wrongly. This time his formula of mentally putting himself into the shoes of the other man and working out what he would have done in similar circumstances did not seem to be working. The place had a deserted look. The layout resembled roughly the map of Rumania. They could be anywhere in it.

He got back into the car and drove slowly past the entrance. The road curved and narrowed as if the forest were trying to reclaim it, and the overhanging branches cast such deep shadows that he almost missed the two cars parked side by side under the beeches. He accelerated, although he was positive that no one was in the cars. The men had to be somewhere in the grounds.

It was almost closing time, so they would have to come out very soon. If it transpired that the cars belonged to lovers, meeting clandestinely, he would feel a fool.

He turned the car, sweating slightly as he swung the stiff lock around hard again and again on the narrow road. If he had guessed wrongly and they drove away from Bucharest, he had no hope of following them.

He waited patiently, looking at the tangle of growth beneath the fence that marked the boundary of the grounds of the Village. Between him and the cars was a clump, thick enough and high enough to conceal a man. He moved like a shadow toward it.

He had been lying in the bracken for almost ten minutes according to the luminous dial of his watch when two figures came strolling toward the parked vehicles.

Forsyth breathed quietly through his mouth and strained his ears to catch the harsh flow of Bonneaud's French. The other man was not known to him.

Bonneaud's beaky profile was raised toward the taller man. His hands wove placatory patterns in the air. "My dear Fossard," he said, "who blames you? I have no fears at all. Nothing is altered. All I must decide is when we move him."

"Do you mean that you do not intend to wait until Lupescu gives Rothman the all-clear?"

Bonneaud spat expertly into the bracken. "Lupescu! That quack! He's good enough for filling a syringe, but not much more. I'll wait two days—no more than that." Bonneaud's voice took on an ominous edge. "Fossard!"

"Yes?"

"Something makes me uneasy about Lupescu. I have a feeling . . ."

"No," Fossard protested. "Surely you are wrong. He has been a member of the Society for at least five years. I know his work. I'll swear he is reliable. He is a true communist. I would stake my life on it. With a French wife, his ties with France are strong."

"Maybe . . . maybe. But there is no harm in keeping an eye on him. I wish it were possible to have a second medical opinion, but it would take too long to get a man here. If I thought that his diagnosis was misleading . . ."

Forsyth could picture Bonneaud's face from the ugliness of his tone. If the Rumanian doctor had been less than frank with the Frenchman, even his worst enemy would pity him.

Forsyth pigeonholed the conversation for later consideration. At the moment, he could make little of it. Had the smr injured Rothman so badly that he was dying and now they were trying to keep him alive? One point was clear: Rothman had not yet talked. But if he were as badly injured as the conversation seemed to suggest, how much longer would he hold his tongue?

The two men had lowered their voices, so that Forsyth had to strain to hear. Only snatches of their conversation came to him.

"I'll get back to the villa now . . . phone call to Lupescu . . ."

". . . best I go straight to the restaurant and pay the men . . ."

"Good, Fossard! I'll join you in . . . say, about an hour and a half at Baneasa . . ."

Forsyth pressed farther into the ground as the headlights raked the edge of the grass.

If Bonneaud left first, it would be hard luck.

He waited for the revving of the second engine and the rasp of tires on the road before he moved, keeping as low to the ground as he could. At that deserted spot, it was unlikely that the driver would look in the mirror, but habit might prevail.

Following the car was, after all, a simple matter. Because of the twists and turns in the road, he could keep at a comfortable distance, yet through the trees see the lancing spears of the headlights.

When they passed the road to the forest restaurant, he knew that it was Bonneaud who was in the car immediately ahead.

He felt an anticipatory tingle at the prospect of an encounter with his former adversary. Something primitive in him stirred, so that his hands tightened involuntarily on the wheel. While he watched the road and judged distances and speculated, a deeper layer of consciousness was defending his right to destroy a man who was without morals or scruples.

Yet, because he was an honest man, Forsyth recognized that, even without the spur of the danger to world peace, to Tony Rothman and to an ancient, holy relic, he would still have gone stalking Bonneaud as he was now doing. The personal element outweighed all the others. In this, he was guilty of a cardinal offense against the outfit.

The lights of Bucharest were coming up fast. Bonneaud, he reckoned, would have to leave the main road soon.

Almost at once, the Frenchman turned sharply to the right, swinging into a narrow unlit sideroad.

The crowding trees reminded Forsyth of his arrangement with Nicola Beaufort. A quick glance at the dashboard told him that already she had been waiting for almost an hour. Let the bitch wait! he thought savagely, his anger against her reviving.

He braked sharply and swung the car well over to the left where there was a narrow inshot. Belatedly, memory told him that there had been two white posts, crowned with stone pineapples, at the entrance to what he had mistaken for a side road. He was on a private road, leading to a house. In moments, he would probably have come out at the front door. Silently, he cursed his carelessness. He might as well have handed Bonneaud his visiting card.

Carefully, he considered the car's position. Anyone driving in from the main road would see it at once, but it would be invisible to anyone coming from the house. A cautious survey of the road ahead convinced him that he had no choice.

Methodically, he loosened his jacket and checked his gun. He pushed the tiny, leather-covered cosh on the strong elastic band well above his right wrist. The head was smaller than a billiard ball, but one quick jerk would bring the specially loaded weapon immediately into play. He would, he decided, hate to use it on Bonneaud. When he caught up with him, he wanted the sod to know what was happening to him.

Mechanically, he patted the side pockets of his jacket and froze. Nicola Beaufort's gun had gone.

In a moment of lucid comprehension, he recalled the incident in the gift shop when, fractionally, he, Nicola and a tough-looking customer had collided. It had happened then, but which of them had taken it? The man or the girl?

It was foolish to waste time now on anger or surmise. Quietly, he emptied his pockets of loose change and put the coins on the ledge under the dashboard. He was ready.

The trees stopped abruptly at the edge of a wide lawn fronting the house. The road widened and swung to the right in a long graceful arc that ended a little beyond the left wing of the building in what appeared to be a motor yard paved with stone.

Bonneaud's car was standing at the entrance to an impressive white frame building. Yet the house was impressive solely because of its size and because of the wedding-cake decorations around and between the numerous dormer windows. The original block was three stories high and towered above the two-story wings that, at some later date, had been clumsily added to each side. It lacked the grace of the flowery terraces that were characteristic of Rumanian houses. It looked functional, ugly and deserted.

Forsyth was so intent on taking in every detail before darkness blotted the house out completely that he almost failed to notice the cattle grid at the end of the tree-lined road. He halted abruptly. His eyes followed the curving line of white-painted posts along one side of the drive. Presently he spotted where the thin cable emerged from the grid to thread the posts like a dark streak just clear of the ground.

The pressure of a foot on the grid would have rung an alarmbell in the house. He decided that he would be wise not to underrate Bonneaud's precautions. Recently, he told himself grimly, there had been just too many examples of carelessness on his part.

The grid, he calculated, was almost six and a half feet wide. Fleetingly he regretted the indulgence of the last three months. He stripped off his jacket, rolled it into a bundle and tossed it to the opposite side of the grid.

His shoes followed. Because of the curve in the road, he could not get a good run at the jump, but he filled his lungs with air, ran as hard as he could in his stocking feet on the loamy ground and took off. He landed on top of one of his shoes and cursed briefly, knowing that his carelessness might have cost him a twisted ankle.

Since I met that girl, he told himself furiously, *I've been behaving like a rank amateur. She's jinx material.*

He surveyed the innocent stretch of lawn. There was no cover, so there was nothing for it but to go boldly forward. He crouched and zigzagged, hoping that, if spotted, in the half-light, he might be taken for a large dog enjoying a gambol.

Once on the paved section, he drifted silently toward a

ground-floor window where a single chink of light threaded the gloom. He could make out part of Bonneaud's figure, seated at what was presumably a desk.

Suddenly, the Frenchman turned his head and bellowed at someone out of sight, "Haven't you got that number yet? Don't take all night."

"No, Monsieur Bonneaud. There is no answer at the moment. I will keep trying on the hall phone, so that the ringing does not disturb you."

It was a cheerful, comfortable voice with no trace of obsequiousness. A servant-cum-colleague, Forsyth conjectured, wishing he could get a look at him.

He studied the blank windows and wondered if Rothman was in one of the rooms.

Well, he told himself philosophically, there is only one way to find out.

He moved quietly along the front of the house, but each window was closely curtained. Someone was obviously very security conscious.

Forsyth skirted the side of the house and found himself in a patio dotted with tubs of flowers and white-painted garden furniture. Before he could stop himself his hand touched the arm of a long, canopied seat and set it rocking gently. To his relief, there was no telltale creaking, but he did not trust himself to touch it again to stop the movement.

He pressed close against the wall where curtained French windows led on to the patio. The sound of a car starting up brought his head up alertly.

Dammit! he thought, *That's probably Bonneaud leaving to meet the man Fossard.*

He hesitated, wondering whether to follow at once or to search the house for Rothman.

It was all very well to be smart, but an operator needed some point of reference. He might as well stick a pin in the map of Rumania and start looking for his colleague wherever the pin came down. So far, all he had was the name of a doctor and Bonneaud's occupancy of this house.

He decided to investigate the house.

As he was on the point of moving, one side of the French doors opened and a cat stepped delicately onto the patio.

Out of the darkness, the cheerful voice said, "Ten minutes only, Tommy! Then I close this door and you are out for the night."

There was the heavy sound of receding footsteps.

The cat purred and wove sinuously between Forsyth's legs. "Don't forget your watch, Tommy!" he admonished it silently. It disappeared into the darkness.

Either the man was an idiot or it was an invitation to enter. Forsyth looked at the gently swinging hammock seat and smiled. His hand tightened on the gun.

He stood for a moment inside the darkened room and waited. It felt empty. He moved cautiously forward, found the door and stepped into the passage beyond. The long, tiled corridor was dimly lit. He had an impression that it bisected that part of the building. Forsyth looked ruefully at the doors on either side of the passage and decided that a complete search was out of the question. It would be best to concentrate on locked doors.

He began a systematic trial of door handles, moving swiftly until he came to the central hall, an unexpectedly beautiful place of cool green and white tiles and soft green bronzes. A long, shallow, copper trough, set diagonally on a circular marble table, spilled flowers in a riot of color.

Forsyth paused. Somewhere there was a woman around.

He moved toward the back of the house where he judged the servants' quarters would be.

Light spilled from the open doorway of a bedroom. Practically opposite was a life-size statue of some saint set in a deep alcove. Forsyth squeezed behind the statue and studied the room. He smiled. This was not the usual servant's room. Soft lamps cast a rosy glow over the ivory furniture. The broad expanse of bed was covered in richly quilted ivory silk, but someone had pulled the white pillows from underneath the spread and piled them on top of the cover at the head of the bed.

A young woman crossed the room and sat on a brocade-covered chair. Gleaming black hair was piled high on her head, as though she had just come from her bath, or was preparing for it. She had a pale, pretty face, with a generous, smiling mouth. As she studied her pink-lacquered toenails, she hummed softly, then began in a sweet, true voice to sing what Forsyth recognized as an old Gorj lullaby:

> *"Don't cry, Mary, little mouse.*
> *Better mind your little house.*
> *And our little children heed.*
> *We are badly off indeed . . ."*

She stopped the *doina* abruptly, as if she had lost interest, and stood up, tossing her dressing gown behind her onto the chair. Her body made a white arc and her breasts lifted as she unhooked her bra. She stretched out on the bed and swung her arms up to loosen the coils of hair. It fell in a dusky, voluptuous cloud over the white shoulders and breasts.

Her eyes closed and she seemed to listen, turning her head to the right. Presently, she called in a patient, fluting voice, "Ready, darling!"

From somewhere deep in the room, the cheerful voice answered, "Coming! Coming! Just one moment!"

Forsyth breathed deeply. He had been mistaken, after all. The swinging of the hammock had not been noticed.

Feeling the worst kind of voyeur, he squeezed from behind the statue and went softly back to the hall, moving slowly and cautiously in the dimness. He could, he reckoned, count on at least half an hour.

The last door that he tried was to the left of the entrance

and led, he calculated, into the room where he had had the tantalizing glimpse of Bonneaud. It was locked. That pleased him, for obviously the Frenchman had something there that he wished to hide.

Forsyth went silently to work. Within minutes, the door swung quietly inward. He stepped confidently into the blackness, pulling the heavy wooden door gently behind him.

The smash of the cosh on the side of his head sent pinwheels and rockets whirling madly, throwing off sparks of agony that exploded behind his eyes and died in a darkness that was shot with crimson.

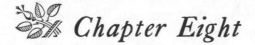

Chapter Eight

THE top of his head felt as if it had been blown off. For a pain-filled moment, Forsyth remembered the naked woman on the bed and the cold feel of the statue under his hand. After that, there was nothing.

He looked muzzily at the smiling face of the little man standing in front of the door which was still ajar. The room was flooded with bright light which hurt Forsyth's eyes, but he forced himself to keep them open and look steadily at Tommy's timekeeper. Instinct made him note every feature and detail of his dress, although it now seemed very unlikely that the knowledge would be put to any practical use.

The man was well below average height, with a grossly swelling paunch that gave him the look of Humpty Dumpty. From the crown of his pink bald head to the tiny feet, he exuded friendliness, but it did not quite reach the needle-sharp gray eyes. A leather-covered cosh swung from the wrist above a pudgy hand, and Forsyth guessed that the bulge in one pocket was made by a gun. He tried to guess his nationality. From some mid-European country, he surmised. What interested him was that beneath the childish, unformed features rippled a knowingness that made the flesh crawl.

He said interestedly, "How did a midget like you manage it?"

"No difficulty." He waved a hand to a spot behind Forsyth. "There's a second door there, as well as an exit from the bathroom behind the bedroom, where you had the bad manners to spy on my wife. I nipped in here, stood on a chair and waited for you. Most tall men are stupid, so I was quite confident, but even a genius hasn't much chance against a gun."

For Forsyth, the most humiliating aspect of the affair was his ignominious position on the floor, trussed up like a chicken. Fatty did not look like a man who would tie a "granny" knot. He hoped that Bonneaud would take a long time over dinner. There was little doubt about his own fate when he returned.

The little man's voice hardened. "Now we'll have the answers to some questions. Who are you and what are you doing in a private house?"

"I came to read the gas meter, Rosebud."

At the weary insolence in Forsyth's voice, a fleck of foam appeared suddenly at the side of the pursed mouth. A foot shot out and Forsyth heard the sharp crack of a rib. The wave of pain gathered and broke in beads of sweat on his forehead.

The shrill voice went on and on, telling him obscenely what was in store for him.

He looked steadily up at the suffused face. Suddenly the expression changed. A look of surprise spread over the soft features. The jaw stiffened; the eyes bulged and the fat body dropped heavily across Forsyth's knees.

Nicola Beaufort stood in the doorway. Her gaze went in dazed horror from the fat body on the floor to the tiny gun in her hand. The hand was steady, but the great eyes were blank with shock.

"Is he dead, do you think? Have I killed him? It is not supposed to, you know." She looked pleadingly at Forsyth. "The woman too . . ."

"Don't stand there like Banquo's ghost," he said harshly.

"Get this damned weight off my legs and get me out of this rope outfit. If Bonneaud gets back here unexpectedly, we won't need our return tickets to London."

She looked wildly round the room, saw the scissors on the desk and ran across to fetch them. As she went, she tucked the gun into the bag that dangled from a wrist, almost as if it were a handkerchief that she no longer required.

When she flopped on her knees beside him, Forsyth saw with relief that she was in control of herself.

She tugged futilely at the fat man's shoulders.

Forsyth advised, "Try pulling him by the feet."

"No. I am afraid that might touch you." She pointed to what looked like a thick pin sticking out from a fleshy fold of the neck.

"Is that what you shot him with?"

"Yes. It is covered with a derivative of curare. I know it is supposed to paralyze, but not to kill. What I don't know is how long the effects last."

She put both hands on the swollen paunch and pushed, gritting her teeth in distaste. The weight rolled off Forsyth's legs. In moments, she had freed him.

When he tried to get up, he groaned in agony. The room spun slowly round and round. Her voice seemed to come from a long way off.

She said with a kind of anguish, "You're hurt. That kick—"

"Probably nothing worse than a busted rib. It's a nuisance. I won't die." He made a tremendous effort to rise.

"Wait," she said imperiously. "Don't move. I know what to do."

She was gone in a flutter of silken garments.

When she came back, she was carrying a long Continental-style bolster case. Working fast, she loosened his shirt and bound up the rib cage tightly.

As she worked, he studied her intently. Obviously she

was dressed for dinner, in a jade silk evening suit. The effect was lush and unpractical. The jacket was heavily encrusted with multicolored jewels and the jewels were repeated on the slender heels of the matching shoes. The lamps caught the sparkle of dozens of rhinestones, so that she seemed to be encased in light. Her face under the soft radiance had the improbable beauty of some legendary princess in an ancient Eastern manuscript.

He said stonily, "That's a helluva outfit to wear when you go burglaring."

There was a flash of humor in her eyes, but she simply said quietly, "That's exactly why I chose it. Very conspicuous. Besides, I don't possess a pair of dungarees."

He made a quick gesture to silence her. He whispered urgently, "Get back to the door and keep out of his range of vision. I should have thought of this—he may be able to see and hear. I don't want him to be able to identify you. I'll tie him up. You do the same for the woman."

When she came back, she had a relieved look. "At least she is breathing, though in a funny, constricted sort of way. I hope she'll be all right."

"I'll remember to cry about her tomorrow."

Deliberately, he made his tone brutal. It would be disastrous if she went to pieces now. He handed her the fat man's gun. "If anybody comes back, give him a permanent paralysis with this. Don't stop to philosophize."

He looked around for his own weapon and found it on the settee where the small man must have tossed it while he was tying him up. Thankfully he pocketed it and eased the band of his cosh farther down his wrist. Fatty had overlooked it.

"Where are you going?" She sounded very calm.

"To search for Rothman. It shouldn't take long."

He went quickly through the house, but found nothing of interest, other than some papers in Bonneaud's bedroom that showed that he had rented the villa two years previously and that the lease ran for five years. The house was the Villa Florica. It had nothing further to tell him.

He had his hand on the girl's arm to lead her through the main door when she said, "Did you notice the map on the desk?"

Without a word, he went back. The fat man's eyes followed him across the room.

He opened the folded map and spread it on the tabletop, where it overlapped the edges. It was a full-scale map of the country with hundreds of names encircled in blue ink. The circles started at the borders of Yugoslavia, Hungary, the USSR, Bulgaria and where the Black Sea washed Rumania's shores. They moved inward, as if the intention was to cover the whole of the country. The unmarked area looked very small, as though the project, whatever it might be, was almost completed. Forsyth found it disturbing that Sinaia was practically at the center of this blank area.

Frowning, he folded the map and stuffed it into the large, inner, poacher-type pocket which his tailor made in all his jackets.

A retching sound came from the fat man. Forsyth crossed the room and dropped on a knee to examine him. He was fully conscious, but his face was puce-colored. The gag had slipped back and was choking him.

Forsyth plucked it out and put a hand behind the man's shoulders to support him and let him breathe more freely. The flat gray eyes hated him. The mouth pursed and ejected a stream of saliva at Forsyth's face. It landed below the knot of his tie and crept viscously down the silk.

Expressionlessly, Forsyth removed the tie, bundled it up and forced it into the fat man's mouth.

"Choke on that, Rosebud," he said unemotionally, "and don't be in a hurry to hit a tall man again. He might retaliate like this." He brought the cosh down on the side of the bald head and walked out.

Anger at the incident and at his oversight of the map made his voice sharp as he thanked the girl.

"One more item to attend to and then we go," he said.

When they were outside, he left her for a moment while he cut the telephone wires. That should slow Bonneaud up for at least a little, he thought.

Together they went quickly across the grass and walked over the grille. This time, nobody was going to do anything about the bell.

In the glow of the car headlights, he looked at her curiously. "Did you know about the alarm bell?"

She nodded.

"Then how did you get across?"

She widened her eyes. "Very easily. I found out the name of the next villa. Then I drove up to the Villa Florica in a taxi; got the driver to get out and ask directions to it from here, while I sat back and powdered my face. In this outfit, who would have doubted that I was simply keeping a dinner date? I paid the driver off just before we got to the grid and I got out, telling him I would walk through the grounds. Presumably, the bell would ring in the house as the taxi left. Simple!"

"Yes," he said drily. "I'll give you this month's paycheck. I don't seem to be doing so well. So you were already inside when I got to the house? How did you find the place?"

It was difficult to concentrate and something had happened to his vision. He was seeing double.

He thought she was going to say "Simple!" again. She hesitated, then went on as they were getting into his car. "I knew that a man called Bonneaud was in some way involved with Tony. I phoned around and he wasn't booked in at any of the hotels. Then I got on to the main office of Carpati and explained that my friend, Monsieur Bonneaud, was in Bucharest, but that, unfortunately, I did not know where he was staying. Pretty please! would they find him for me? They came up with the Villa Florica."

"Good going. Move to the top of the class." Did she have to outsmart him on every count?

In a small voice she said, "Don't you think that I should drive? The less you move that rib, the sooner it is going to heal." She was out of her seat and at his side of the car without waiting for a reply. He slid over into her place, trying to control a wave of nausea.

"Now I'll take you to dinner at the Baneasa-Pod. It's on the main Bucharest–Ploesti highway. I'll direct you." He glanced at his watch. It would soon be too late for dinner even in a Rumanian restaurant. "When you're around, nobody in the restaurant is going to take two looks at a slightly pregnant man." He had the impression that something had pleased her and that she was smiling in the darkness.

When they parked at the restaurant, she said in tones of surprise as she got out of the car, "I'm starving. That's astonishing."

"No. They say that sex and fear always do that—I wouldn't know."

He had the queer feeling that the only time he had really shocked her was when he had failed to assist her to her feet at Heathrow. The females of the species were nutty.

A sudden thought struck him. He halted abruptly. "About that gun—one barrel shoots out cyanide, the other a curare derivative. Correct? There is no bullet mechanism?" Was he falling into Brett's way of talking?

"No. I thought you knew that."

"It seems I know damned little." His tone was bitter, as he thought of Neville's mocking smile. Naturally, Valmy must have phoned him immediately. Why the hell had he added that unnecessary sentence?

The girl said timidly, "Is something wrong?"

"No. Some cases have a jinx on them. This is one. I

suggest that you and Rothman go to the Antipodes for your honeymoon and give me a break."

She preceded him into the restaurant and he saw the proud stiffening of neck and shoulders. All eyes were on the male singer who stood under an arc lamp, so nobody paid any attention to them as they sat down at a table set far back under the trees.

She looked about with lively interest. Through the trees, she could see the quicksilver glint of water.

"There's a string of beautiful lakes in this area," he explained. "Lake Herastrau . . . Floreasca . . . Tei . . . Fundeni . . . and some marvelous fish restaurants. I don't mean to be impertinent but, really, Tony Rothman should bring you back here someday."

Her face closed up and she gazed steadily down at the crimson tablecloth.

To their right, under ancient white poplars, a couple of peacocks strutted, spreading their tails like emerald-studded fans and startling the diners with their nerve-shattering screams.

Under ordinary circumstances, Forsyth would have enjoyed the meal. The girl was a stunner; the night was balmy; the setting, romantic; the food and wine, just adequate. But each breath sent a hot flash of pain through his side. His head ached dully and he knew that he was suffering from slight concussion. He should have been in bed. Most of all, he was full of self-disgust, feeling that he had mishandled the entire operation.

Nor had he yet picked out either Bonneaud or Fossard from among the diners, and had he been able to do so, he doubted if he could have benefited in any way. He was not entirely displeased that Bonneaud would eventually learn from the fat man that he was on the operation. It might trigger off some action. He ate with a little better appetite.

The male singer was back and the thin clear notes of a flute soared and broke in unbearable sweetness in the *doina*, the song of longing. The forest seemed to hold its breath as the singer raised his voice in the unsurpassed *Miorita* ballad.

"What is it?" Nicola Beaufort whispered.

Forsyth forced himself to sound pleasant. "It's a folk suite called *The Story of the Shepherd Who Lost His Sheep*, very old and much too long for my taste, but it works like a charm on Rumanians. Never known it to miss. I suppose you are lucky to hear it."

"I wish I could follow Rumanian. Translate as much as you can, please."

"Well, it's from the Galatz region. There are mountain pasturelands where the peasants take their cattle and flocks to winter up in the mountains. So they don't need to cart the hay down the hills in their sleighs which they draw over the grass." His eyes kept up their restless search for Bonneaud. "Each flock is guarded by a single man for months on end. The singer is telling about three shepherds from Moldavia, Transylvania and Vrancea."

The voice soared,

> "*Where the mountain ends,*
> *And to heaven bends,*
> *They are coming, lo,*
> *And downhill they go,*
> *Flocks of fair sheep three . . .*"

The diners under the trees were silent, caught and held by a tragic voice from their past. The entire restaurant was under a spell.

Forsyth whispered, his head heavy with pain, "Two of the shepherds plot to kill the third. A ewe warns the shepherd, but he isn't afraid. All he wants is to be buried beside the sheep pen."

The liquid notes pleaded,

"There at my head let be
The beechen shepherd's flute,
It sings such lovely tunes . . .
It wakes the flutes to song . . ."

Forsyth looked curiously at the girl, marveling at her resilience. The events of the day seemed to have left her untouched. Her expression, as she watched the singer's face intently, was absorbed and happy.

A candle on a table flickered wildly and drew Forsyth's attention. The table was almost directly opposite, but was on the outer rim of the circle of diners and was almost hidden by the drooping branches of a tree. Bonneaud's head was bent close to Fossard's. The light caught the feral gleam of his eyes.

It seemed to Forsyth that the Prague affair had robbed the Frenchman of none of his wiry strength or cunning. In comparison, he felt sluggish and diffident.

Nicola Beaufort said urgently, "Tell me the rest."

He said impatiently, "He's only halfway through the story. These people like their drama long and strong. It bores me. Well, the ewe is warned by the brave shepherd to say nothing about the murder, but to say only what the man is singing now." *What the hell was Bonneaud planning?*

The singer pleaded,

"And tell them downright this:
That I am wed henceforth to one so proud and fair,
The fair bride of the world . . ."

Bonneaud and Fossard were on their feet. Forsyth said hurriedly, "I'll be back. I've spotted Bonneaud, but even if he is leaving, I won't follow him to the villa. Just wait for me."

As he rose, he picked a glass from the table and thrust it into a pocket. The song followed him, soaring in ecstasy,

> *"The bridal wreath was held*
> *By sun and moon alike,*
> *And fir and maple-tree*
> *Were wedding guests to me . . ."*

A sound like a great sigh came from the diners, a sigh of recognition for the final triumph of simple goodness. It pursued Forsyth like an accusation.

Bonneaud and Fossard had disappeared.

He said quickly to a waiter, *"Unde este toaleta?"*

The man pointed to two doors, hung with crimson curtains. Above one was the sign *Barbati* and above the other, *Femei*. Forsyth knew that there was rarely an attendant in Rumanian toilets. He took a rapid look around. No woman was going to leave that seductive voice if she could possibly help it. He went behind the curtain marked *Femei*.

From the other side of the thin partition, there was the sound of a toilet being flushed.

Forsyth put the glass against the wall and listened.

Fossard said irritably, "Which is which?"

"Rece is the cold tap and *cald* the hot." Bonneaud sounded amused. "Why don't you try them? Trial and error, you know." His voice sharpened. "Hurry it up. You are as fussy as an old woman. I want to get back to the villa and have another look at the map. I've always found that it pays to play hunches. While we were eating, I had one." He sounded smug. "I'll be furious if I find that I've spent two years pouring out money for men to do a search for a place that I could have arrived at by logical thought."

"Do you mean that you think you really know where it is hidden?"

"Not so fast. I think I know where to concentrate the search, but it was always agreed that when we got to that stage only you and I would do it. I think we've got there."

Fossard swore excitedly.

"Well, *mon vieux,* where would those pampered Nazi swine be liable to make for? Not Bucharest—too many people around and too many chances that the crown might be stumbled upon. No . . . a quiet place, but a comfortable place . . . a very German place. What about Peles Castle . . . German Renaissance . . . home of the Rumanian monarchy which was for so long drawn from the Hohenzollern dynasty? Eh? What about that, *mon vieux?* The old idea of hiding a leaf in a forest."

Fossard sounded doubtful. "You might as well say it's at Pietroasa, where the famous Golden Hen and Chicks treasure was discovered. You know—hide a treasure where a treasure has already been found."

"No. I'm sure I'm right. I have a friend who has a small but comfortable villa at the foot of Mount Furnica. We'll be less conspicuous there than in Sinaia itself. I'll phone him first thing in the morning, pick you up about seven o'clock and make for Sinaia."

"And what about Lupescu? Do we stop there?"

"No. He is moving Rothman tomorrow, after dark. The following night will be time enough to make that bird sing. If we've already got the crown, Lupescu can simply turn the key in the lock and forget him."

He laughed and the sound made even Forsyth's blood run cold.

The curtain rings rattled and a fat woman waddled in. Her face was a picture of outraged modesty.

Forsyth pushed past her with a muttered, *"Scuzati-mă."*

Back at the table, Nicola Beaufort looked inquiringly at him but said nothing. He had a feeling that much of her dislike and fear of him had been left behind in the Villa Florica. Trust a woman to have a soft spot for failure!

To his astonishment, he found himself saying, "I was

not completely birdbrained tonight. I took this from Fatty's telephone pad." He showed her the page which he had taken from the pad in the hall. "It's a Cimpina number, as you see—the one, almost certainly, that belongs to Dr. Lupescu. My guess is that he has Rothman at his house or nearby."

Her eyes twinkled as she drew a notebook from her bag. She opened it and slid it across to him. He looked at the Cimpina number.

Almost apologetically, she said, "I noted it while you were getting the map. Perhaps I was overcautious, but I thought it might be better to leave the page, so as not to alert Bonneaud to the fact that we had the number."

He got silently to his feet. "Come on!" he said.

When she had settled herself behind the wheel of the car, he said comically, "I surrender! You've earned your place on the team. I wouldn't put it past you to get Rothman out singlehanded. Just remember that I'm still the boss even though I have been stumbling around as if I had two left feet."

"Yes, *sir!*"

He gave her a worried look in the darkness. "I'm such a big tough guy that all I want at the moment is to find a nice sympathetic doctor to take care of me, tuck me in a comfortable bed for a week, and put a big NO VISITORS sign on my door."

"Instead? . . ."

"Instead, I'm going to ask you to drive me back to the Lido Hotel where I'll pack, check out, study that map and make for what is laughingly called the Pearl of the Carpathians. If my luck continues to run as it has been doing, I'll be in time to have a ringside seat when Bonneaud collects the crown and gives your boyfriend the old one-two." His tone softened. "Luck changes. I think it is just about my turn for the good variety. Relax for a couple of days and I'll do my best to give you the chance to play queen for a few minutes and incidentally kiss lover-boy."

"Not on. You can't drive, especially once you get up into the mountains near Sinaia. I know the kind of roads to expect. What do you think all that twisting and turning would do to your rib? I have the impression that if you have a meeting with Bonneaud, you'll not only need your wits about you, but you'll need all your physical strength. I can pack in fifteen minutes. Let's go!"

Back at the hotel, he packed swiftly. As he felt the dart board at the foot of his case, he reflected that there had not been very much time for playing games. The darts were in two tumbler-shaped plastic boxes, one white, one green.

He broke the seal on the box of hypodermic syringes. There were twenty in the box. The label read: *Administer every four hours.* It pealed off easily. The close-printed instructions on the one underneath read: *Temporary paralysis requires patient be chair-borne. Double dose fatal. Use only if Rothman noncooperative.*

Slowly, he put the top label back in place.

The girl was waiting for him in the entrance hall of the Inter-Continental. She had changed into beige slacks and a bulky white polo-necked sweater and had caught her thick mane of hair back in a white ribbon. Her face had a look of composure, with nothing of the feverish excitement that he had seen on the plane. She handed him a pink cashmere cardigan. "It's all I've got," she said apologetically. "You'll look ridiculous, but there'll be nobody to see and you'll be glad of it once we start climbing up into the mountains. I've got brandy and some food."

"Now I know why soldiers used to take their wives when they went to fight. I never knew that it was to *feed* them." He laughed.

She gave him an offended look.

He picked up her baggage. There was an airflight case

and a clumsy round leather box with a strong leather band across the top, forming the handle. It felt empty.

He swung it lightly. "What the hell is this?" he inquired.

"It's a hatbox. I bought it from one of the girls on night duty. It cost me a fortune, but I think it was worth it. It's for holding the crown."

He looked at her with awe. "Christ!" he breathed. "The faith that moves mountains!"

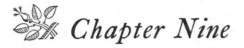 *Chapter Nine*

IN the light from an occasional passing car, her face had a curious serenity. Forsyth watched it and the competent way her hands dealt with the wheel. She was a good driver, keeping up a steady sixty on the straight stretches as soon as they had left Bucharest behind. Once they began the steep climb up into the Carpathians, progress would be slow.

The enclosed space of the car and the humming silence created an atmosphere of intimacy. It was difficult to keep track of time or location. It was almost like being in a time capsule, launched into outer space. Probably he was a little lightheaded, for he found himself saying, impulsively, "Mother . . ."

He looked at the girl in horror, but she did not seem to have heard him and he wondered if the conversation had been going on only in his head. At intervals, he speculated about Bonneaud's cold rage when he found that his headquarters had been brazenly entered. He would come after them very, very soon. When the Carpati office opened, at the latest.

This time, he felt, one of them would have to die. The thought produced only a great weariness.

"You realize," he asked suddenly, "that I could be miles off the beam? I've been behaving as though, as sure as God made little green apples, the crown is in Sinaia, but I could be as crazy as a coot in my thinking. Maybe Rothman knows something more than I do and we'll have to wait until we catch up with him before we find out." His voice petered out in a grumbling mutter.

"It's there." She spoke soothingly, as if to a sick child. Her confidence enraged him, but before he had time to marshal the wounding, skeptical words, he was asleep, hunched uncomfortably against the door.

When he awoke, he felt completely disoriented.

"Cigarette?" she asked, as he stirred.

The pain in his side was so bad that he could only shake his head in refusal. She must have guessed the cause, for she peered out at the street lights. "According to Bonneaud's map, we should be in Ploesti now. I'm going to stop for a few minutes."

She pulled up at Spatari 17, where a ribbon of light from a café spanned the blackness of the street.

While she was away, he allowed himself the luxury of a deep, pain-filled groan. His physical condition worried him more than he was willing to admit even to himself. He could picture the astonishment of the outfit if they could see the tough Forsyth folding under a crack on the head and a kick in the ribs. It *was* time to get out.

When she came back, she handed him a glass of water and a codeine pill. As he was swallowing the tablet, she grinned and said, "I think I'll go on the stage when I get back to London. You missed a good performance. If my pantomime act went over, I have found out from the barman that there's an hospital just around the corner. Mind you, it could turn out to be the zoo. In the end, I think it will be time well spent to have a professional job done on those ribs. Better think up a good story to explain the injury."

She was with him when he took off his shirt for the doctor. There was the sheen of tears in her eyes when she looked at the ugly, spreading wound. He wanted to laugh at the idea that, while she had been prepared to kill him, the sight of a bruise made her turn pale. He was aware of the sincerity of her compassion now and of the reality of her womanly shrinking from the sight of his pain. Baffled, he gave up the attempt to equate it with her unexpected attack on him in Bucharest. Only illness could account for it.

In an effort at levity, he said in an aside to her, "My wrist was worse," and was immediately sorry when he saw her painful blush.

They got back into the car in silence.

Sometimes a wattle-roofed cart would loom suddenly out of the darkness, jogging along with a timeless air of going nowhere in particular. Festoons of baskets and brooms were obviously the stock in trade of the gypsy owners. From underneath the curving roof, lying full-length on the piles of goods, children with wild, dark eyes and elfin faces peered out.

There were few villages to break the monotony of the seemingly endless straight road. He sighed. It was going to be a long, hard drive, though at least until now they had been able to make good time. In daylight, because of the good road as far as Ploesti, Bonneaud could eat up the miles. Inevitably, the time was fast approaching when their advantage over him could be only marginal.

She said suddenly, "I know that we are in the oil region, but isn't that delicious perfume the smell of the tobacco flower?"

The car was full of it and, through the open window, came the piney breath of the woods.

"It's a pity it isn't daylight," he said. "The corncobs are worth seeing in this area and the walnut trees will be simply hanging with fruit."

At once he thought, *I'm talking like a damned travel guide.*

But his mood had lightened and the worrying double

vision had gone. Even his dislike of the girl had undergone a change to an indifference that accepted philosophically the danger to her from Bonneaud. Had he dwelt on that problem, he would have said quite literally, It's her funeral. She had had her chance to go and had chosen to stay. What happened to her was her own responsibility.

When they skirted Cimpina, both fell silent, their thoughts busy with the problem of Tony Rothman. Forsyth tried to think of him quite impersonally and not as a colleague or as a suitor for Nicola Beaufort. As that analytical mind marshaled the few facts available, Forsyth's suspicions of the blond giant increased and crystallized. How could an agent of Rothman's experience and ability fall so easily into communist hands? How was it possible for an operator of his intelligence and resourcefulness to leave behind in his room, not merely a clue to the wherabouts of the Crown of Hungary, but the vital and apparently the only clue that had turned up in twenty years? Rothman was incapable of such crass stupidity. It had to be a planted clue.

The muscles of Forsyth's stomach tightened as he worked out the full implications of the instructions under the label marked *Insulin*. In the darkness, his mouth became a hard line. The Department might be bastards, but they did not, under any circumstances, kill their own operators. There could be only one explanation for their instructions to him. Rothman was a double agent.

Carefully, he examined that conclusion. What else, he asked himself, would explain the necessity for a paralyzing drug to get Rothman out? The label made it clear, moreover, that while Rothman was to be brought back to London, there was the strong possibility that he would resist rescue. Rescue? How could it be a rescue, if Forsyth's orders were to kill Rothman if he put up any serious resistance? Paralyze him to rescue? Kill him if he resisted rescue strongly? Why, in the name of God, would a British agent resist rescue unless he were working for the other side? Rothman simply had to be a traitor.

Hunched in his corner of the car, Forsyth seethed with anger against Neville who had quite obviously known that while they were eating breakfast in his kitchen. His deepest anger was aroused because the head of the outfit had not trusted him to put out his best efforts to bring back a traitor. In reality, he reflected cruelly, there were always special reasons for getting a double agent out. Rothman was certainly going to go back to that room in Swiss Cottage.

For the first time, he felt a treacherous pity for the girl beside him. She was in for a bad shock.

Did Bonneaud know of Rothman's treachery? Unlikely . . . very unlikely. The whole setup smelled of the KGB.

Pieces of the puzzle were falling into place. Both Britain and the USSR, it appeared, had sent Rothman after the Crown of Hungary. Somehow he had found the clue of the holy picture of Saint Jude. The significance of the tiny inscription, PRINTED IN RUMANIA, had obviously struck him, as it had Forsyth. Once recovered, the crown was to be planted in London, while the Russians produced faked evidence to show that Britain was inciting a movement to restore the Hungarian monarchy. Meanwhile, in Moscow, Rothman was to be babbling out his carefully manufactured confession of Britain's treachery.

At any other time the thought of the KGB and the SMR in opposite camps would have been hilarious.

He said silently to the quiet form of Nicola Beaufort, *Yes. I'll bring you back lover-boy . . . in very small pieces. You won't have much use for him when the Department has finished with him.*

She shivered as if he had spoken aloud. They had left the town behind and were on the outskirts of Cimpina, bowling along an attractive walnut-tree-lined road.

"Do you think we should stop and eat?" she asked.

"Good idea. Slow down. Turn the car in at that opening ahead. The owner has been dead since 1907 so he won't mind if we have a picnic in his drive."

Once out of the car, she stretched wearily. He could see the smooth line of her raised breasts and the long, slender curves of her thighs where the beige pants clung. Although her shoulders drooped, she turned a gallant smile on him, as if denying her tiredness.

The air had a sharp clarity that cleared the mists from their brains. He was glad of the cardigan, which he wore like a scarf.

As they walked back and forth across the lawn, Forsyth was surprised and slightly amused to find his attitude toward her mellowing. Had the tablets given by the Cimpina doctor to ease his pain anesthetized his emotions? He felt much less hostile, much less indifferent to her fate, much more aware of her as a person who would suffer cruel disillusionment soon. He made no attempt to hang on to his earlier hard feelings. Indeed it was difficult to recall his very recent angry dislike of her. Getting soft in my old age, he told himself.

He said to her suddenly, "How do you feel about brown towels in a bathroom?"

She looked puzzled. "Sounds ghastly to me. Why? Is it some kind of test?"

"No. It's just that I'm thinking of changing my color scheme."

They went back to the car.

As they ate chicken sandwiches and she took carefully abstemious sips at the brandy flask, she peered up at the attractive white house with its fretted wooden balcony and quaintly canopied chimneys.

"Who was he?"

"The Rumanian painter Nicolae Grigorescu. He used to live here, but the place is now a museum for his work." He looked across the lawn, silvery with dew. "By ten o'clock, this place will be swarming with tourists. If you are a praying woman, put in a request now that Bonneaud gets tangled up with them. We are going to need lots of luck to find the crown and get away with it before he starts breathing down our necks."

He found her hand creeping over to take his. It didn't surprise him when his own closed over hers. His confidence was at such a low ebb that he would have taken comfort from the devil himself. Maybe Rosebud had given him a harder knock than he had realized. Head injuries, he knew, could be tricky.

"I can always try a prayer to the saint of the holy picture." Her voice was light, but he knew that she was telling him not to give up the ship.

A fierce irritation swept through him as he thought of Bonneaud's rictal sneer at his lack of confidence. He felt a crying need to get drunk and so blot out the whole messy business. With his feet soaking up damp in a garden in a remote corner of Rumania, it was ludicrous to try and convince himself that he or Rothman or Bonneaud or anybody had anything to do with world peace. *It was a tale told by an idiot . . .*

He said tiredly, "Let's get the show on the road."

The quality of the light had changed, as if someone had drawn aside veil after veil on a vast stage.

Nothing but a long sleep was going to ease his bone-tiredness, but at least the pain in his head had subsided into a dull throb and he was aware that the doctor had done a good job in supporting his ribs. He settled down to plan each move to be made once they reached Sinaia.

As they climbed upward through the Prahova Valley, they could hear the breathy snufflings of cows grazing near the roadside. The mountain scenery was superb but he cut across her murmurs of pleasure as though continuing a long discussion with her.

"Rumania is the logical hiding place for the crown. Cardinal Mindszenty's long stay in the American Embassy in Budapest probably gave some patriot the idea that Rumania was convenient, not strikingly pro-Soviet and had an unmatched outlet via the Black Sea. We may never know the full details, but, frankly, I don't care as long as we collect the crown and get it back to London. Incidentally, do you have a hat?"

"No. I don't possess one, even at home."

"Buy one in Sinaia. It doesn't have to be a Paris model, but it must have a brim that will just fit into the hatbox and no more. A large crown—about a size seven and a half I would think. It has to fit over and cover Saint Stephen's Crown."

Sinaia loomed up, enshrined in the wide gap in the southeastern Carpathians and dominated by lofty peaks. The town clung to the side of the mountain like an illustration in a German fairy tale. It was so stunningly appropriate as the hiding place for a priceless treasure that Forsyth almost laughed aloud at the sheer corniness of the whole situation. The look of good-humored disdain that the girl had first seen at Heathrow was firmly back in place.

As they bumped over the steep cobbled streets, Nicola Beaufort exclaimed in delight.

"How very Germanic!" She was clearly enchanted. "Just look at those gingerbread houses! I've never seen such a mixture of spires and balconies and cupolas and beamed mansions. I must have execrable taste, for I love it!" She was like a little girl turned loose in Toytown.

Forsyth looked at her shining, weary eyes and felt an unfamiliar twist at his heart.

Bloody women! he told himself cynically. *Trust them to go starry-eyed, when they should be sharpening the knives!* He glowered at her and got a sunny smile in return.

They checked in at the Palas Hotel and ate breakfast in one of the large dining rooms overlooking the grandiose panorama of the mountains. When they had finished eating, he said, "Now I'll go and make arrangements for buying a wheelchair and a couple of traveling rugs."

"A *wheelchair?*"

"Yes. I don't expect to find Tony in the best of health. But we may not need it."

"But where on earth will you find one?"

"No problem. There are men and supermen. A good hall porter belongs in the latter category. I've had a look at the man here. He's the type who will take this sort of request in his stride."

One part of his mind was worrying away at the problem of Bonneaud, trying to guess his possible moves. He felt her eyes on him and, for an incredible moment, seemed to read in them the same air of loving concern that he had seen so often in his father's gaze. He hesitated and lost the thread of his thoughts.

Uncannily, she asked, "How can Bonneaud possibly know that we are in Sinaia? We could be anywhere."

"No. We can only be in the Palas Hotel in Sinaia. Have you forgotten that you require a permit to move anywhere in Rumania? All Bonneaud has to do is to phone Carpati in Bucharest and, in minutes, they can tell him from their files where we are."

"Oh."

"Yes. That's why it looks as if we will be sleeping in the car tonight. I suggest that you go and buy that hat now and enough food for at least a couple of days. I don't expect to be patronizing any hotels after we leave Sinaia. We'll be roughing it until we get on a plane for London."

"And what will you be doing now?"

"Practicing darts." She gave him a puzzled look, but he did not enlighten her.

When he left her, he went to his room, took out the dart board and spent fifteen minutes practicing. To his annoyance, the adhesive bandage round his ribs affected his aim. He continued to try for a double top until he could do it nearly every time. He was back in form.

By now, he reckoned, Mass would be over and the church deserted. He would not quite allow himself to believe that the relic was there.

An instinctive delicacy made him leave the gun behind. Atheist as he was, it did not seem right to take the weapon into a church. He recognized and accepted the genesis of this feeling, but could not justify to himself his taking the girl's leather hatbox. He had a broad grin on his face, as though he had been caught in an act of faith.

While Charles Forsyth was holding his breath to allow the doctor in Ploesti to wrap the adhesive bandage tightly round his ribs, Vasile and Chantal Lupescu were sound asleep in the bedroom next to Rothman's. His wife's early return from Sinaia had aroused in Lupescu an unexpected upsurge of sexual desire. Now they slept heavily, fulfilled and comforted by each other's warmth.

The phone rang harshly from the hall, jerking them both into complete wakefulness.

In the next room, Tony Rothman came groggily out of his sedated sleep to peer at the luminous hands of his watch. He snapped on his bedside lamp and looked vaguely round the room, rubbing a hand irritably over the short stubble on his head.

At least, it was not time for that damned farce of the shaving.

The ringing went on and on.

Chantal Lupescu sat bolt upright in bed, her spine rigid against the headboard and the sheet pulled high against her rosy-nippled breasts. She said urgently, "Answer it, Vasile, answer it. Something has gone wrong. I know it. Perhaps we should get the cases and go now."

She swung the sheet back and got quickly out of bed. Her arms hugged her breasts as though she were cold.

Vasile Lupescu was already halfway across the room, clutching his robe and trying to get into it as he walked. His expression was composed and alert.

"Get dressed," he said curtly over his shoulder, "and don't open the Englishman's door. Maybe he is still asleep."

When he lifted the receiver, his voice was calm and noncommittal, but his eyes became wary as Bonneaud's voice came reedily over the wires.

"Your patient should be moved immediately." He might have been a consultant advising a general practitioner. "I will leave you to make the arrangements with your colleague, Fouquet."

"Has something gone wrong?"

Lupescu heard the click as the receiver went down in Bucharest.

He stood looking at the instrument as though it might give him the answer to a difficult question. His hand was out to lift the receiver when Fouquet's voice came from the stairway.

Lupescu spun round to face the Frenchman.

"What goes on?" Fouquet was aggrieved, as if it were Lupescu's fault that he had been disturbed.

Lupescu looked with distaste at the other's pajamaed figure and bare feet. "We have to get Rothman into the cell now. You know what to do. Get started. I'll attend to him at once."

He went swiftly up the stairs and into his bedroom.

His wife was already dressed in a pale-gray woollen frock with a white collar. It gave her a nunlike look, though her thin blonde hair still hung in two long braids over her shoulders. Her face had a pinched appearance which could have been either from fear or cold. She watched her husband steadily as he dressed, waiting in a subservient way for his explanation.

"Fouquet and I will be taking the Englishman over to the museum now. As soon as we have gone, phone Danilenko and let him know this. For some reason, which I don't know, Bonneaud has changed his plans. A pity, that. Ask him if we can expect him tomorrow. I mean, today." He halted on his way to the door, struck by a sudden thought. "I've just remembered. The museum is closed to the public the next day. There would be no need to wait for darkness then. Ask him what he thinks. Let him fix a time and we will be ready."

He went out without a backward look. She followed him into the upper hall and stood listening anxiously when he went into Rothman's room. At first, there was the sound of angry voices, then silence. Satisfied, she went back into her own bedroom and, in a burst of nervous energy, began to make the bed and to tidy the room.

When she had finished, she went next door. The room was empty and the chains and dog collars had gone, but the air had an elusive odor of hospitals and disinfectant. She threw up the window and set to work to obliterate all traces of Rothman's occupancy. In her nervousness, she knocked over a tin of talcum powder and stood rigid with anger as the powder billowed and settled on furniture and floor. She looked despairingly at the clock and began frantically to sweep and dust.

She was almost sobbing with frustration when she ran downstairs and lifted the receiver to phone Bucharest.

Danilenko answered at once, as if he had been awake and waiting for the call.

She was so intent in pouring out the message to him that she did not hear the gentle sigh of the swing door leading from the kitchen.

Sitting on the edge of his disordered bed, the Russian listened patiently. When the spate of words had stopped, he said evenly, "There is nothing very bad about this. You have the number of the hotel in Cimpina. A message there will reach us. We will leave now. If there is no message, we proceed as planned. Understood?"

"Yes, yes. Vasile will let you know if Bonneaud—" She spoke Russian.

"Quiet, woman!" Danilenko was annoyed. "Speak Rumanian. You are sure that you are ready to move out at a moment's notice?"

"Yes, I assure you. The cases are packed. We can be with you in minutes. That is no problem."

"Good night, then." Danilenko hung up quietly.

She sat for a moment, staring blankly at the pattern of fat rosebuds on the wallpaper. Two arms crept softly around her neck and there was a chuckle in her ear.

"Don't, Vasile!" she said absently.

The hands crossed to grasp the ends of the dangling braids. They pulled violently upward and backward. Behind her, the man panted with effort as again he crossed and twisted the braids.

Her heels drummed on the floor and her nails raked desperately at her throat, leaving bloody trails.

The biceps of Fouquet's arms stood out like billiard balls.

When the pounding heels were still and her arms had flopped to her sides, he left to switch on the light in the adjoining room. This was still kept as Lupescu's surgery for the patients who never came now. There was a small sink in one corner with a glass-fronted medicine cabinet above it. Behind the scuffed desk and the swivel chair was a steel cart with a collection of instruments and stainless-steel dishes. An armchair for patients faced the desk. The couch along one wall was littered with old medical journals. Behind the door hung the surgical coat and mask.

Fouquet looked quickly around and crossed the room to jerk the curtains close. The moment of fright and anger in the kitchen might never have been. It had been replaced almost at once by the detached quick thinking which had earned him his place high in the echelons of the smr. Now his considering look around the room was that of a stage manager evaluating the possibilities of a stage setting.

When he lifted the garotted woman, he grunted under her weight. The bulging eyes glared fiercely at him and the protruding purple tongue moved slightly as he staggered into the surgery.

Even in the short interval of time, she seemed to have shrunk, to have become at once smaller and heavier. To prop her upright in the chair, he had to pad out her back with some of the periodicals and put her hands on the desk. She had the air of an obscene object trying to get out of the chair.

By now, Lupescu would be restless and worried. In fifteen minutes the anxiety would be insupportable.

Rothman was deeply unconscious and should not waken until mid-morning. He was no problem.

Lupescu would come to the house to find out why he had not returned with the pentathol.

Fouquet squeezed behind the chair to study the instruments on the cart. He selected the largest scalpel. As he lifted it, there was the gurgle of escaping gas from the body, but he did not turn his head. Death and its indecencies was no stranger to him.

He cleared the papers from the corner of the couch nearest the door, glanced across the room to the desk, then switched off the light.

He went back to sit with the instrument in the darkness and wait.

Alan Bonneaud had phoned the Doftana villa from Fossard's hotel room in Bucharest within an hour of his return to the Villa Florica.

When he had left Fossard earlier at Baneasa, Bonneaud had been in excellent spirits. He had no reason to believe that his plans, formulated fully two years ago, were not about to come to fruition.

The merest chance had taken him back to his birthplace on the Taldy estate, where the sycophantic whisperings of an old servant had sent him probing and digging into the past. Like a pig snuffling after truffles, he had dug up one tenuous lead that connected the Holy Crown of Saint Stephen with Rumania. It was enough.

He had no scruples about employing the considerable resources of the SMR in an operation which he intended should be ultimately for his private benefit. Nor did he feel that his allegiance to communism was in any way besmirched by his plan to make a deal with Moscow. It simply meant that, this time, what he had to sell was infinitely more valuable and, therefore, understandably more costly, than anything he had been able to offer his fraternal colleagues on previous occasions. The stakes were high, but the reward promised to be of dazzling proportions.

He had chosen his team carefully, men who were brave, ruthless and as tenacious as terriers. He was too wise to cheat them or to trick them. If successful, they would be rewarded with princely generosity; if they failed, through stupidity or cowardice, they would be eliminated without mercy. Treachery was, of course, unthinkable.

Tony Rothman's intervention had not been entirely unexpected. Bonneaud had a respect for the British Department's Intelligence team that acknowledged the inevitability of its pursuit of the relic. He laid his plans to seize whatever operator they sent out and was a little disappointed that his catch had not been Charles Forsyth. He was still smarting from his punishment at the Englishman's hands at Prague. But his time would come.

Long experience had taught him the futility of dwelling on setbacks. Rothman's precarious state of health was a matter of cynical indifference to him. At least, the British

Department was now temporarily out of the game. By the time they put in another operator, Bonneaud hoped and expected that the crown would be in his possession. He was confident that they would never find Rothman in the old Doftana prison and if, by some million-to-one chance, they did, it would be a simple matter to arrange that Rothman be of no use to them.

He whistled a bawdy Marseilles bordello song as he parked his car and strolled toward the front door of the Villa Florica. The alarm bell operated by the grille had given warning of his approach. The door should have been open, with his secretary, Pietru, waiting for him. Impatiently he rang the bell. The frown deepened as the seconds ticked away and the door remained closed. Clearly something was wrong. Moving like a ghost, he went round the side of the house and found the open French window. He kicked with savage accuracy at the head of a cat that appeared suddenly at his feet.

He found the woman first. Her eyes filled with tears of relief that spilled and ran in crystal drops down her cheeks. He put a hand out and cupped one of her breasts, then drew a finger automatically down over the swell of her belly. She shivered and her eyes glazed with pleasure.

"Later, Magda," he murmured, "later." His eyes were on the thick pin sticking out from the top of her right shoulder, just above the arm socket.

He went into the bathroom and returned with a bundle of tissues. Using them, delicately he picked out the pin, examined it carefully and, wrapping it in the tissues, put it in an inner pocket. Only then did he pick the gag from the woman's mouth and begin to cut the bonds. As he worked, he questioned her softly, calming her with his detached manner and unhurried movements.

"Who did it?"

"I don't know."

He frowned uncomprehendingly at her reply.

She poured out the story of the intruder and of how Pietru had instructed her to trick him.

"But he didn't shoot that thing into me. I am sure of that. He was making for the front of the house then. I swear it."

He shrugged it aside. "Stay here," he commanded. "Either Pietru has him or he has gone by now. There is nothing to fear." He went out quickly and moved noiselessly toward the hall.

He looked coldly down at the suffused face of the man on the floor of his makeshift study. His first glance had told him that the map was gone.

Almost absently, he plucked out the saliva-sodden gag and went quickly toward his bedroom. He would have been amazed if Pietru had called out or had appealed for help. The room, he realized, had been searched by a professional.

He packed rapidly. All his possessions went into one case which he placed in the hall close to the door. He tried the telephone, but he did not expect it to work. He had no means of knowing that a page had been torn from the pad.

When he returned to the front room, he went down on one knee beside his secretary. With his hands deliberately motionless on the knots at the pudgy ankles, he commanded, "Tell me about it."

As if his thoughts were far away, he sat back on his heels and considered the story.

"Who did he claim to be? Describe him. He was not alone? You are certain that you did not see his companion?"

The questions were rapped out and the answers carefully considered. When Pietru described his paralysis, Bonneaud covered his fingers with a tissue and plucked the pin from the thick neck. He put it with the other in his pocket.

For a moment, he looked into the pale eyes below him

and then spoke softly. "You realize, Pietru, that you have behaved like a fool. I chose this villa very carefully, since I intended it to serve not only for this operation but for many in the future. It was to have been my headquarters in Europe. It has cost me much time and much money. Now all that is lost because of your carelessness. I have no alternative."

The man did not beg, but the expression in the eyes would have struck terror into most hearts.

Bonneaud's left hand shot out and seized the man's nose. He forced the jaws apart and, with an expression of disgust, rammed the soaking gag well down the gaping throat.

He walked swiftly to the woman's bedroom. She was standing in the middle of the room in her slip as though her trembling fingers had prevented her from dressing quickly.

He gave her a brilliant smile, as he went past her into the bathroom. "I will be with you in a moment, *chérie*. I must wash my hands."

When he came back, he took her very gently in his arms, cradling her head against his shoulder until the trembling stopped. The face she raised for his kiss was blank with adoration. She did not hear the tiny click of the switchblade knife, nor feel the thin blade as he thrust it strongly upward between her ribs, before giving it the final twist to let air into the wound.

His arm caught and held her as she fell. Methodically, he removed and cleaned the knife before pocketing it. He put her quickly on the bed and walked smartly along the tiled corridor to the hall to collect his case. He thought for a moment, then went back along the passage to secure the French window. Satisfied, he left, closing and locking the front door behind him.

With luck, it would be weeks or even months before the bodies were found.

When Fossard opened his bedroom door to him, Bonneaud looked just as usual. He said at once, "I must make a call to Lupescu."

When he had done so, he told Fossard what had happened.

"It sounds like the pig Forsyth," Fossard said explosively.

"You are wrong, *mon vieux*. Forsyth is no pig. Pigs are stupid and Forsyth is not. That one, I think, came out of the head of Zeus and it will be a long time before it opens up again. It is a pity about the Villa Florica, but it is not the end of the world."

"What do we do now?"

"Until morning, we sleep. I will stay here. We can do nothing until the Carpati office opens. Then I will find out where Forsyth has gone. Once before, when he was in Rumania, he called himself East. It will be so again."

He stretched himself out on the second bed and was almost instantly asleep. Fossard's eyes were bright with respect.

In the morning, when an official at Carpati had informed him that Mr. John East had arranged to stay at the Palas Hotel in Sinaia, Bonneaud's hand tightened for a moment on the receiver.

When he turned to face Fossard, his expression was unreadable. "We leave now for Sinaia," he said quietly.

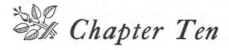

Chapter Ten

AS CHARLES FORSYTH climbed briskly up the main street in Sinaia, his thoughts veered away from the prospect of actually finding the crown somewhere ahead. It was as if he dared not allow himself to believe that its discovery was possible and imminent. The atmosphere of the mountain town helped to preserve his feeling of detachment, and he found himself concentrating on its sights and sounds to the exclusion of what really mattered to him.

He saw, as if it were immensely important, the cloud-wreathed "Cota 1,400" Alpine Hotel, resting like a snowflake on a peak of the Bucegi Mountains. His eyes followed the heart-stopping, upward crawl of the small khaki-colored jeep which acted as the local bus. He ought to have boarded it and let it take him past the entrace to Peles Castle and a short way into the woods, where he would find the little church.

Instead, he negotiated laboriously the dizzy hairpin curves and goatlike climbs, feeling the pain in his side knocking like an angry reminder of his folly. As he toiled upward, he would willingly have hurled the leather hatbox into the undergrowth. It reminded him too clearly for comfort of Nicola Beaufort and of her vulnerability in the Palas Hotel. Unconsciously he quickened his pace.

Meanwhile, high in the woods, Father Damian waited in his study as if he expected a guest.

The women in his congregation took it in turns to look after him, dividing their time between the presbytery and their own homes. He could not afford to pay, and they would not have expected it. This week Eva Bastouni was in charge.

To his annoyance, she flicked a duster across the spotless pile of books on his desk and said in the indulgent, bantering tones of a young woman addressing an old man, "Are you expecting somebody? Shall I make some fresh coffee?"

"Yes . . . no . . . oh, thank you, no." He rubbed a thin hand helplessly across his forehead. She must think that he was a fool, but he had awakened at dawn with that odd feeling of expectancy and it was still with him. He gave her the smile of blinding sweetness that reminded her of the picture of the Christ child in the church. She was not sure if it was a proper thought to have.

She gave him a troubled look. She and her husband, Zev, worried a great deal about Father Damian. Everybody knew that he was too old and too frail for the work of the church, but what would become of him if he could no longer say Mass, and what would become of all of them if they had no priest?

Fear and anger sent her stomping out to the kitchen where she collected a bowl and some vegetables. Today there was no meat. She placed a chair outside, so that she could prepare the vegetables in the sun-drenched light and at the same time watch the entrance to the church. Nobody had ever stolen or damaged anything there and they had few visitors, since the tourists were, in the main, communists; but the church was theirs, so she kept a proprietary eye on it.

In the dimness of the house, the old priest sat motionless in the straight-backed chair, deliberately denying himself the comfort of the shabby easy chair with the wings that supported his head so well. Nature, he knew, was preparing him for the grave. The flesh was disappearing from his bones, so that his face and hands had a transparent look. Try as he might, he could not keep his spine erect, so that it sometimes seemed to him—and the thought amused him —that he was returning to the fetal position. Eating had ceased to be a pleasure and was now a duty which he owed to the good souls who prepared his food so carefully. He felt guilty when he fed most of it to his cat and when he saved part of his bread allowance for the birds.

A great blessing was that his eyesight was surprisingly good and that, while he often became confused and forgot whether he had had his lunch or not, the words of the Mass and of his Office remained crystal-clear in his memory.

His days were long and pleasant as he waited for God.

He was a humble man, who saw nothing especially praiseworthy in his long service to the church under particularly difficult conditions. When he thought about himself at all, it was to feel wistfully that, in his eyrie in the Carpathians, the great dramas in the church had passed him by.

So there was no reason at all for this restlessness that made it difficult for him to sit quietly reading his Office. *Be still, and know that I am God,* he quoted often to his congregation when the pressures of poverty and politics seemed insupportable. Now he whispered the words to himself, seeking a serenity that never really left him.

When he had finished reading, he closed the scuffed black leather book, patted it like an old friend and placed it carefully on the top of his desk.

It was time for his stroll in the garden adjoining the church.

Two doves flew down, almost at his feet, twittering nervously and so beautiful in their gray and rose and blue softness that at first he did not hear Eva Bastouni's loud whisper.

"There's a man. He has just gone into the church. Shall I find out what he wants?"

He gave her an amused look. "No, thank you, my dear. I imagine his business is with Our Lord. I think we can trust Him to bid him welcome." Sometimes, in moments like this, his Rumanian had the Italian lilt of his native Celena where he had attended the same school as Pope John XXIII.

He walked slowly along the path, breathing the sweet earth smell and listening to the wind far off in the mountains, lightly moving the pine branches. High up in the sun a lark was singing and the priest paused to listen, remembering how the throat vibrated in an explosion of sound. He wondered how the great old trees would look to the bird, whirring and poised in the blue.

A butterfly, its orange wings streaked with gray, alighted on a stone. He paused to watch it and to admire the gold fans of the ferns, but Eva's voice followed him accusingly, like a hissing in dried weeds, "The man looked tired. Are we so poor that we cannot give him a glass of milk, a cup of coffee?"

His left hand patted the air in a gentle wave of assent. Behind him, he heard the rustle of her skirts as she went into the house.

In the church, he bowed his head and genuflected. The dark, wise eyes went to the figure at the other end of the aisle and he prayed, "Comfort this man, O Lord, and take from him the trouble that is in his face."

He went to meet him.

Close up, the man was not as young as he had thought. The deep lines in his face were like the marks of physical suffering and the blue eyes, that should have been frank and merry, had the guarded look that Father Damian had seen so often in the eyes of his flock. But the mouth was good—well formed and humorous, with a hint of kindness deliberately suppressed. Father Damian decided that he liked the face, just as he liked the purpose and strength that he sensed in the quiet figure.

The man had been examining the picture of Saint Jude on the right wall of the church, but he turned his head alertly to watch Father Damian's approach. He had been holding a leather box. Now he put it down on the nearest seat as if embarrassed by it.

He said in excellent Rumanian, "I have been admiring your picture of the saint. Isn't it unusual? I don't think I have seen one before."

The priest smiled. "There is nothing unusual about it as a painting. It has no great monetary value and I hope the artist will forgive me if I say that it has no great artistic merit. But my people and I love it. Saint Jude is good to all of us. And we are honored to have it, because I do not know of any other in this country."

The man, he sensed, was not at ease in the church. Clearly he had not come to pray, yet Father Damian felt that he was not a tourist. He waited, as he always waited for his parishioners to tell him their troubles.

The saint looked placidly down at both of them and, crazily, without conscious intention, the priest found himself on his knees, praying aloud the familiar prayer: "Saint Jude, glorious Apostle, faithful servant and friend of Jesus, the name of the traitor has caused thee to be forgotten by many, but the Church honors and invokes thee universally as the patron of hopeless cases—of matters despaired of . . . Come to my assistance in this great need . . ."

When the formal prayer had been concluded, he paused momentarily, then continued: "Grant that the purpose that has brought this man to seek Thy aid may be fulfilled. Bless his task and bestow upon him the grace of perseverance and the courage to work for the greater glory of God and of His saints."

When he got to his feet, the man was standing very stiffly, with a strange expression on his face.

"You were expecting me," he stated.

"Yes," said Father Damian. "I think I was. What is your name?"

He thought the man hesitated for a moment before he said, "I am Charles Forsyth. I am English and I would like to ask you some questions, but it is only fair to warn you that there may be danger for you if you answer them, and danger if you even talk to me."

The priest smiled. "At my age, there is little left to be afraid of. How can I help you?"

Forsyth took the tattered holy picture from his wallet. "Can you tell me if this came from your church?"

The priest examined it carefully. "I am certain that it did. You see here," he pointed to the lower left-hand corner, "the name of the printer. He lives in Brasov and still does this work although he is very old. But this was printed a long time ago, perhaps—I am not certain—more than twenty years ago. I did not come here until 1952. There were no such holy pictures then, though our painting of Saint Jude was here. Recently, about a month ago, we were able to have the little cards again."

Forsyth put the paper back in his wallet. He got down on his knees and examined the wooden floor carefully.

The priest said tranquilly, "If you want to know if that floor has been tampered with, we have only to ask Zev Bastouni. His father laid it and, as a boy, Zev helped him."

"It is tongued and grooved," Forsyth said thoughtfully. "I am sure it is just as it was originally laid down. I would like to look at the outer wall."

They went out together. The air smelled of sweet grass and the great gong of a frog boomed at them from a small pond half hidden by the trees.

Forsyth had paced the distance from the picture of the

saint to the door. Now he paced the same distance along the outer wall. He halted at the trunk of an odd-looking tree.

"What is it?" he asked.

"A Judas tree—it gets its beautiful red blooms first of all and then the leaves."

Forsyth laughed. "A Judas tree! How appropriate!" He seemed to come to a decision. "Would you mind very much," he asked, "if I were to dig it up? I promise to put it back again as carefully as possible." He looked round the immaculately kept garden. "I know that I am asking a great deal."

The dark eyes twinkled. "Mr. Forsyth, you will be digging up my conscience and that isn't a bad thing to do. Whenever I have felt that my faith needed strengthening, I have walked up and down by this Judas tree and always felt the better for it. Then my conscience would trouble me that I found my consolation outside and not inside the church." He laughed merrily. "Saint Jude has had a hard time with me."

The wise old face sobered. "We will go indoors and you will drink a cup of coffee and make up your mind as to whether or not you want to tell me why you must dig up my garden. Meanwhile, I will send Eva Bastouni for her husband, Zev, and young Barbu. They are woodcutters and very strong. They will do what you want in half the time that you could do it. Come, my son."

This time Father Damian sat in the winged chair so that his guest might sit at ease in the one opposite him. The two men studied each other and smiled as if they had reached a mutual understanding.

Charles Forsyth then broke a Department rule and told Father Damian the whole story.

As he listened, the old man's face was suffused with such a look of joy that Forsyth's voice stumbled in its quiet recital and finally was silent. He saw the trembling of the waxy hands and the frank spilling of tears from the innocent eyes.

"I walked and was comforted and strengthened! The holy relic of Saint Stephen is assuredly there! O God, I thank Thee that I have been, though unworthy, the guardian of Thy treasure!" He got up from his chair and went unsteadily across to Forsyth. He kissed him gently on the forehead. "You have been chosen to be the instrument of God's grace. He always desires the peace of the world."

He clapped his hands sharply together. "Now we must be practical. The men will be here soon. I must tell them something of this, but they are to be trusted. It is as if it were the Body of Christ Himself. They will be careful and reverent. Forgive me, but I cannot stay here. Let us go back to the tree."

It was probably the strangest moment of both their lives when they watched the first spadefuls of soil being thrown up.

The two woodcutters were powerfully built men with calm eyes and unhurried movements, but they looked moved when Father Damian touched them lightly and said, "The great Princes of the Church have not had the privilege that Our Lord has vouchsafed to us. May He bless this work!"

While they waited, Forsyth fetched the leather box from the church and carried it into the priest's house. He brought out a chair and made Father Damian sit while the men worked.

They had dug down more than a meter when Zev Bastouni said hoarsely, "It is there!"

His spade had split the padlock that secured the lock on the black metal box that he hauled out and placed in the middle of the path.

For a moment, Forsyth and Father Damian looked at it in silence. A bird sang a piercingly sweet song over and over again.

"I think we should get it into the house as quickly as possible," Forsyth said.

"No!" Father Damian's voice was strong and authoritative. "Not the house—it must go to the church first." He turned to Barbu. "Carol, fetch a bedsheet as quickly as possible. There is no time to clean the box properly. You and Zev must place the box on the sheet and carry it into the church. It must be put on the table at the door. Zev, light the candles on the altar and come back here."

He turned almost apologetically to Forsyth. "This will not take long. You must understand, my son, that this is a holy relic which has been desecrated by theft. The church lays upon me the obligation of carrying out the ceremony prescribed for such circumstances."

So Forsyth the atheist lifted from its hiding place the Holy Crown of Saint Stephen and followed Father Damian to place it on the altar.

While the words of the Latin service flowed over him, he and the two Rumanians looked incredulously at the enormous jewels winking in the candlelight, at the massive gold of the rounded crown, at the tilted cross and the dangling pendants. Above it, Father Damian's face shone with a joy that seemed to give his features a new youth and a new strength.

Thundering into Forsyth's mind came the words, *As He died to make men holy, Let us live to make men free! . . . And His soul goes marching on!*

Glory Hallelujah, indeed!

With hands that trembled with emotion, the old priest carried the crown and headed the strange little procession back to the presbytery. He led Forsyth to his study.

Father Damian saw the Englishman look impatiently at his watch and frown. With a pang, he watched Forsyth place the crown in the leather box and square his shoulders as if he had an unpleasant task to perform. Clearly it was time for him to leave.

From the kitchen came the deep rumble of voices. For Eva and Zev and Carol, as for him, this time of wonder could not—must not—be over. But the great moments in life always called for a correspondingly great faith. This was one of them.

He said gently to Forsyth, "Do not be afraid, my son. You will finish your task. There will be angels about you, although," the dark eyes twinkled, "they may come in the unlikely guises of my friends, the woodcutters. I think you need them still. What were your plans?"

"I must get the girl, but I know that it would be dangerous to drive now to Cimpina. The man Bonneaud must be very near and we might meet him. I can't risk that while I have the crown. That I must get back safely to London." He hesitated. "I have no say in what becomes of it then, but I imagine that it will be sent to the Vatican."

The priest closed his eyes.

Forsyth continued, "The two Frenchmen will come here. That is certain. You must understand that these are evil men." He looked despairingly at the gentle old face. "You will be no match for them. I think you must get away from here before they come."

The priest laughed. "My son, you forget that I am an expert in dealing with evil. I have been fighting the devil all my life." His face sobered. "Of course, I am afraid of evil. Christ Himself prayed to be spared temptation, but . . . this is my job. Leave me to do it."

Forsyth thought for a moment. "Then," he said, "don't attempt to deny that I have been here. Tell them that I have taken the crown, but that you do not know where it is. The girl and I will drive out to Busteni and stay there until after dark. By then, Bonneaud should have gone back to Cimpina. To convince him, give him this." He handed over his visiting card. "Tell him that his business is with me and that I invite him to come and settle it."

Father Damian looked at the card doubtfully. "I do not

like this." He eyed Forsyth sternly. "It is not good to mix up God's work with the settling of personal scores." He looked with those surprisingly alert eyes into the younger man's worn face. It was as if he felt in his own body the bone-weariness and heartsickness that had been growing in Forsyth like a mortal illness. He leaned forward and handed the card back. "I will not let you spoil this good work now," he said firmly. There were centuries of authority in the old voice. "I do not have the ability to read much in English. It is a labor for me, but once I read about the famous cleric who was murdered in a cathedral and I have never forgotten what the poet wrote." He hesitated, searching for the quotation. "Forgive me. I do not recall the exact words, but the meaning was that it is treason—the greatest treason—to do a good action for the wrong reason. Intention is important. Sound theology, my son!"

Forsyth smiled, looked down at the scrap of cardboard and crushed it absently between his fingers.

"We should have met sooner," he said. "I am sorry, but now I must go."

"No. It is better to hide up here in the woods. Busteni is small and very, very quiet. You would be seen. Let me think." He pounded his two tiny fists against his brow. He got up abruptly and went into the kitchen. When he came back, he looked relieved. "It is settled. Tonight you and the girl will stay in the Bastouni cottage. It is a poor place, but there you will be safe."

"But I must make arrangements for the car. I can't bring a car up into the woods here."

"The cousin of Eva is the hall porter at the Palas Hotel. He will take care of everything. Now Eva will go and fetch the girl. While we wait we will drink a little *ţuica*." He laughed. "I am tempted to drink a lot of *ţuica*, but it would be a pity to blot out any of my memories of this morning. There will be rejoicing in heaven today. Let us join with the saints."

As Father Damian collected the glasses and the bottle of plum brandy, Forsyth wrote a note to Nicola Beaufort:

Leave the Palas as quickly and quietly as you can. Pack both cases and leave them in your room. Wear warm clothing, strong shoes and an anorak, if possible. Bring both traveling rugs, my gun and half of the food. Mission successful. Join me earliest. The woman is completely trustworthy.

When Eva Bastouni had left, both men sat and stared at the box containing the crown. Their thoughts were very different. Even the day of his ordination had not brought the priest the sense of holy joy that now filled his whole being. At times it was as if his body could not contain so much emotion. In a sense, it would almost be better when the young man had taken the relic away. Then he would be free to dream and remember and speculate.

It was strange, he thought, how quietly the Englishman had come into his life and how briefly their paths had crossed and yet, because of him, he, Father Damian, would never be the same again. He was conscious of being very tired. Perhaps even the small glass of *țuică* had been a mistake.

For Charles Forsyth, it was a time of intense frustration. When the tin box had been opened, he had had a moment of blinding triumph tinged with incredulity. Now the feeling of satisfaction had gone. His impulse had been to move quickly out of the area as soon as he had checked that he had really secured the treasure. Now it was as if he was being held by invisible bands that irked him and undermined his singleness of purpose.

What the hell was he doing sitting drinking when he should be showing Bonneaud a clean pair of heels? How had the girl managed to maneuver him into a position where he felt that he could not move without her? He got suddenly to his feet feeling that he had to assert himself and convince himself that he was firmly in charge of the operation. He began to fasten the lid of the hatbox.

"I think I should walk to the edge of the road and wait for the women there." He patted the box. "The sooner I get this away from here, the happier I'll feel. I won't try to thank you for your helpfulness. I'm grateful."

Father Damian escorted him to the door of the study and opened it. "Go with God," he said. He watched his visitor departing as quietly as he had come. Then he went back to enjoy his thoughts and his confused prayers.

He was asleep in the wing chair when Bonneaud came.

From Bucharest with Sergio Eliasberg at the wheel, the car sped off through the darkness heading for Ploesti. Once they had crossed the thin trickle of the Dumbovitza, the Russian whipped the car along the highway past Lake Caldarusani. He drove with a skill that allowed Yuri Danilenko to sleep peacefully beside him. It was a strange, lonely journey, as if there were few people in the region.

When Eliasberg saw on his right the beginnings of the archways of centuries-old silver poplars, he knew that he was at the edge of the Rucasa Forest and that soon the road would climb into the mountains.

He sped through a small white town of enchanting old belfries, imposing white houses and dreaming gardens. At his side, Danilenko stirred in his sleep and settled more deeply into the car seat. The gun in his pocket brushed lightly against the door.

As the dawn wind rattled the pane of Father Damian's bedroom window on the day that was to be the most exciting in his life, Danilenko woke as if an alarm bell had gone off in his brain. His right hand automatically checked his gun. Satisfied, he eased his legs in the confined space of the car while his eyes noted the fugitive lights springing up on the outskirts of Cimpina.

He had been trained to sink grayly into the background, so it would not have occurred to him to pass this day exploring the town. In that way he might have invited attention. But two men spending the day in their bedroom were just as liable to spark off gossip. That must be taken care of.

How could they pass an entire day without attracting attention? What possible reason could they have for remaining in the privacy of their room? Danilenko saw a solution. If Eliasberg were seen to be ill, the problem was solved. He would not risk asking his comrade's consent.

He said easily, "Pick a suitable spot and stop."

"Good," said Eliasberg. "I have a call of nature." He eased the car gently into the side of the road and got out, yawning and stretching comfortably. Then he began to walk back toward the spot where a thick clump of bushes threw a deep shadow across the road.

At the back of the car, Danilenko quickly opened his valise and found the leather case with its array of bottles, tablets and syringes. His hand went unerringly to the square brown bottle with the label marked *Spirit of Ipecac.* He had transferred the bottle to his pocket and was back in the car when Eliasberg returned, fumbling with his buttons.

"Take your time," Danilenko commanded good-humoredly. "We must waste a little time. By eight o'clock, people will be busy over breakfast. It would be best to check in at the hotel then. Nobody will pay much attention to us."

He noticed without appreciation how the masses of the honeysuckle vines had crept from the fence line and cast silver-violet shadows on the grass. The fallen walnuts were sooty black. He disliked the country and looked forward to getting to Cimpina. Although he did not know the town, he realized that he would feel more at home in it than he did on this windy country road.

Casually, he added, "I do not think I can wait much longer to eat. How do you feel? There is bound to be a café for workers before we get into Cimpina. Drive slowly and I will look out for one."

Almost as soon as the road surface changed to become the cobbled streets of the town, he saw what he wanted.

Both men felt at home among the truck drivers and the steel workers. They sat at a zinc-covered table and ordered coffee and the thick wedges of bread which they saw on the plates at the other tables. Danilenko chose a table at the back of the room and sat with his back to the wall where he had a good view of everybody. Through an arch covered with a long crimson curtain was the entrance to the café, where there was a counter with a poor assortment of sweets, wines and cigarettes.

As the sleepy waiter was approaching the table with their breakfast, Danilenko patted his pockets. "Tch! Tch! No cigarettes. Be a good fellow and fetch me some. Any kind will do." He pushed some money across the table to Eliasberg, who got up good-naturedly and went out through the curtain.

As soon as the curtain folds had settled into place, Danilenko drew the brown bottle from his pocket. There was a dropper attached to the stopper. His hand above Eliasberg's coffee might have been adding sugar. With his eyes apparently on the room, the Russian managed with incredible speed to drop fifteen drops of the emetic into the strong black coffee.

As Eliasberg took his place opposite him, Danilenko paused in the act of raising his cup to his lips. "You'll need half the basinful of sugar. Their coffee is vile. But drink it up. We never know when we may get a meal again. In our business, ulcers come as regularly as our pay." They laughed with the confidence of healthy peasants who had never experienced a day's serious illness.

Eliasberg tossed off the coffee and grimaced. He made

an obscene suggestion about the origin of the coffee which amused them both. Danilenko's pale eyes watched him thoughtfully. Within a couple of hours at the most his companion would be fully restored.

They had finished their meal and were about to light their cigarettes when Eliasberg began to feel sick. Waves of cold sweat broke out over his body. With an anguished look at Danilenko, he heaved himself up from the table and went in a blundering rush through the curtain marked *Barbati*. He was just in time. When he leaned, still retching and trembling against the wall of the toilet, his face had a startling pallor.

After a time, Danilenko heard his groans and went to look for him. He had to support him to the car, where he sprawled, sweating and shuddering.

At the hotel in Cimpina, the receptionist took one look at his livid face and waved aside the formalities until the poor sick man was safely in his bedroom. As he waited downstairs for Danilenko to come down with their passports and permits, he remarked to the hall porter, "They are booked for two days. That pair won't be moving far from their bedroom or I miss my guess."

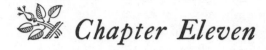

Chapter Eleven

A T MID-MORNING, near Mount Furnica, Bonneaud's Porsche 911S turned in at the white-painted gates fronting a broad drive. The house could be seen very clearly from the main road. It sat in icing-sugar splendor high on a hill. So it commanded an excellent view of the encircling mountains and the narrow fissure that marked the beginning of a cleftlike valley.

Bonneaud's considering gaze took in the impressive location, the sturdy compactness of the villa and its disarmingly pretty appearance. It was like a doll's-house version of a Rhineland castle. Almost imperceptibly, he nodded as if satisfied. It was farther from an airport than he would have liked, but that was not a major drawback. When the affair of the crown was over, this would do very well as a base for future operations in mid-Europe. He surveyed the center of his new kingdom benevolently.

As Fossard brought the car gently to a halt at the front door, Bonneaud was busy calculating just how big a slice of the profits from the sale of the crown he would have to surrender.

Mihnea Jordanes, the owner of the estate, had more than his share of the greediness of the very rich. He would drive a hard bargain. Bonneaud smiled cynically. What his friend Mihnea would not be able to resist was the power that the association would bring him. The serpentlike cunning and total corruption that had enabled him to retain his wealth and influence in communist Rumania would be worth a fortune to them. Eventually, Bonneaud determined, the funds of the SMR would reimburse him. The money was not important. Not for nothing was Bonneaud known as the Red Wolf.

Fossard whistled enviously at the sight of the porcelain-white Lamborghini Espada parked askew a few yards away.

A man in chauffeur's uniform came around the side of the house, gave them a hard look and moved quickly toward them. There was something truculent and threatening in his attitude. Fossard braced himself with feet apart and let his hand drift gently toward the gun in his pocket.

Bonneaud ignored the man and pushed the bell of the front door. He said over his shoulder, "Wait in the car. I won't be long."

Fossard heard a voice saying, "Ah! Monsieur Bonneaud, how good to see you again! Monsieur Jordanes is in the library. He will be delighted."

The chauffeur heard it also and turned away.

Half an hour later, Bonneaud and Mihnea Jordanes had come to terms. They would be partners in all future SMR operations and the villa would be the new center for such operations.

Afterward, during the recital of the full story of the Hungarian crown, the Rumanian's brain had ticked away like a computer, evaluating his chances of cheating Bonneaud.

The Frenchman said coolly, "Don't try it, Mihnea. Steal from me and—." He made a chopping movement with his left hand over his right wrist.

Jordanes laughed. "One always explores the possibilities, my friend." He stretched across the desk, extending his hand. "Let us shake hands on our partnership. And now tell me about the man Forsyth. Can I assist you there?"

"Thank you, but no."

He described Forsyth briefly and Jordanes listened intently. "He sounds a dangerous man. The sooner you get rid of him the better."

Jordanes was a muscular man in the late forties, with a mop of prematurely white hair above a youthful, tanned face. He had an alert, bright-eyed look like an intelligent adolescent, but now the eyes flattened curiously, as if he were contemplating unspeakable horrors.

Bonneaud knew that he enjoyed cruelty for its own sake and despised him for it. For himself, violence was something to be used efficiently and only when necessary. When there had to be embellishments, he left it to underlings.

There was a sound behind him. He got quickly to his feet as a girl came into the room. The man behind the desk did not stir.

Bonneaud's eyebrows climbed. She had lasted longer than usual. She wore the customary uniform. The white cat-suit emphasized her height and slimness and strikingly complemented the gleaming pompadour of black hair and the slanting green eyes. His eyes slid over the voluptuous curves.

From behind the desk, Jordanes watched them both.

The girl crossed the room and leaned a hip against the corner of the desk. She regarded Bonneaud amiably, with the same considering look that Jordanes had given her.

Bonneaud grinned at her. He understood her perfectly.

"Chi-Chi is as delighted as I am that you will be staying overnight. She has hopes." Jordanes laughed with no amusement in the sound. "She is doing her best to blush, but Nature omitted to furnish her with the necessary mechanism."

He got up and walked around the desk. One hand tilted the girl's chin up. The other cupped her breast and Bonneaud saw the fingers tighten cruelly. The blood drained from her face.

Bonneaud got to his feet. "Thanks for the show, Mih-nea." His voice was a lazy drawl. "They do it better in a *boîte* in the 7th *arrondissement*. I must take you there sometime. If you do not get some new ideas, I will pay for our entertainment." With his hand on the doorknob, he looked with genuine amusement at his friend. "I see that I have come at the right time. You are bored, *mon vieux*. I hope that over dinner this evening, I will have something to show you and to tell you that will dissipate your ennui. *A bientôt!*"

Before he got into the car beside Fossard, he spat on the ground, as if he had a bad taste in his mouth.

He was silent throughout the journey until the Porsche crawled up the main street of Sinaia. It was slowed almost to a standstill by the town jeep.

"*Merde!*" said Fossard explosively as the jeep ground to a halt immediately opposite the entrance to the Palas Hotel. He parked the Porsche at an awkward angle behind it.

Bonneaud looked with interest at the two women standing on the pavement, obviously waiting for the clumsy vehicle. One he dismissed immediately. She was a peasant with a sturdy body and walnut-brown face. She could have been any age from thirty to fifty. She was clutching a bundle of dark-colored blankets and stood protectively over what looked like a box of groceries.

Probably the girl's housekeeper, he thought.

His gaze lingered appreciatively on the younger woman. She had that to-hell-with-the-peasants air common to some American and English women. Normally, he did not like women in trousers, but the beige slacks suited her and the polo neck of the white wool pullover made a becoming frame for the clear cameo of her face. Her eyes were hidden behind enormous sunglasses, a fashion he deplored. The glare from mountain sunshine could, he allowed, be uncomfortable. Nor was there anything incongruous in the blonde anorak draped over her arm. But two items in her equipment brought a curl to his lips. She was holding an old-fashioned gray felt hat, decorated with a ridiculous bunch of glossy red cherries. The other hand held a dart-board.

An *original,* if ever there was one!

At his side, Fossard said angrily, "I must move the car. I'll be back as quickly as possible. No one seems to know where the hall porter has gone. Smoking or drinking somewhere, I'll guess." He got back into the driver's seat and waited for the jeep to move off. "At least the man at the reception desk seems bright enough." He added humorously, "Don't dispose of East until I get back."

Bonneaud smiled and entered the hotel.

He emerged shortly afterward, looking thunderous. Swiftly he went back down the street to meet Fossard and said curtly, "We've missed him. Reception seems a bit hazy about his movements. The sum total of their knowledge seems to be that he has checked out and his stuff has gone from his room. He had a car, but it is no longer in the hotel parking place. A great big zero of information, it seems."

"He can't have come to Sinaia and practically turned around and left," Fossard said. "That doesn't make sense. Could he be at Peles Castle?"

"I don't think so." Bonneaud cocked his head and listened absently. The local train was making its way down the valley, its whistle reverberating in the mountains like the grandiose echoes of a Wagnerian chorus. "There was just one thing. The man at reception overheard him asking the hall porter where the Roman Catholic church was." He tapped his lower teeth thoughtfully with a forefinger. "Perhaps I will ask the same question."

When he returned, his face had the preoccupied look that Fossard knew meant that it was unwise to attempt conversation. Together they went back to collect the car and drove up the main street. When the Porsche could go no farther, Bonneaud got out. "Wait here," he commanded. "The priest is old, I understand. Two of us might alarm him." He looked at his watch. "If I am not back in half an hour, come after me." He disappeared along the mountain path.

When he came to the church in the peaceful, sundappled clearing, he had for the first time a pang of doubt. Impossible to associate one of the great treasures of a country with this backswood building!

He prowled restlessly through the church, glancing indifferently at the painting of Saint Jude. It meant nothing to him.

He stood for a moment in the entrance looking around, then turned impatiently and went into the garden. Almost immediately he saw the newly turned earth and halted, rigid with shock.

"Two men did it. The foreigner watched them."

He pivoted around.

A ragged boy of about ten years of age stood at the end of the path, poised as if ready for instant flight. He looked neglected and dirty and the dark eyes had a vacant look.

The village idiot! Bonneaud thought disgustedly. He schooled himself not to move. "Hello!" he said gently. "That was clever of you to see it. Did you know who they were?"

He spun a coin in the air. The quenched gaze followed the gleam of its flight. The boy waved a hand vaguely in the direction of the woods, leaped like a fawn to catch the falling coin and was off among the trees before Bonneaud could stop him.

His mouth set in a grim line. The thought that Forsyth had outwitted him filled him with a rage that brought the dark blood pounding in his forehead. He willed himself to be calm.

The priest must have been a party to it. The next move was to talk to him.

He moved between the clumps of flowers to the presbytery. The door was wide open. He could see a shabby hall with two doors on either side and one facing him. Nobody answered his ring.

After a moment, he walked softly into the hall and turned the handle of the first door on his left.

A very old man lay asleep in a wing chair. At first, Bonneaud thought he was dead. The face and hands were waxy, and when Bonneaud put a finger lightly on his cheek, the flesh had the chill of marble. The scraggy, corded neck reminded him of a plucked hen's. As he watched, the lips moved.

Father Damian was dreaming of his father who had been long since dead. He was a small boy again. He could see his father's dark Latin face and hear his kindly voice saying, "My son, never argue with the devil. He's too clever for you. Say your prayers. That defeats him every time!" And his father's joyous laugh had boomed out.

In a burst of impatience, Bonneaud seized the frail shoulder and shook it gently.

Father Damian's eyes flew open. Vaguely, he saw the controlled face above him.

The aura of evil was unmistakable.

"Where is the Englishman?" Bonneaud strove to keep his voice pleasant.

"He could not wait," the old voice said mildly, "but he left you a message." His fingers fumbled beneath his soutane, searching in his trouser pocket for his rosary. Strength seemed to flow to him from the worn beads.

Bonneaud's mouth tightened impatiently.

"What did he say? What was the message?"

"That he had found the crown and had taken charge of it. I can assure you that it is not here. It would be pointless to look for it."

"But where is he now?" Bonneaud saw the distant look

in the priest's eyes. The old man was remembering his father's warning. To Bonneaud, the face looked senile.

The wavering voice began, "My soul doth magnify the Lord . . ."

The Frenchman cut across the prayer. "You were with Forsyth when he took the crown. Where has he taken it?"

Father Damian began to recite the Nicene Creed.

With difficulty, Bonneaud restrained himself.

"I will go unto the altar of God," chanted Father Damian, "to God who giveth joy to my youth . . ."

The veins on Bonneaud's forehead stood out like ropes. "You old fool!" he gritted and struck the priest a resounding blow on the face.

"Te Deum," caroled Father Damian feebly and his eyes twinkled as they followed Bonneaud's progress out of the room.

As he wiped away the trickle of blood from the corner of his mouth, he was deeply happy. Shortly, he would drink a little *ţuica*.

As he helped Nicola Beaufort from the jeep, Forsyth's eyes went approvingly to the hat and incredulously to the dartboard. Was the girl *mad*?

He saw her eyes on the hatbox, as if she expected him to open it there and then.

"Any trouble?" he asked.

"None."

They began the laborious, intricate climb to the Bastouni cottage. The air smelled of sweet grass laced with the pungency of fungi. Occasionally they passed a woman sitting by the side of the path, her hands busy with the tatting from which she hoped to earn a few *lei*. Sometimes a woodcutter would edge past, carefully protecting them from the crude, swinging coat hangers or carved boxes that he would try to sell to the tourists in the town.

Forsyth was full of an unusual sense of peace which he in no way confused with the satisfaction following a job well done. From the beginning of the operation, it seemed to him that he had stumbled from situation to situation in an unprecedented way. He had brought to the job little of his customary coolness and efficiency, and the fact that the crown now hung weightily from his hand owed more, he felt, to an obscure waiter than to him. Moreover, the rescue of Tony Rothman now had an alarming lack of urgency in his mind. That mood would have to be altered sharply. Now that Bonneaud knew where the crown was, Rothman was expendable.

He began to plan, the moves slotting smoothly into place like the meshes of well-ordered gears.

From behind him came a rhythmic whispering thud as Nicola Beaufort's large white shoulder bag struck her hip as she strode.

Once he glanced over his shoulder at her and was startled by the tension in her face. The light caught the gleam of perspiration along the hairline and upper lip. He made an excuse to stop as though winded.

Her breathing was slow and untroubled, but he frowned as he saw her fumble in the handbag and swallow a capsule. His hand shot out and grabbed the small bottle before she could replace it. The label was marked *Serenace o'5m.* The prescription had been issued by a Wigmore Street chemist almost two weeks earlier.

"Why the devil is a healthy young woman like you swallowing tranquillizers?" His tone was deliberately offensive.

Her chin went up. "I suggest you leave the care of my physical functions to me." Her tone was icy.

He gave her a defeated look and resumed the plodding climb. Unwillingly he acknowledged to himself that her well-being was important to him, not because her illness might endanger the assignment, but on a purely personal level. Was she ill? His thoughts worried away at the question and he had to make a determined effort to put it aside. What he could not control was his deepening sense of compassion for her.

Presently they followed a narrow track that snaked between the firs and brought them out in front of the Bastouni cottage. It was a substantial two-story log cabin with a deceptively opulent look.

"These people are much poorer than the people in the marshlands of the Danube Delta," Forsyth explained quietly to the girl. "Looking at this kind of house, you wouldn't think so, but these mountain folk have ample resources for building at hand. I hope you brought plenty of food. These poor souls have nothing to spare."

His eyes were taking in the terrain round the house. He moved quickly to the back and found that the back half was a single story. The roof had an odd appearance as if it had been split in two. There were two shuttered windows in the two-story part and below them the roof sloped down sharply. At one side, under a lean-to, was a huge pile of logs and a mound of brushwood.

He went back to join the others in the house. There was a fairly large living room, dominated by an enormous blue-tiled stove which was sending out a gentle heat that made the room cozy. The furnishings were sparse and appeared to have been made by Zev.

The woodcutter saw Forsyth gazing at the thick rope which hung from an iron ring in the wooden ceiling and had its end twisted round an iron latch on the wall.

"That works the trapdoor into the loft," he explained. "Someday I will make two rooms there and a proper stairway. The flooring and the walls have been completed, but God has not sent us any children, so there is no hurry. Eva and I will sleep there tonight." He looked troubled. "We have only one bedroom." His eyes went doubtfully to the girl.

"No." Forsyth was firm. "Miss Beaufort and I will sleep

there. We have blankets. In any case, we will leave during the night—by two o'clock at the latest. I think we are safe here until then, but if the Frenchman should come, I want to be able to get out over the roof."

Bastouni accepted the arrangement. He opened the trap-door and a ladder swung down into the room. He jumped and pulled it down to floor level.

When their few possessions had been taken into the loft, Nicola Beaufort handed Forsyth a spectacle case. "You forgot your glasses," she said. "I thought you would need them. I also brought your night binoculars and—"

"And that damned dartboard. What possessed you to bring that?"

She looked at him blankly. "But I thought it was important. Even after that horrible man kicked you in the ribs and you were in pain, you practiced. You told me so."

"Of course I did." He explained patiently. "The board is standard equipment in my job. A good eye, whether it is for shooting, lobbing a grenade or what-have-you, is essential. Playing darts is like a musician practicing scales—dreary, but necessary." He omitted to mention the green darts, stuffed in the binocular case. He hoped she had not found them.

She looked crestfallen.

"We'll be stuck indoors until we leave for Cimpina. A few games will help to pass the time." He put a hand under her elbow and led her to the front door.

When he removed her sunglasses and replaced them with his spectacles, she drew in her breath in amazement.

"Fantastic! I've never seen anything like it. Why! Surely I'm seeing around corners!"

"Actually what you are having is a wide-angled view. These glasses operate like a wide-angle lens."

Eve and Zev Bastouni tried them and looked at the glasses as though they were bewitched.

Forsyth explained patiently, "More than one hundred

and fifty years ago, a Frenchman called Augustin Fresnel invented a thin-edged lens to focus the flashing beams of lighthouses. In 1970, two great advances were made on this work by the Optical Sciences Group in America. First of all, they developed a stepped lens that produced a much clearer image. Secondly, a computer-controlled ruling machine made the production of these lenses practical."

"How marvelous! Are the lenses used only for glasses like these?"

"No. You can buy what's called a lensor. It looks like a thin plastic disc for a record player. It's made of optical grade polyvinyl chloride which has been asphericized to eliminate spherical aberration. It is a piano-concave lens with a diameter of eleven inches and a focal length of minus twelve inches. If it were made of conventional glass, its edge would be four inches thick, it would weigh fourteen pounds and it would be expensive."

Nicola Beaufort looked slightly stunned.

"To think I might have dropped them!" she said.

Forsyth laughed. "If they don't earn their keep before we get back to London, you have my full permission to smash them. Now," he added crisply, "we eat and then you and I sleep. Barbu and Bastouni will be keeping a lookout for Bonneaud and his friend, so we can relax. He won't leave Sinaia without trying to find me, but he'll also expect me to go after Rothman as soon as possible. Bonneaud will be beating it back there to grab the crown and, incidentally, me, when I get close to wherever he is holding him in Cimpina. Let's make the most of this chance to rest."

He saw her shivering. "You've done very well," he said stiffly. "Get some sleep and concentrate on the thought that in about three days' time you'll be back in London, planning your trousseau."

She turned abruptly away and climbed the ladder to the makeshift bed in the loft. He thought that her eyes were full of tears.

Before he followed her, he trimmed the rim of the felt
hat. Feeling faintly sacrilegious, he fitted the hat over the
crown. It covered the glowing mass of gold and jewels
completely. No one opening the box would have suspected
that it held anything other than a collection of rather
dowdy hats.

His last waking thought was that he had not shown the
crown to the girl and she had been too proud to ask.

"You mean that all you have to go on is a wave of the
hand from a boy you thought looked a bit touched?" Fossard sounded disgruntled and incredulous. He was tired
and hungry and quite convinced that their search of the
woods was an impossible task. But the habit of obedience
died hard. Even as he protested, he followed Bonneaud
closely along the mountain track.

Bonneaud halted. He was in magnificent physical condition now, fully recovered from the beating he had endured
from Forsyth in Prague. He knew that he could keep up
the search for many more hours. "Forsyth is still here," he
explained patiently. "His next move is to try to find Rothman. He didn't pass us on the road, so he has to be here.
What the boy added is simply confirmation of that. He'll
try to move south as soon as it gets dark. We have to find
him before then."

"And if we don't?"

"Then I'm afraid Mihnea Jordanes will have to do without our company tonight. We'll get back to Doftana and
wait for Forsyth to find Rothman." He laughed. "It might
be necessary to make that easy for him, but not too easy or
he'll smell a rat." He looked at the shadows lengthening
along the path. "We'll keep it up until it gets dark. After
that, it will be a waste of time."

"Agreed! Then before we start back, what about trying
to buy something to eat? I'm starving. They won't have

much in these woodcutters' cottages, but at least they should be able to let us have some cheese."

Bonneaud lengthened his stride, careful not to let Fossard see his contempt. To be within reach of a fortune and to bleat about food! Patiently, he tried to think his way into Forsyth's mind.

At that moment, Fouquet's mind was also on food—on the problem of feeding Rothman, who had been alone all day.

After killing Lupescu, Fouquet had tried to phone the Villa Florica, knowing that it was of the utmost importance that Bonneaud should learn at once that the KGB were involved and of the treachery of the Lupescus. He was puzzled and worried by the fact that the exchange informed him that the phone appeared to be out of order. Bonneaud's plans covered just such an emergency, but the system seemed to have broken down.

Bonneaud, he reasoned, would try to get in touch with Lupescu when he failed to hear from the doctor, so it was essential that Fouquet should stay within reach of the phone.

He was faced with a dilemma. In order to attend to Rothman, it was equally essential that he should have been in his cell below the public part of the building before eight o'clock that morning. That was when the keepers of the museum came on duty. But because of the telephone vigil, that had not been possible. Consequently, he had been forced to leave Rothman to his own devices for the entire day, since he had not dared to go to him before half past five at the earliest. By then, visitors to the old prison would have gone.

Fouquet was on edge. The basement cells were closed to the public, but there was always the chance that some inquisitive visitor might find his way there. For the first time, he longed for Fossard's sarcastic presence.

Baffled and uneasy, he prepared a meal in the Lupescu kitchen, ate his share quickly and went swiftly across the meadow with Rothman's portion.

For the first time, he was struck by the eeriness of the place.

Understandably, the Englishman was in a vile temper.

"Where the hell have you been all day?" he demanded, as soon as Fouquet entered.

Fouquet ignored him as he placed the meal before him.

Rothman had regained consciousness sooner than Lupescu had predicted. By eleven o'clock, he had been aware of the change in his surroundings, of his hunger, and of the odd fact that, for the first time, Lupescu had not appeared to shave his head. Like all prisoners, he found any change in routine deeply disturbing.

He had quickly realized that he must be in a cell in the base of the old Doftana prison. Naturally, his view in the mirror had shown him nothing of this particular part. His comfortable bed, the warmth from the stove and the light in the cell, from what must be an emergency electrical supply, puzzled him.

For the first time, Rothman felt really afraid because he could find no logical explanation for the strange combination of circumstances. He had been looking forward to seeing Lupescu and was disappointed when Fouquet appeared. He relieved his feelings by cursing the Frenchman roundly.

"Where the hell's the doctor?"

Fouquet looked up sharply. "Why? Do you feel ill?" It would be the devil if Rothman had an attack now. He thought the Englishman looked grotesque, but better than he had looked for days. It would be a triumph if he could get him to talk—to tell him where the crown was. Shortly, he would go back and try once more to get in touch with Bonneaud. Meanwhile, he settled down to question Rothman relentlessly.

While Rothman was becoming dangerously angry with Fouquet's questioning, Forsyth woke in the shadowy loft, feeling fresh and alert. He saw the neatly folded blankets and realized that Nicola Beaufort was already in the room below.

As he swung himself through the trapdoor, he saw the remains of a meal on the table and that the two women were giggling happily over their attempts to throw darts at the board which they had set up on one wall.

Forsyth had a bad moment until he saw the white flights of the darts.

They looked up guiltily as he descended the ladder.

"Where's Zev?" he asked.

"Gone to find out where the car is and to ask if Carol Barbu has seen Bonneaud." She began to help Eva Bastouni to clear away the used dishes and to serve Forsyth with a meal. "Eva is practically certain that her cousin will have put the car at the back of the Palace of Culture, but Zev wanted to make certain, so that we wouldn't be stumbling around in the dark." She gave him an impish look. "Not bad to have made that out without the benefit of Rumanian!"

They exchanged friendly grins. She looked better now, with more color in her face, and she seemed more relaxed. He felt relieved about that, though he had to admit that she had given him no trouble.

While he ate, she and Eva Bastouni resumed their game of darts. Neither was very good at it. He called out instructions in Rumanian and Eva Bastoni laughed happily as she tried to obey them.

There was a loud knock at the door.

Fear leaped in Nicola Beaufort's eyes.

Like a cat, Forsyth was on his feet and snatched the dartboard from the wall. He signaled imperiously to the girl to pick up the darts, then pointed to the loft.

She was up the ladder in a trice.

"When I am up," he whispered to Eva, "open the door. It will be suspicious if you don't."

She closed the trapdoor behind him and went to the door.

Forsyth cursed silently as he realized that his gun was useless. He could not open the trapdoor from inside the loft and the timbers were too thick to allow him to shoot through them into the room below.

Behind him, in the darkness, Nicola Beaufort was silent and immobile.

He put his ear to a space where two planks did not quite meet.

Bonneaud's voice was unmistakable.

When the Frenchman stood in the doorway and asked courteously if he might buy some cheese, he had given up hope of finding Forsyth. His eye took in the table set for one. Probably the woman had been in the middle of her meal. His gaze went casually around the room. The woman was bundling up some bread and cheese from the table. She looked nervous, but these bucolic types always were when the routine of their lives was changed.

She came toward him with the package and her features struck no chord of recognition.

There was a crunching noise and both looked down at the mangled dart that she had tramped on.

She looked terrified.

Bonneaud took a step into the room. He had a clear picture of the aristocratic girl with the dartboard.

Why the devil had Fossard chosen to stay out of calling distance?

He cursed his own stupidity in assuming that Forsyth's companion was a man. His brain raced, rejecting as mere coincidence that the girl had checked out of the Palas Hotel soon after Forsyth. What would such a girl be doing in a woodcutter's cottage?

And where was she?

The casual glance followed the path of the rope from the wall to the iron ring in the ceiling.

He knew beyond any shadow of doubt that Forsyth and the girl were in the loft.

He smiled brilliantly at Eva Bastouni, thanked her courteously as he pressed the *lei* into her hand and stepped back into the darkness.

Forsyth heard the slam of the door and let his breath go in a sigh of relief.

Automatically, Eva Bastouni lifted the crushed dart and thrust it into her pocket.

Nicola Beaufort wanted to leave at once.

"No." Forsyth was firm. "He had no means of knowing that we are here. We don't want to blunder into him in the dark. He will have given up. Besides, we must wait for Zev. We don't know where the car is." But he looked restively at his watch.

"I shall go to get Zev. You need him to find your way down. It is too dark to see the trail." Eva Bastouni pulled off her apron and tossed it toward a chair. It fell on the floor covering the dart which had dropped from the pocket. She pulled a thick black shawl around her head and shoulders. As she paused in the doorway, she said doubtfully, "Wouldn't it be better to go into the loft until we came back? If the man returns, it would be safer."

Forsyth considered it. He was convinced that Bonneaud had gone, but if he had not, Eva was right. In any case, they could always get out by the roof.

When they were in the loft, she closed the trapdoor and went quickly and surely out to the trail.

Bonneaud watched her go.

He and Fossard had worked fast, gathering up the brushwood from the pile. They went silently into the cottage and heaped two great armfuls of it on the floor beneath the trapdoor.

Fossard brought a pannikin of water and tossed it over the dry brushwood to keep it from flaming up. Bonneaud had no intention of burning them to death, nor of setting the forest on fire. In five minutes, the house would be full of dense smoke and by that time Forsyth and the girl would be suffocated.

When he and Fossard went out to the front of the house to wait, he closed the door carefully to avoid creating a draft. He dare not risk losing the crown. In moments, the first ribbon of smoke went curling upward.

Forsyth was face downward at the crack, straining to hear and to see. He raised his head alertly. "I smell smoke," he said. "Quick! Get to the window. Keep close to me and do exactly what you are told."

He grabbed the hatbox and the night binoculars, finding both very quickly in the darkness.

The girl crowded close behind him.

While they were on the roof, there was a bad moment when he thought that he could not halt his slide down the steep slope. He tucked his right leg under his left hip, leaned back on the palms of his hands and came down slater-fashion. Zev had made sturdy gutters which ultimately stopped him. He caught the girl as he braced himself on the edge of the roof. She had imitated him perfectly.

He passed her the hatbox. "I'm going to drop down now. Count ten, then drop the box exactly where I've gone over. Then count fifteen and let yourself drop. I'll catch you, but if I miss, bend your knees and roll." He paused. "If anything goes wrong, grab the box and run like hell toward the front of the house. That's where the path is. Zev can't be far away. Good luck!" He was gone.

She obeyed him to the letter. Billows of smoke were pouring from the house as she dropped into his arms. He held her close against his aching ribs and felt the thumping of her heart against his chest.

He had a heady moment of exultation, though common sense told him that they had merely exchanged one danger for another.

He put a hand against the softness of her cheek to pull her ear close to his lips. He whispered, "Grip the back of my jacket and don't, for the love of God, let go. I'm going to try to circle around to cut onto the trail farther down. In an emergency, give two tugs at my jacket, but don't talk."

She moved like a ghost behind him. He was so encumbered by the box and the dangling binoculars that he considered throwing the glasses away. In the end, it was the slap of a branch against the hatbox that told Bonneaud where they were.

He began to stalk them.

Mihnea Jordanes waited impatiently for his guest. Finally he had to recognize that Bonneaud would not be dining at the villa that night. He shrugged. He would probably turn up sometime during the night. His hand closed viciously on Chi-Chi's forearm as he led her into dinner.

Throughout the meal he eyed her somberly. This evening she wore a scarlet cat suit and he noted that there was a matching spot of scarlet high on each cheek. Tonight the green eyes glowed with the unpredictable fire of a sulky tiger. The unexpected show of spirit excited Jordanes. During the meal he baited her unmercifully, taking pleasure in watching how the delicate, scarlet-tipped fingers fumbled with the cutlery.

She ate nothing.

When her uncertain movements sent her wine glass toppling, he watched in complete silence the slow spreading of the stain on the damask cloth. Utterly unnerved, she sat, rigid with fear, then, unable to endure the silence any longer, she pushed her chair back and rose from the table.

"Ah! Chi-Chi," Jordanes said silkily, "you are like a pretty little scarlet pussy."

His arm shot out and swept plates, glasses and cutlery from the table. He ignored the debris. "Get up on the table, pussy, and let me see you lap up the wine."

His eyes met hers coldly. Like a mesmerized rabbit, she pulled herself up and crouched on all fours above the wine which had by now completely soaked into the cloth. Her head drooped in an agony of despair and humiliation. Small, mewing sounds of distress came from her throat.

Jordanes got up slowly and came to stand beside her. He smiled, almost tenderly. "My dear, do you know how cats and dogs are trained? You rub their noses in their mistakes."

His hand shot out and pushed her head violently down, grinding it against the table until she screamed.

He laughed, his good humor restored.

Smiling, he made his way to the library, content to wait for Bonneaud's arrival. He got out a portfolio and arranged the papers on the desk. He would probably stay up all night and go to bed at dawn. When Bonneaud eventually arrived, it would be amusing to tell him about his fun with Chi-Chi.

That night, only the Russians enjoyed a restful sleep.

Fully recovered, Eliasberg had eaten heartily and now slept, replete and comfortable, snoring spasmodically. In the neighboring bed, Danilenko lay neatly on his side, untroubled even by dreams. Neither was the type to lie awake worrying about eventualities.

Had he been asked to outline the position, Danilenko would have said that the KGB's plans were functioning perfectly. Lupescu would phone some time in the morning. If, for some reason, he was unable to do so, Danilenko would still make the move at four o'clock exactly. Daylight would help the operation. The fact that the prison would be closed to the public tomorrow had, of course, been taken into account by his superiors. They had planned well.

Within the bounds of his instructions, he felt secure and powerful.

Had he allowed himself the luxury of expressing a preference, Danilenko would have hoped that Rothman would reveal that the crown was hidden in the mountains. As a townsman, he was curious about mountain scenery, half repelled and half attracted by it. Wherever it was, he would have admitted that he hoped that the crown was not too far away. The sooner they were all on the plane for Moscow, the better. Every detail of the journey had been clearly explained. Once they were airborne, there would be Beluga caviar and good Russian champagne for all of them.

He and Eliasberg would get leave and a substantial bonus. For him, the greatest treat would be his reunion with his little dog, Pushok.

Rothman would, of course, be treated like a tsar.

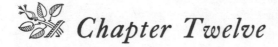

Chapter Twelve

FORSYTH caught the girl's hand and pulled her forward, less in order to speed their progress than with the queer intention of protecting her by his closeness. He thought he could hear voices behind him, speaking fast and angrily. Ahead and to the right, there was an eruption of sound, a crashing in the undergrowth as if someone were blundering into the trees. A rifle cracked from the direction of the house.

Beneath their feet the ground was soft and wet in places. He veered to the left, seeking dryer ground where there would be no squelching to betray them. There was a pain like a knife being turned slowly in his side. As if she knew, the girl tugged at his arm and pointed to where the ground dipped into a shallow leaf-filled hollow. As they dropped into it, the beam of a flashlight cut between the trees a little ahead. Fossard's angular figure showed up clearly. Out of the darkness behind him, Zev Bastouni's massive form loomed menacingly. His arm shot out, spun Fossard around and, as he yelled, "You fire my house!" his clenched fist came down like a battering ram on the top of Fossard's skull. The crack of the shattered bones was like the sound of a bullet in the quietness. Before they could move, Bastouni had dropped Fossard like a puppet and disappeared among the trees.

Then Forsyth heard it—the stealthy thud of feet running

on the telltale earth. Bonneaud was very near. Suddenly and coldly he knew that for the Frenchman and himself the Crown of Saint Stephen was an irrelevance. All Bonneaud really wanted was to kill him. He felt the slow, insidious influx of fatalism.

As if she sensed the strength of the death wish in him, she prodded him fiercely. He glanced back. Bonneaud's flashlight beam moved steadily to left and to right, covering the ground swiftly and systematically. In seconds, he would see their footprints and be on them.

Forsyth heaved himself upward like a diver surfacing. The girl was like an extension of himself. She ran easily and effortlessly beside him, her breath no more than a sigh in the darkness. Boldly he cut across his tracks, staking everything on the belief that the direct path to Sinaia was ahead.

Her voice in his ear breathed, "Look!" Immediately below them the lights of Sinaia thrust their bright golden points toward them. With hands clasped tightly like children, they slithered and slipped downward.

They stumbled through the gardens at the back of the Palas Hotel and Forsyth saw the dim outline of the car behind the Palace of Culture.

Silent as an Indian, Barbu came to them out of the shadows. He pushed the ignition key into Forsyth's hand, but it was clear that he was anxious to be away.

When the girl was in the passenger seat, Forsyth put the hatbox on the floor between her feet. It was as if he had laid down an intolerable burden. He turned the ignition key and began the journey toward Tony Rothman.

He said suddenly, "Bonneaud was really inviting me to shoot at him there in the woods. Crazy man!"

"You're both crazy," she said wearily. "You're like little boys who have begun a fight and now you're stuck with it. Neither will give in." Her voice grew stronger. "You are both whipping up an emotion that neither of you really believes in. Maybe it began as patriotism, but it isn't that anymore." She sounded as angry as she had been when he had first met her on the plane.

He said pacifically, "Come now! It's our job. If we stopped to examine motives before every operation, we wouldn't get anywhere. Besides," he sounded amused, "strange as it may seem, this game of espionage does have some rules. Countries don't mow each other's spies down regardless. There's an implicit understanding that this type of work has to go on. Recruitment would fall off sharply if spies were shot on sight. In the course of an operation— well, that is different."

She cowered into her anorak, pulling the hood over her head. "Men can talk such drivel," she said explosively. "Perhaps Bonneaud was inviting you to take a potshot at him, but not from any *taedium vitae.* He may have been trying to draw your fire, so that friend Fossard could mark you down as soon as you fired. You should be rendering thanks to Zev, instead of philosophizing about Bonneaud's motives."

He laughed and said, "Don't let's quarrel." He put out a hand and pressed her knee. She stiffened and seemed to withdraw.

To cover the awkwardness, he said lightly, "We should be two very happy people. Do you realize that in a few days we've done something that has defeated many of the best brains in the world for over thirty years? I've made myself a cast-iron promise. As soon as I get back to London, I'm going to get drunk to celebrate." He waited, but she said nothing.

Rebuffed, he concentrated on the driving.

"That rifle shot!" she said suddenly. "Bonneaud was running away from it. He wasn't thinking of either of us then. He wasn't even looking for us. He and Fossard were both running away from the woodcutters, but Fossard didn't make it."

"You're right. I wonder if Bonneaud made it. That could make a very big difference to Tony Rothman." He strained forward over the wheel and listened.

"Is something wrong?"

"I don't know," he said, "but the car is not pulling well." He peered into the darkness. "This would be a helluva place to have a breakdown."

As he spoke the engine coughed and died. The car came to a shuddering halt. Forsyth restrained an impulse to curse. There was no need to alarm the girl unnecessarily. He got out and struggled to release the hood.

Nicola Beaufort rolled down the window on her side. "I can see two pinpoints of light over on the left, but they seem pretty far away."

Forsyth straightened and looked around. About a quarter of a mile away on his right was another light. He called out cheerfully, "It looks as if we are in luck. Either somebody is feeding the baby or raiding the larder. I don't care which it is as long as they have a spare can of gasoline. That seems to be our trouble. Our paragon of a hall porter forgot to fill her up." He went around to stand beside her window. "I don't have a choice. We can't walk to Cimplua and this road isn't exactly crowded with gas stations." He pointed in the direction of the light. "A house as isolated as that one must run to a car and that suggests extra supplies of gasoline to me. It looks as if it is our only chance. I'll be back as quickly as I can."

He had taken a few steps when a thought struck him. He went back and said evenly, "I think I should leave you the gun." He thrust it through the open window. "I don't think I'll need it as a calling card and there is just that remote chance that Bonneaud may still be running in this direction. If anybody tries to rob you of your spring hat, shoot him."

He moved quickly off in the direction of the light.

When he reached the house, he was relieved to see the

dim shape of a car parked a little to the left of the entrance. The building was in darkness except for one room to the right of the front door where light blazed from an uncurtained window.

Forsyth hesitated, unwilling to ring the bell and arouse the whole household. He went crunching over the gravel to tap on the window. Before he could do so, a voice called from the room, "All right! Just coming!" There was the screech of a chair being pushed back.

Forsyth smiled and went back to stand at the door. He heard the sound of light footsteps and the turning of a key in a lock. He stood blinking, momentarily blinded by the flood of light from the hall. When his eyes focused, he saw a youngish man with very white hair examining him carefully.

"It's unpardonable to disturb you at this hour," Forsyth said pleasantly, "but I'm completely stuck. I've run out of gas and I've been hoping that you might be in a position to let me have some."

The man stepped aside and waved him genially into the hall. "Come in! Come in!" he said jovially. "This is a great pleasure. I'm practically a hermit, so I'm delighted that you chose my part of the country for your misfortune. Gasoline? Naturally! But I can do better than that. Come in and have a drink."

Forsyth followed him into the lighted room. The man had obviously been working at his desk which was covered with papers. He went toward it now. "My name is Jordanes —Mihnea Jordanes. And you are? . . ."

"John East." He smiled easily. "I'm a tourist, gawking at your lovely country. I've learned a lesson tonight—not to underrate the mileage. I feel a fool."

"You *are* a fool, Mr. Forsyth. A fool and a liar. I do not like men who come into my home and try to deceive me." The blue nose of a .22 Walthner pointed at Forsyth's chest.

Behind Jordanes's head a door opened a crack and an eye gleamed in the opening.

Forsyth sat very still. He thought regretfully of his quixotic gesture in leaving the gun with Nicola Beaufort. It was highly unlikely that she would come charging to his rescue once again. He watched the white-haired man warily. There was something off-key about him—an unstable personality, Forsyth surmised. The thought worried him.

"We have a mutual friend," Jordanes continued. There was a gloating expression in the baby-bright eyes. "I am expecting Alan Bonneaud very soon." He strolled over to stand in front of Forsyth.

Come a little closer, Forsyth was imploring him silently.

Jordanes's hand snaked out and the gun crashed on the side of Forsyth's head.

A train was screeching loudly, the wheels sending great sparks of light off into the darkness that crept up and up . . .

He came to in the chair, but, while he had been dreaming of trains, someone had tied him up tightly. He thought about that, then looked vaguely at the girl who was kneeling before him. She was dressed very oddly in what looked like a scarlet one-piece jersey garment. Forsyth thought that it was immodest. She should have been pretty, but her mouth was badly swollen and there was a big black-and-blue bruise on her forehead. She was frantically cutting the ropes. All the time, she was sobbing, "Oh please wake up! Please! Please!"

He said politely, "Glad to oblige."

She looked up, startled, then said frantically, "He could be back at any minute. He'll kill me. You'll have to kill him. Do you think you can do it?"

"*Very* glad to oblige." He got groggily to his feet.

"I was supposed to watch you," she said, stammering with fright. "Have you a gun?"

"No." He was beginning to feel more normal, but he had the alarming feeling that all his movements were dangerously sluggish. No gun. No cosh. No *brains,* he told himself disgustedly.

The girl fluttered about the room like a scarlet butterfly. She came back and thrust a small erotic bronze statue of a woman into his hands. "Hit him with this," she said tensely.

Women seemed to keep giving him orders.

Forsyth rubbed a hand shakily over his face. For an alarming moment, he thought he was going to be sick. He hefted the bronze in his hand and took up a position behind the door through which he had come.

The phone shrilled from the desk behind him. The girl flew to answer it. She listened. "Yes," she gasped, rolling great green eyes at Forsyth. "He's still out." She listened again. "I'll come at once."

She replaced the receiver. "He's in his bedroom. I have to go up," she whispered.

"Right," said Forsyth. "I'll be a step behind you." He had a thought. "Are there any servants?"

"Yes, but they are at the back of the house—too far away to hear." She went padding into the hall. Forsyth deposited the statue on the desk and lifted his own cosh which Jordanes must have taken from him while he was unconscious.

He followed the girl up the curving stairway and pressed himself against a wall while she went into a bedroom, leaving the door ajar.

Cautiously, Forsyth edged forward and peered in. The room was empty, but Jordanes's voice came from the bathroom beyond.

In a flash, Forsyth was across the room. He hit Jordanes as he was coming into the bedroom. The Rumanian fell crashing back into the bathroom and rolled into the bath which was sunk in the floor. The girl stood on the other

side of the bath with her hands pressed against her mouth
as if to choke off a scream. Her eyes were enormous in a
paper-white face.

It was a large room with walls, door and ceiling completely mirrored, so that Forsyth saw the scene endlessly
repeated—his own tall figure swaying drunkenly above the
prone figure in the bath and the girl like a scarlet flame in a
classic attitude of shock.

He tried to throw off a feeling of unreality. What was
real and dangerous was that Jordanes seemed to have been
speaking the truth. Bonneaud might indeed turn up at any
moment. The girl in the car was a sitting pigeon. The
danger to the crown escaped him entirely.

He seized a fine linen guest towel and used it to gag
Jordanes. The blow had not been a particularly heavy one
and he was afraid that the Rumanian would waken up very
soon. He went quickly into the bedroom and found what
he wanted. He trussed Jordanes up with the silk cords used
for holding back the heavy brocade curtains. The bath, he
decided, was as good a place as any for him. With luck,
Bonneaud would not find him immediately.

Forsyth still had the gasoline problem to solve. He had
no desire to sit on Jordanes's doorstep for very much
longer.

"Get a coat and we'll go," he said to the girl.

"Aren't you going to kill him?" She sounded surprised
and disappointed.

"No," he answered shortly. "Maybe another time . . .
This isn't my week for killing. Let's go."

"I'm staying," she said slowly, "but thank you for the
offer."

He gave her a worried look. "Are you sure you will be
safe?"

She smiled, as if he had not been too bright. "Perfectly
safe, I assure you. Good luck!"

He shrugged and left her standing in the beautiful bathroom, dozens of her, getting smaller and smaller, in endless repetitions.

Outside, he drew deep gulps of the air, fresh and pure and innocent of evil.

He looked with relief at the dangling keys of the white Lamborghini Espada. As he gunned the car down the driveway, he had a strong conviction that Jordanes would not be reporting its loss.

Jordanes came slowly back to consciousness. He looked vaguely down at his pajamaed body, stretched out in the bath. A muffled gurgle came from behind the gag.

Chi-Chi sat back on her heels, her knees on a level with his waist, and watched him interestedly. She had changed into a yellow cat suit and the color seemed to please her. She got quickly to her feet and, holding on to an imaginary barre, went through the warming-up movements of a ballet dancer.

Jordanes watched her with growing awareness.

She went back to kneel beside him. "Poor Mihnea!" she cooed. "You look *so* uncomfortable, but Chi-Chi will fix you up nicely."

She padded on her little yellow kid slippers into her bedroom. From her pink-and-white bathroom, she brought back a heart-shaped, frilly bath pillow. Carefully, she moistened the rubber suckers and fixed the pillow behind Jordanes's head. His eyes were terrible.

She chattered brightly. "Scarlet nails are *so* wrong with a yellow cat suit. What would you suggest, Mihnea? Copper? Bronze? Deep marigold might be fun."

She tripped back to her bedroom and brought back a little pink-brocade footstool. She sat on it like a tall pixie, with her long legs almost touching her chin. "This is cozy, isn't it, Mihnea? I'll do my nails while we talk. You and I never seem to talk."

The large green eyes reproached him. He forced the hatred out of his and implored her silently.

She looked at him with exaggerated surprise. "Poor Mihnea!" she crooned. "You want your bath! That's it, isn't it?" She went to the foot of the bath, put the plug in position and carefully turned on the water.

Jordanes's eyes were fixed on the flow from the tap. The bath would not fill quickly.

She went back to the stool and began to remove the scarlet nail polish. "I never liked cat suits," she told him confidentially. "I think I'll give them up. What do you think, Mihnea?" She frowned over a nail. "I think I need calcium. I must get some tablets."

The water was lapping his shoulders. Though it was cool in the bathroom, sweat poured down his face.

The soft, gossiping voice went on and on as the water crept higher and higher. . . .

Chapter Thirteen

NICOLA BEAUFORT accepted the Lamborghini, as she had accepted everything else, with an equanimity that verged on indifference. A tiny finger of fear touched the back of Forsyth's neck. Her detachment was unnatural, even allowing for the not-unexpected dulling of her emotions by the fatigue and tensions of the past hours. He eyed her thoughtfully, recalling with an icy clarity some of the comments of colleagues attached to the Narcotics Division. He could not, would not, accept that she had willingly experimented with drugs. Pity became a vast pain that beaded his forehead with sweat. In that moment, to his astonishment, he recognized that he had accepted that whatever her problems might be, they were now also his. He looked at her with sudden insight, amazed that the strength of his compassion had not somehow reached her.

"Better than a can of gasoline," was her sole appreciative remark.

Forsyth decided to keep the story of Jordanes and the girl in the scarlet cat suit to himself. *Maybe I dreamed it*, he told himself wryly, but the renewed pain in his head and side contradicted him. What did not trouble him in the slightest was the knowledge that, by leaving Jordanes alone with the girl, he had murdered him as surely as if he had shot him. Characteristically, he did not speculate about the method she would employ.

He worked swiftly, transferring their possessions to the Lamborghini. Sweat was pouring from his face by the time he had strapped the wheelchair into position.

The girl eyed it doubtfully. "It's very clumsy. What a pity the porter couldn't have got a folding affair!"

"No. This is exactly what I wanted. I was incredibly lucky to get it. It was practically made for the job. You'll see."

She was clutching the hatbox. In the light of the head-lamps, she was a tall, weary child. His heart contracted suddenly with an unfamiliar emotion.

"This is a helluva time and place to be trying on hats, but, madame, we have a fetching gold model that won't be around ten minutes from now. Would madame care to try it for size?"

It was a strange and awesome moment when he stood facing her on the dark and lonely road, holding the Holy Crown of Saint Stephen between them. Her eyes were great amber pools of light. Very gently, her forefinger traced the uneven line of pearls along the base.

"The Empress Maria Theresa wore it," she whispered.

"And now you'll wear it," he smiled, "even if I have to bust another rib putting it on your head."

He moved closer to her as she bent her neck to receive the crown. The soft fragrance of her hair and her subtle woman-smell was in his nostrils. For a moment, their breaths mingled, as she looked at him in speechless delight. Stiffly, he bent his head between his raised arms and kissed her gently on the mouth, feeling her lips moving under his in delicate response.

Abruptly, he stepped back, but the radiance in her face stopped the cynical words almost before he had formed them. She followed him wordlessly to the back of the car and held the crown while he fumbled with the seat of the wheelchair.

"What on earth are you doing?"

"It's a commode, or, as some people call it, a portable nightstool. I grant that it isn't the most dignified container for the Hungarian crown, but, under the circumstances, it's certainly the safest."

"You mean," her tone was horrified, "that you are going to put the crown in *that?*"

"Yes, and Rothman, I hope, is going to sit on it until I get them both to London." He had an inexplicable urge to defend himself. "What the hell do you think I should do? Declare it to the Rumanian Customs officials? The Rumanian authorities wouldn't have any alternative—they would have to commandeer it. And what a headache that would be for them! It wouldn't exactly endear them to their Russian brothers."

He raised his head triumphantly. "Look! Tailored for the job! Now let me have your hat and your pink cardigan." He stuffed the soft cashmere round the crown to protect the jewels and placed the gray felt hat on top. "Now, if anybody gets inquisitive, you have an eccentric taste in hatboxes."

He was aware that he had offended her but her fastidious recoil from the commode seemed to him both childish and unreasonable. Savagely he repeated, "What the hell should I have done?" and felt that he was attempting to justify the act not only to her, but to Father Damian.

Angrily he picked up the hatbox. "We won't need this anymore. I'll get rid of it." He strode back through the darkness and tossed it over the hedge with more force than was necessary.

He helped her into the Lamborghini in moody silence.

As soon as she felt the comfort of their new acquisition, Nicola Beaufort discarded the anorak and stretched her long, beige-covered legs out luxuriously.

"I think I'll sleep now," she said contentedly.

Presently her breathing grew deeper and slower. She was sound asleep. At times, she moved convulsively and moaned so piteously that Forsyth felt himself swept by such an intense grief that his grip tightened painfully on the wheel.

Once he let the car glide to the side of the road, then stop, while he pulled her comfortingly against his shoulder. She sighed and nestled against him like an exhausted child, but her brow remained furrowed and the tender mouth drooped forlornly.

"Hush!" he whispered, rocking her gently. "There's nothing at all to worry about."

"I'm not worried," she murmured, sweetly and dreamily, as if she had heard and understood.

When he edged her back against her seat, his arms felt empty and he looked down at the sleeping face with a baffled expression.

What is so special about Rothman, he wondered, *that he can evoke such love and anxiety?*

Forsyth did not recognize the swift pang as jealousy.

Resolutely he concentrated on Bonneaud and tried to estimate how close he might be to them. The Frenchman would certainly head for Rothman, and he had the advantage of knowing where the unknown Dr. Lupescu lived. In the darkness, Forsyth sighed as he worked out how much he would have to do in the next hours.

Meanwhile, he had abandoned at the side of a country road a valuable piece of Rumanian property. He had stolen a car; was, he was fully convinced, involved in the murder of its owner and was attempting to smuggle out of the country a treasure of such political significance that most diplomats would have had heart attacks at the prospect of being found with it in their possession. His spirits rose. This was something he could and would deal with.

The silver wings of insects starred the blackness of the

windshield. Presently the ebony outlines of the mountains became silver-blue and the girl awoke as the landscape became filled with warmth and light and perfume. The shell-pink breasts of doves shimmered among the trees and great masses of white blossom spilled from the hedges.

Forsyth turned his head to smile at her and she gave him a look of radiant happiness, quickly clouded by some freak wind of memory. She hummed determinedly, and he had the feeling that she was trying to keep up her courage. Probably she was aware, as he was, that Rothman's fate must be settled before the day was over.

"You would make a good operator," he said consolingly, as though he were presenting her with a lover's accolade.

The car was filled with her laughter and Forsyth grinned sheepishly.

He peered at the landscape. "My guess is that we are approaching Doftana, which is just northwest of Cimpina. Let's have a five-minute break. I need to stretch my legs."

He watched her as she strode briskly up and down the country road, pausing occasionally to look at the crimson masses of poppies on the banks. She was tall, tired and beautiful, and as strange to him as an unexplored country. He wondered how he would have felt about her if he had met her in London under normal circumstances.

When she stretched out on the grass at the side of the road, he said, "There's a building just ahead. It looks like a small inn. I'll see if I can phone Bucharest from there." He riffled through a sheaf of papers. "Here's what I want— 14.51.60."

Her brows climbed inquiringly.

"The number of the Carpati Rent-A-Car service. They won't be too pleased to learn that I have abandoned their Mercedes 200A on the public highway. Ah, well, they can only put me in the Rumanian version of the salt mines." He halted abruptly and the smile left his face.

"What is it?" She looked at him curiously.

He shook his head, concentrating on the name, *Doftana*. Excitement tightened his stomach muscles. "Come on!" he said sharply.

When she looked doubtfully at the wheelchair, he said impatiently, "If anybody guesses that that contains the crown, my chances of getting it through Customs would be nil anyway. It's safe."

The inn was a poor place, but the proprietor led them both eagerly through the small front-entrance hall to an equally small room at the back where the telephone was housed.

"We had better have coffee here," Nicola Beaufort whispered, "but let's eat at the car. We have plenty of food."

Forsyth handed her the tattered telephone book. "While I talk to Carpati," he suggested, "see if you can find Lupescu's number and address."

The official in Bucharest was polite and almost ingratiating. "It's good of you to call, sir, but Madame Jordanes has already reported the matter. We'll arrange to have the car picked up. Just let me check one point—you have borrowed one of her cars, so there is no need for us to make arrangements for transport for you?"

"That is correct," Forsyth said slowly. *Madame Jordanes!* His voice revealed nothing of his surprise.

"What a tragedy!" the official continued chattily.

"Tragedy?"

"Yes. Poor Monsieur Jordanes was accidentally drowned in his bath last night. A great loss to the country!"

Slowly Forsyth replaced the receiver. Obviously, the frightened girl in the cat suit had kept her head. Silently he saluted her.

Behind him Nicola Beaufort said, "I've found it! We might have made a ghastly mistake. There's only one Dr. Lupescu—a Dr. Vasile Lupescu. He has the number we got in the Villa Florica, but, while it is a Cimpina number, the house is actually in Doftana." Some of the color left her face as she saw his expression. "Do you think that means that Tony Rothman is somewhere near?"

"Probably." His tone was noncommittal. "Let's get that coffee. It looks as if the gods are on our side."

As they sat sipping the sandy Turkish brew, an old man in the picturesque costume of the area stumped into the room. He handed a letter to the innkeeper.

"*Bună dimineaţa*," he called pleasantly to them.

"The postman," Forsyth murmured, "just the man to direct us to Lupescu's place." He began to talk rapidly in Rumanian.

Nicola Beaufort watched the old man's face. His expression was wary, but as Forsyth talked, she saw the postman's look change. He spoke excitedly and confidentially and she had the impression that he was warning the younger man to be careful. Her heart began to thud painfully.

Forsyth got to his feet, thrust a bundle of *lei* into the old man's hand, patted him on the shoulder and said tersely to the girl, "Let's go!"

As they walked quickly back to the car, she said, "What was all that about?"

"We are on the right track, but we'll have to move fast. The old boy told me that he found a bloodstained bandage in the basement of a deserted house near here. He seems to be an inquisitive old rascal. Then he saw Lupescu carrying bandages and a cylinder of oxygen into his house. He is sure he's got a patient there, but Lupescu is not supposed to practice medicine."

The girl had gone deathly white. She said stiffly, "So that's where he is!"

"Not necessarily. Lupescu's house is in the grounds of the old Doftana prison. My hunch is that Rothman is there or is destined to go there—an ideal hiding place."

"So, what do we do?"

"Visit Lupescu, first of all. But I'll need to get this car

off the road. I daren't have it too far away in case I have to
carry Rothman, and yet I don't want Bonneaud stumbling
over it." He was scanning the road as he drove. They saw
the white house simultaneously. Forsyth applied the brakes.
"Stay here," he commanded. "I'll be back in ten minutes."
He disappeared in the direction of the house.

When he came back, he said evenly, "I think we're in
luck. I'm going to park the car at the back of the house.
There's an ideal parking place behind a high wall of vines.
Unless somebody made a point of looking for it, a car
wouldn't be noticed. My impression is that there is nobody
in the house, but I am going in to find out."

Her chin came up. "I'm going with you."

He gave her an exasperated look, but said nothing.

Before they left the car, he said, "Leave your fancy gun
behind or you might end up killing one of us. You have
Fatty's gun. Take that, but don't aim it in my direction."

She moved the binocular case to get at Pietru's gun, as
he had suggested.

He hesitated, remembering the darts. It would be best to
warn her. "Don't fool around with the box of darts in that
case. They are lethal. Each dart is tipped with poison, so
keep your pretty little fingers away from them. Keep close
to me and don't talk."

They moved toward the back door of the villa.

As Alan Bonneaud hurled the Porsche down the road from
Sinaia to the villa at Mount Furnica, he had very definite
plans for the next few hours. He was tired, hungry and
dirty, but all these discomforts would be taken care of as
soon as he had a quick talk with Mihnea Jordanes. With
that wily bastard lay the answers also to more subtle problems. His new partner was about to win his spurs.

Next on the list of priorities came a phone call to Lupescu with explicit instructions that the doctor and Fouquet must carry out to the letter. Bonneaud glanced at the

clock on the dashboard and made a rapid calculation. Even allowing for a fairly lengthy stop at Jordanes's villa, with luck it would be possible to be at Doftana by early afternoon.

Where the devil is Forsyth? he asked himself irritably. In spite of his coolness, that question nagged at him. He grimaced as he went over mentally all that he must accomplish within a short time. He had to locate Forsyth, give him the come-on with the bait of Rothman and then move in fast to grab the crown and wipe the supercilious Englishman out.

His mouth curved in pleasure at the prospect.

Momentarily, he regretted the death of his colleague, Fossard, but the devious mind quickly saw that in the long run it would suit him very well. In fact, that big woodcutter had probably saved him some trouble. Fouquet was just as brave as Fossard had been, but not quite as astute, a not undesirable shortcoming in an underling.

Always provided that he could catch up with Forsyth soon, things were not going too badly. After all, it was better to know that the crown was definitely where Forsyth was than to have to start digging up half of Transylvania to look for it.

His foot went down hard on the accelerator and the car bounced on the road. Complacently he told himself that Mihnea Jordanes's tentacles stretched wide and far. Forsyth would be quickly located and liquidated.

The clear morning light showed up the Mercedes 200A parked at the side of the road. It had an abandoned look. Frowning, Bonneaud slackened speed and drove slowly past. Belatedly he recalled that Fossard had checked the number of the Englishman's car, but that information lay in the dead man's pocket, high in the Carpathians. He had a quick surge of elation at the thought that at this moment Jordanes might be entertaining Forsyth.

He swung the wheel around, thrusting the car into the

driveway leading up to the villa. There was the totally unexpected squeal of tires on the road. Quick as a cat, Bonneaud hauled the wheel frantically to the right, stamped on the brakes and threw his body backward to avoid crashing through the windshield. The Porsche had remained upright and had come to rest inches from a hedge.

Shaken and furious, Bonneaud scrambled out. He stiffened at the sight of the police uniforms.

"Sorry—no damage done, I hope?" He spoke with rueful courtesy.

What the hell were the police doing there?

The older policeman looked sympathetic. He seemed unaware that he was still clutching a square box. "I'm afraid you are too late, sir. Monsieur Jordanes's body has already been removed. The funeral will be tomorrow."

Bonneaud's mind raced. There was a cold feeling in the pit of his stomach. There simply had to be some mistake. The tremor in his voice was not entirely false when he said, "I can't take it in. What happened?"

The officials exchanged embarrassed glances. "Between ourselves, sir," the policeman lowered his voice discreetly, "Monsieur Jordanes seems to have dined a little too well last night. It was most unfortunate—he drowned himself accidentally in his bath." He coughed. "Maybe a heart attack. Who knows?"

The two men waited until Bonneaud had maneuvered his car back onto the driveway. As he drove slowly toward the villa, they touched their caps and got back into their car.

For a stunned moment, Bonneaud allowed himself to contemplate the collapse of his second plan to center his empire in Rumania. His face looked suddenly old and slumped.

But when he got out of the car at the entrance to the villa, he was again in command of himself. His step as he walked into the shadowy hall was brisk and almost jaunty.

"Madame Jordanes is in the garden at the back of the house, sir." The servant's voice was subdued and respectful.

Bonneaud swung slowly around on a heel. "*Madame* Jordanes?"

The servant's eyes were curious. "It is a great tragedy for a bride of only three weeks. We hope you can comfort her, sir."

The icy feeling was back in Bonneaud's stomach. He went slowly down the steps and around the side of the house. He had the curious feeling that the ground was shifting under his feet. He walked heavily, with his anger against Jordanes growing with every step. It was as if he thought that the man had died to spite him.

But the greatest treachery of all was the Rumanian's marriage to Chi-Chi. Bonneaud's thoughts scurried, as he tried to determine how he could use her, how to retrieve something from the ruin of his plans.

A servant passed him quickly, carrying a bundle of clothing, and was already beside Chi-Chi Jordanes when Bonneaud stepped off the path into a clearing.

The girl watched his approach with no expression at all on her features. The bruised face might have been swollen with grief. That thought amused Bonneaud. He had to admit that the tall figure had dignity and a certain forbidding quality that surprised him.

The eddies of wind that blew down from the mountains had an icy freshness. Chi-Chi was closely wrapped in a full-length cape of black tulip mink. It gave her the look of an avenging goddess.

Bonneaud felt the stirrings of uneasiness.

Between them a bonfire burned fiercely, sending a wavering column of flame and smoke upward through the clear air.

The servant threw the bundle of clothing on the flames

and poked at them with a long stick. As the fire licked at the scarlets, yellows, blues, whites and pinks, Bonneaud saw that the garments were cat suits.

The servant went quietly back along the path.

Amusement grew in the tilted obsidian eyes. "I'm practicing my own form of sutteeism," she said demurely.

He looked at her blankly.

"Tch! tch!" she chided softly. "Even you would scarcely expect me to follow the old Indian custom and burn *myself* on my husband's funeral pyre." She looked blandly at the flames. "So much more sensible to burn an unpleasant part of dear Mihnea's life." She sighed voluptuously. "Fortunately, so much that was good about him remains—his money." She paused delicately. "I mean to enjoy it." Her eyes mocked him. "Dear Mihnea would not want me to grieve or even to dwell on what has gone. I shall do what I know he would have wanted—cut all my ties with the past." Again there was the tiny pause. "Good-bye, Monsieur Bonneaud," she said softly.

For a moment, the red haze of rage blotted out her features. He clutched at control.

"You killed him!" he said starkly.

She considered that. "Yes," she agreed. "I've always wanted to do it—long before we were married. It was simply a question of waiting for the right moment and the right person to help."

The heat of rage had died in him, leaving an icy chill. He did not need to be told who had helped her. He was unaware that his mouth was twisted in a rictus that was a grotesque parody of a smile. This time Forsyth had finally smashed the hopes and plans of years.

His eyes measured the distance between them, watching the flames, imagining how it would be when he slammed that smiling face into them.

She laughed. "You won't do it," she said placidly. Her eyes went to the path behind him, where two policemen strolled in the sunshine. "Officialdom likes to pamper wealthy widows. Besides, Mihnea took a recording of his talk with you last night. I added some interesting parts to the tape." She studied his furious face. "Oh! I knew you wouldn't like it, so I asked the police officials to guard carefully dear Mihnea's last message to me."

With a sick feeling he remembered the box in the policeman's hands.

He turned heavily away. Her laughter followed him.

Chapter Fourteen

THE air was full of bird song as Forsyth worked on the lock of the door of the Tupescu villa. He had said savagely to Nicola Beaufort, "It's stupid to come with me. Much more sensible if you stayed outside and kept an eye open for unexpected visitors."

"I'm coming," she said flatly.

He shrugged and went back to maneuvering a strip of celluloid in the lock.

When the door swung quietly inward, they found themselves in an untidy kitchen. Dirty dishes were piled in the sink and two pots held the remains of food. Flies had settled on the dark masses of beans and meat. They stirred sluggishly, as though sated.

The house seemed unnaturally silent, as though nobody had been in it for a very long time, but Forsyth noted the rim of water on the draining board where someone had rested a glass of water. He ran a finger round the inside of the glass in the sink. It was damp.

His glance at Nicola Beaufort was worried.

He tensed as he went into the dimness of the hall. The trapped heat was full of the sweet smell of corruption. He saw the overturned chair beside the telephone and the tiny splashes of blood on the telephone pad.

The girl saw them too. Her face said nothing, but he felt

that she had turned to ice. He went before her into the blackness of the surgery and turned on the light.

Behind him, she said steadily, "I'm going outside. I have to be sick."

He heard the soft whisper of her departing feet.

The flies had preceded them. They were clustered over the woman's eyes and drifted in and out of the gaping mouth. They lay like a dark scarf along the rusty line of the man's slashed throat.

Forsyth looked stonily from one body to the other, as though he would find the answer to the puzzle in the dead faces.

An ordinary citizen might have done one of two things: got out, or called the police. Being a professional, Forsyth did neither.

The man's pockets were empty, but as he bent over him, Forsyth smelled the faint hospital odor. He would not, after all, be having an interview with Dr. Lupescu.

The woman, he surmised, would be the doctor's wife. He squeezed behind the body at the desk to go through the drawers of the cabinet behind her. He found nothing of interest, other than a small bunch of keys embedded in the heart of a roll of cotton.

He had to move the desk away from the woman to get at its drawers. His face stiffened with revulsion as he caught the swaying body and tied it to the back of the chair with a length of bandage.

The middle drawer on the left side yielded a treasury of information. Meticulously, Lupescu had recorded every detail of Rothman's condition and treatment. Forsyth's brows met in a worried frown. He was not, after all, to have the satisfaction of punching Rothman on the jaw.

He read steadily.

When he had finished, he pocketed the signed order for an ambulance, due to collect a patient from the villa at five o'clock and to transport him with Dr. Lupescu and a nurse to the Bucharest airport. There was a letter from the airport authorities, promising to facilitate passage through the terminal. In view of the patient's condition, all formalities would be waived, but it was essential that the three passports should be readily available. Forsyth pocketed these.

In the woman's right shoe, he found her marriage certificate and a scrap of paper on which had been written an address in Moscow. Forsyth studied that impassively. It was the building that housed those to whom the Russians had cause to be grateful. He left the marriage certificate, but took the address.

On a chair near the window was a crisply starched nurse's uniform, flowing white headdress, white buckskin shoes with laces, a trim dove-gray gabardine coat, gray nylon gloves and a gray suede shoulder bag. A doctor's case was propped against the leg of the chair.

Forsyth moved silently into the hall. He knew as surely as if he had been told that Nicola Beaufort was huddled in the car behind the sheltering screen of vines.

Nothing moved in the house. He went like a cat up the wide stairway to the upper landing. He began a systematic search of the first bedroom. Within ten minutes, he had found Rothman's scratched message on the bedpost.

On the windowsill, a dove cooed with distracting sweetness. His eyes followed the curve of the meadow, took in the outline of the prison and measured the distance between the building and Lupescu's villa. A knife turned slowly in his side, reminding him of the folly of hoping to carry Rothman's bulky form over that distance. Whoever released Rothman from Doftana, it was unlikely to be he.

He went downstairs, righted the chair in the hall and sat at the narrow table to call the Hotel Modern in Mamaia. He had to wait for almost ten minutes before the waiter Jan Balanescu came to the phone, but the brief talk was highly satisfactory. That evening, someone would certainly be waiting at Bucharest airport to hand him the three flight tickets for the BEA plane.

When he had replaced the receiver, Forsyth thought for a moment. If the international lines were busy now, there was just a chance that he might be able to make the call from the airport, but it would be cutting matters very fine. As he lifted the receiver, his expression was grim.

Within fifteen minutes, the phone rang in the Eton Avenue house. Brett answered. Forsyth spoke steadily for ten minutes, rapping out information and directions like a general in the heat of battle. At the end, Brett said quietly, "I'll attend to it," and hung up.

Forsyth released his breath in a soft explosion of sound. He stood up and pushed the chair over on its side as he had found it.

He had reached the doorway of the study when the phone shrilled. The sound was shocking in the stillness. Forsyth looked steadily at the instrument, pondering the possibilities. He glanced at his wristwatch. Whoever was attending to Rothman—if anybody was—would be expected to be in Doftana now. He decided to ignore the call.

In the surgery, he dropped on his knees beside the doctor's case and examined the contents, grunting with satisfaction when he saw the pentathol and the array of syringes. He examined one box of loaded syringes with particular care.

Back in the kitchen, he found two large plastic bags with sturdy rope handles. Into one he put a bottle of wine, a bottle of *ţuica*, and two well-rinsed glasses wrapped in a clean tea towel. He carried the other bag to the surgery where he packed it with the nurse's outfit.

When he let himself out at the back door, he was dangerously encumbered with the bags and the doctor's case. He grinned as he thought of Neville's horrified disapproval.

The phone was ringing again as he walked toward the vines.

When he opened the car door, she started to cry suddenly, a heartbroken sound full of grief, horror and exhaustion. He shed the bags and case and put his hands on either side of her face, forcing her to look at him. She stammered, "I didn't know it would be like that. Death is horrible! Horrible!"

He wanted to hold her, to heal her, to blot out the searing memory of the scene in the surgery. In that moment, he knew that he truly loved her, that she meant more than the crown or Rothman or even the safety of the world.

She looked back at him, at first with an icy terror, but gradually the deep shuddering stopped, her eyes warmed and she raised her face almost desperately for his kiss.

Bonneaud stood for a moment with his hand on the door handle of his car. His eyes swept along the impressive frontage of Jordanes's villa, noted its impregnable position, the way in which the narrow valley ran like a river to the edge of the estate.

Instinct told him that over the years he would meet its new owner at Saint Moritz, in the Caribbean, at Marbella, in Sardinia—in all or any of the playgrounds of the rich. Her mocking gaze would follow him everywhere.

His hand tightened on the handle. It was a nuisance, but soon he would have to return to kill the girl in the black mink. Getting the box from a bunch of country bumpkins would not be such a problem. What would be more difficult would be making Forsyth pay adequately. But even that would be done very soon.

He drove carefully down the drive and turned into the highway, heading for Doftana. His physical needs had not changed. Rest, food, a bath—because they had been denied him by Chi-Chi they had now become a clamant necessity. At the same time, his hatred of Chi-Chi demanded a victim. He was in a dangerous mood when he caught a glimpse on his left of the roof of a house among the trees. He slackened speed and pulled the car gently over to the opposite side of the road.

The house was a surprise. For a moment he imagined that he had come to a woodcutter's home, but the long, low log cabin had an indefinable air of opulence. It was, he decided, the shooting lodge of some tycoon from Ploesti or Bucharest. His lip curled in appreciation of the elastic consciences of the communists.

The lodge sat among the cool aisles of pine trees as though it had grown out of the ground. A thin curl of smoke hung like an interrogation mark above the roof. Fat pink geraniums spilled from windowboxes.

So there is at least one servant, Bonneaud concluded.

His eye traveled to the wooden double garage on the left. The doors were open and the garage was empty.

As he was about to leave the car, he hesitated. He studied his face in the mirror and rasped a hand over the blue stubble of his beard. At best, he knew that he was not a handsome man. Good grooming and an indefinable animal magnetism had helped in his conquests. Now the face in the mirror looked villainous.

He sighed, rolled down the window at his side and gently pressed the horn three times.

Within moments, the door of the lodge flew open and a woman appeared. She was small and slender with a pert little face under a springing mass of dark curls. The merry dark eyes and the curving happy mouth cheered Bonneaud immensely.

He relaxed and examined her closely.

She was older than he had first imagined. Probably thirty-five, he estimated, but she had preserved the taut lines of her figure and the costly olive-green suede pants suit helped.

She's a fool, he thought contemptuously, as she walked confidently toward the car.

Close up, she smelled of some expensive perfume which he did not recognize. He remained seated in the car and was careful to keep his hands in full view.

"Don't come too near!" he laughed. "I didn't want to alarm you, but I must look like the devil's brother and," his smile was rueful, "I'm afraid I don't smell too clean."

She grinned at him like a friendly puppy. "You look like my husband when he has spent a night in the woods. At the lodge, we don't expect people to look like *Buçaresti* diplomats. Do come in."

"That's exactly what I have done—spent a night in the woods, but I certainly didn't plan to do so. I got lost near Sinaia and I'm afraid I was not meant to be the rugged type. I don't mind admitting that I'm dirty, hungry and exhausted. I'm damned glad to get back to civilization."

She giggled adorably. "And to think that Fernando and I imagine that we are getting away from it here! I'll soon fix you up."

She led the way into the pine-scented living room.

Bonneaud began to ride on a wave of euphoria. He settled down to enjoy the experience. The aromatic pine forest, the grassy patch fronting the house thick with autumn crocus, the spilling gaiety of the windowboxes had pleased him, but the interior of the lodge delighted him. It had the understated perfection that money wisely spent can achieve.

A log fire, recently lit, burned in an enormous stone fireplace. A glass screen, engraved with hunting scenes in the Limoges style, broke up and multiplied the reflections of the flames until the glass looked like a sheet of dancing ruby constellations. The stellate light cast a rosy glow over snowy-white fur rugs scattered on the pale pine floors. There were deep caramel-colored leather armchairs and settees. He noted the David Cox prints, the Steuben glass, the English linen curtains with the gay hunting scenes.

This would do very nicely.

He sank gratefully into a settee in front of the fire.

His hostess said prettily, "I'm Alida Ramirez. My husband, Fernando, and I are South Americans, but we have lived in Rumania for five years. He's in iron, so we have to be within commuting distance of Ploesti." She made a moue of distaste. "I get very bored and lonely here. I enjoy our apartment in Bucharest much more. This morning, Fernando left for Bucharest. He won't be back till tomorrow night and our man is sick, so I am alone."

She looked at him from under her eyelashes. Bonneaud grinned inwardly. This *would* do very nicely.

"I'm Alan Bonneaud, very much at your service, madame." They exchanged contented smiles.

"Alida and Alan—our names are in harmony, don't you think?" The wings of curling hair had been trained to curve round her ears in order to show the diamond-studded earrings. "It is a pity not to use them. I shall call you Alan."

Her smile was enchanting, he decided.

"If you permit me to wash and shave, I shall call you Circe—the sorceress who made her guests feel that they never wanted to leave."

She pouted. "Wasn't she the one who changed men into swine by giving them a magic beverage? Wasn't the drink infatuating and degrading?"

With a lacquer-tipped finger, she pressed a button on the underside of the low table before them. A bar, gleaming with glasses and bottles, rose slowly. She smiled triumphantly. "I shall do better. You will choose exactly what you want. Just enough to keep you happy while I make you some breakfast. Then—when you have eaten—a long, long soak. I shall prepare your bath myself." Her eyelashes lay on the rosy cheeks like fans, then swept upward to reveal the laughter. "After that—you sle-e-e-p!"

Bonneaud smiled inwardly. It was all so predictable! In moments, she would tell him that her husband was too old for her. She would give him a very strong drink, followed by a good breakfast. Inevitably, she would join him in the bath, before sharing her bed with him. He reproached himself. He had forgotten the music. Inevitably, too, there would be music.

Well—why not?

He stretched his tired legs luxuriously. There were worse ways of spending a couple of hours than with a pretty little sex kitten. In fact, it was regrettable that the time would be so short. Perhaps an arrangement might be made. After all, he would be returning almost immediately to Rumania to have a last word with Chi-Chi.

But he must disappoint Alida in one respect.

Her hand hovered over the vodka bottle and her eyebrows climbed.

"No," he said firmly. "I rarely drink." There was a large jug of tomato juice sitting in a bowl of crushed ice. The glass was beaded with moisture. To his smoke-parched throat, it would be nectar. He nodded in the direction of the jug. "Lots of that, please. But let me fix your drink first."

She brought forefinger and thumb almost together. "That much brandy, please! Usually, I keep that jug of tomato juice filled and drink it practically all day. Good for the figure! But today," she patted her diaphragm delicately, "I have a little acidity. I am better off without it."

Expertly Bonneaud fixed their drinks.

Under his fingers, his glass was icy. He raised it in a toast.

"To us and to many happy meetings!"

The huge dark eyes were wistful, with a hint of sadness

in their depth. She touched another button on the underside of the table.

Above the fireplace was a large collage, striking in its surrealistic design and color. What appeared to be great clumps of agate, amethyst, cornelian, amber and obsidian were intertwined with bands of multicolored copper and gold. Bonneaud pursed his lips and nodded in smiling admiration. It concealed stereo equipment.

The room was filled with the haunting music of "Our Love Is Here to Stay." He waited expectantly for the next move.

Alida Ramirez got fluidly to her feet. She crossed the room to a revolving bookcase on which there was a photograph in a heavy silver frame. She brought the photograph back and presented it to Bonneaud.

There was a wry twist to her mouth as she said, "Most of the music we keep at the lodge is at least twenty-five years old. As you see, my husband is of a different generation."

Bonneaud drained his glass and studied the photograph. The man, he decided, was over seventy years of age. He was small and paunchy with a shining bald head which the photographer had neglected to dim down. The fringe of white hair looked wispy, but the eyes behind the heavy horn-rimmed glasses had a youthful, kindly gleam.

All in all, Bonneaud decided, considering the size of her diamond solitaire and the padded comfort of the lodge, maybe Alida Ramirez had not done too badly.

He searched for the right words. He had a long list of phrases for precisely this type of occasion.

"You must add so much to his life," he murmured softly, "your youth, your freshness . . ." He allowed his voice to die away. It was almost boringly corny. "But, alas! you must lose so much too."

She got briskly to her feet. "Bring your glass and your

jug," she commanded. "You can wash your hands, get drunk on that wild tipple and watch me cook for you."

The American kitchen was a housewife's dream.

As he leaned against the sink, drying his hands, Bonneaud felt strangely relaxed and content. The pretty woman preparing the ample quantities of bacon and eggs at the freestanding cooking area looked at once domesticated and seductive.

He filled his glass and examined her dreamily. The music insisted gently that while the Rockies might crumble and Gibraltar might tumble, their love would last.

There was something about the old tunes, he decided. . .

While he ate, she chattered pleasantly in her little-girl voice. "This place would drive an architect mad," she smiled. "I think you'll grant that it is comfortable and beautiful, but it is a hopeless mixture of styles and periods. Fernando gave me a free hand and I've had fun fixing the place up. You'll see when you have finished eating."

"If the living room is your handiwork, the rest will be lovely."

"I restrained myself there. As a child, I lived on a ranch at the foot of the mesa near Taos, in New Mexico. Fernando swears that some of the mystical qualities of the mountain got into me and that I keep trying to get them into my surroundings." Her eyes laughed at herself.

As he swallowed the last morsel of bacon and drained his coffee cup, Bonneaud felt restored. He allowed the quick patter of her words to flow over him while his mind went back to his own affairs. He glanced at the clock above the kitchen door. It was time to get in touch with Lupescu.

He waited until she had finished her account of the Millicent A. Rogers Memorial Museum with its collection of Indian arts and crafts. *Who the hell,* he wondered, *had Millicent A. Rogers been?*

"May I use your phone?"

"Of course." She led the way back to the living room.

"There's a phone in the kitchen. You probably noticed it, but you'll have more privacy here. I'll clear up in the kitchen and by then you'll probably be ready for that shave and soak."

She touched the paneling of the wall beside his chair. It swung out. On a shelf was a telephone with several telephone directories on a second shelf beneath. As he lifted the receiver he heard the quick pad of her feet going toward the kitchen.

He listened carefully. *Nobody*, he decided, *was on the extension.*

The phone in the Lupescu villa rang and rang. He frowned impatiently and glanced at the English carriage clock on a nearby table. He would try again in a few minutes. Probably Fouquet and the Lupescus were with Rothman in the cellar of Doftana. The fools should have arranged that at least one of them remained in the villa to take phone calls. His brow darkened at the inefficiency.

He reached for a directory and quickly found the number of Otopeni Airport. His fingers beat an irritated tattoo on the table. Fouquet should have been doing this.

Bargaining with the Russians from London would give him, he reckoned, a decided psychological advantage. He would be within easy reach of two possible rival clients—British and American. The prospect of playing the nations off against each other was deeply satisfying. He pulled a pad toward him to note particulars of flights out of Otopeni.

"Let me be sure that I have got it right," he said pleasantly to the girl at the other end of the phone. "There is a last direct flight tonight, Bucharest to London, BEA Trident Flight 719? Takeoff 19.30 hours? How long does it take? . . . Four hours, twenty-five minutes? Good! Yes—I have it, thank you. In the unlikely event of my missing that, can any other line get me to London?" He listened intently. "Via Brussels? Good!" He issued a crisp instruction and put the phone down, satisfied that his plans were falling beautifully into place. Given an hour's sleep, he would be more than ready to tackle Forsyth.

He tried the Lupescu number again. When there was no reply, he decided that he would wait until one of them, probably Chantal Lupescu, went back to the villa to prepare a meal. There was no immediate urgency.

He went back to the kitchen in a happy frame of mind.

Alida Ramirez had kicked off her shoes as she stood at the gleaming steel sink. The green suede jacket had been tossed over a chair and she had rolled the sleeves of her cream silk blouse high above her elbows. Hands and arms were covered with suds. She flapped her hands toward the refrigerator. She looked wholesome and disarmingly friendly.

"Finish up your tomato juice," she commanded, "and I'll wash that jug. You'll find a fresh lot in the refrigerator. Take it into the bathroom with you. My idea of bliss is a hot shower, punctuated by long drafts of icy tomato juice." She gave him a wicked look. "I'm a sybarite—Olympic gold medalist standard."

Balancing the jug, he followed her to the bathroom. Childishly, she slid along the polished wood of the passage on her stockinged feet, casting him a mischievous glance over her shoulder. "My husband's things would be no use to you," she gurgled. "You'll have to drape yourself in a bath towel—toga fashion—and sleep in the raw. You have the figure for it," she added comfortingly.

"See you later," she said as she ushered him into the bathroom.

He pursed his lips in a silent whistle. Though smaller than Mihnea Jordanes's private bath, it outdid his in opulence. Like his, the room was entirely mirrored, with walls and ceiling endlessly repeating the plate-glassed twin shower cabinets; the long pink marble vanity, dotted with crystal bottles and jars; the white padded massage couch under the ultraviolet ray lamp; the double pink marble bath mounted on a green onyx platform reached by three shallow steps.

It looked as if Chi-Chi had done him a favor.

He undressed swiftly.

He was absently massaging the Monsieur Rochas after-shave lotion into his face with one hand and watching the water run into the bath when she came in. Her figure was even better than he had thought. Carefully, he deposited his empty glass on the rim of the bath and moved toward her. Their bodies met and fused. She was fire and ice and a synthesis of all the best of all his encounters with women.

"*Chérie, chérie, chérie . . .*" he heard himself whispering urgently, over and over again.

In the big four-poster bed, set in the middle of the shadowy bedroom, he was gentle and expert, but he must have been more tired than he had thought. Her limbs, under his, seemed to him to move languidly like those of a swimmer under water. With his lips on her breast, he drifted into sleep.

Once he thought he heard the ringing of a phone, but he went farther into the comforting darkness.

When he wakened, she had gone. Momentarily that disturbed him and he had a quick flash of fear that he might have allowed his emotions to become involved. That brought a smile to his face. He was too dreamily content to worry about anything. Apart from the thirst he had suffered since the smoke from the woodcutter's cabin had poured out, he had never felt more peaceful nor more relaxed.

Disdaining the glass, he reached for the tomato juice and took a long draft from the jug.

"Mmmmmm!" he murmured.

A ray of light from the clock on the bedside table threw the figures of the time on the ceiling almost directly above him. He pulled himself high on the pillows. Somebody must be in the villa now, preparing a meal. He cursed his languor.

The phone was at his elbow. At the third ring in the Lupescu villa, Fouquet's voice answered. He cut short the man's protests and complaints.

"Give me a synopsis," he barked.

As Fouquet's voice droned on, Bonneaud crouched in the bed as if turned to stone. He said impatiently, "Of course you were right to kill them." His lips went back in a snarl. "I doubted Lupescu. I should have done something about it at once." He listened intently. "The KGB?" There was a sick chill deep inside him. His thoughts raced. "Let me think," he gritted.

Not for a moment had he suspected that the Russians knew anything about the crown. Had he known that they were after it, he would not have dared try an independent operation. This put a totally different complexion on matters. Like a cornered rat, his mind drew on reserves of desperate courage.

Forsyth still had the crown. If the Russians were able to get it from the Englishman, there was nothing that he, Bonneaud, could do. He was convinced that Forsyth would be hoping to be on the BEA plane that night. It might still be possible to snatch the crown from him at the airport. The Russians then would have even more reason to be indebted to him. The game was not yet lost.

Bonneaud forced himself to relax against the pillows. He said crisply to Fouquet, "This is what you do. Get back at once and kill Rothman. That gets top priority. He must not fall into Forsyth's hands. If you have the bad luck to meet Forsyth, don't kill *him*. He won't be running around with the crown in his hand. Kill him and we might never find it, so don't get carried away. Leave Forsyth to me. Next, it is essential that you get away from that villa as soon as possible. I don't want you anywhere in the area when those bodies are found. The Rumanian police are not fools.

They'll soon find a connection between the Lupescus and us." He thought for a moment. "Find out when there is a flight from Otopeni to Paris. If you can't make that today, take any flight to anywhere in the West, but *get out of Rumania*. Meet me in Paris a week from today. No mistakes, please. Repeat what you have to do." He listened. "Good!" He replaced the receiver.

As he settled himself more comfortably against the pillows, Bonneaud felt no real anxiety. The news of the KGB involvement had been a jolt, but he was a realist. It might still be possible to do business with them. He was certainly not fool enough to run counter to them. As for Forsyth— there could be no violent confrontation at the airport. Without the assistance of Fossard, Fouquet and Lupescu, Bonneaud would have to rely on his own brains and he had perfect confidence in his ability to use them.

He was still tired. There was time for a sleep, time even for a little lovemaking, and he would still be at Otopeni well before the plane was due to leave.

His eyelids drooped. The soft rise and fall of his breath was the only sound in the shadowy room. . . .

When he wakened, he was fresh and alert. His eyes snapped open and he saw the time clearly on the ceiling. He came fully awake. He had slept much too long. There was still adequate time to get to Bucharest, but there was none to be wasted.

Alida Ramirez sat placidly sewing in a chair near the window. In the glow of the lamp on the table beside her, she looked rosy and enchantingly pretty. Bonneaud regretted the hours spent in sleeping. She was dressed in a set of white-and-gold hostess pajamas with high-heeled gold sandals on her tiny feet. She had the contented air of a young wife happy in the company of a much-loved husband.

Bonneaud threw back the clothes.

She came to meet him and put her arms round his waist,

pressing her head against his naked shoulder. He put her gently aside. "*Chérie,* I must wash and dress at once. You made me too comfortable. Now I will have to hurry. I ought not to have slept so long."

Her eyes brimmed with tears. "Shall I see you again?" she whispered.

"Of course!" He found to his surprise that he meant it.

She followed him into the bathroom.

As he splashed water on his face, he said, "Write down this address and telephone number, as well as those for your Bucharest apartment. Put the paper in my jacket pocket." He thought quickly. "I don't expect to be free for at least two weeks. After that, you can expect me any day. I promise."

She trotted off obediently.

As he dressed, he was full of the euphoria that he had experienced from the moment he had stepped into the cabin that morning. He was not a superstitious man, but if he had been asked to analyze his feelings, he would have said that he was convinced that Alida Ramirez had brought him luck.

He was whistling lightheartedly as he went out to his car.

Looking down at the rather forlorn little face, he remembered with amazement his savage intention of making the first woman he met pay for Chi-Chi's treatment of him. He smiled indulgently. She had been nothing but a brainless zero, though she would still pay for her presumption.

He drove off, seeing, with something approaching a pang, Alida's figure growing smaller and smaller in his driving mirror.

When the car was out of sight, Alida Ramirez went briskly into the house. First of all, she put her father's photograph into a cupboard. She went through to the bedroom, threw up the windows, as if she could not get sufficient fresh air into the house. When she had stripped the bed, she bundled the bed linen with a grimace of disgust into a container in the laundry room. That night, and for many nights, she would sleep in another bedroom.

She collected the almost-empty jug from the bedside table. Before she emptied the last of the tomato juice down the kitchen sink, she sniffed at it. Even if a concentration of the tetrahydrocannibinol had collected there, it was still odorless and tasteless. It pleased her that she had judged the amount so skilfully that a man as abstemious as Bonneaud had not detected it. She smiled at the thought that he had accepted totally the nature and length of his sleep.

Her next task was to adjust the clocks. The pink tip of her tongue crept along her lips, as she turned the hands forward carefully to the correct time. It took her almost ten minutes to reset all the clocks—in the kitchen, living room, bathroom and bedroom. With luck, not until Bonneaud reached the airport at Bucharest would he realize that, although the times on his wristwatch and dashboard clock matched, they were slow.

She sprayed the bathroom with disinfectant, giving an extra angry squirt to the bath, though she conceded reluctantly that the man was an expert. It was almost a pity that he was such a complete stinker.

Under the shower, she soaped herself liberally and scrubbed vigorously, as if to rid herself of more than the odors and sensations of the day. This time, her expression in the mirrors was genuinely forlorn.

When she had sprayed herself with Imprévu and gotten into her favorite apricot silk evening suit, she was ready to report to Chi-Chi.

She tucked her feet under her in the big caramel-colored chair and lifted the phone.

"Chi-Chi, you are a witch! The whole thing went like a dream. He came—he saw—I conquered!"

"Has he gone?"

"Yes—a little over three-quarters of an hour ago. I'll

swear that he hasn't a clue that he was conned from the moment that his wheels stopped turning at my door. Do you wonder that I've never married? Men!" She spat delicately.

"But tell me about it. Give! Give!"

"It went just as you said it would. Bonneaud has a nose for comfort and a woman. He came like a homing pigeon to the house—not too remarkable since there isn't another for miles. He looked as if he was spoiling for trouble, but I turned on the full battery of innocent charm and he melted, though I have to give the tetrahydrocannibinol a good share of the credit. How did you know that he would take the tomato juice?" Her voice was curious.

"He doesn't trust himself to drink much. Today I was positive he would keep to tomato juice. He's predictable. Most men are." Chi-Chi sounded bored.

"What have you got against him?"

"The fact that he's alive." Chi-Chi's tone was vicious. "You can guess his type from the little I told you this morning. Full details when I see you. But the important thing is that I owe a man a big favor. You've helped me to pay a little of it back. You name your price."

"I'll think about it, darling." Alida Ramirez's voice was a pleasant gurgle. "I was so damned bored today that it was a pleasure to do it. I'm beginning to look like one of the trees here. Would it be too utterly unseemly if you and I took off for distant parts next week?"

"Darling, with our kind of money, you and I *set* standards. Start packing!" Chi-Chi's voice sobered. "Alida!"

"Yes?"

"You've been fantastically good, but don't slip up now. It would be fatal if you forgot to make that telephone call, but it is essential that you don't make it too soon. The timing is most important." She laughed wickedly. "Mine will be made tonight also. Between us, we've made certain that Bonneaud will never trouble us again."

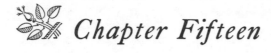 *Chapter Fifteen*

FORSYTH found a grassy, saucer-shaped hollow midway between the highest point of the meadow and the prison building. He grunted with satisfaction. It was an excellent vantage point. From it he could see the Lupescu villa, the entire stretch of the Doftana institution and, what had previously been hidden, the broad sweep of the drive from the main road to the front entrance of the prison.

He could scarcely, he told himself, have been more fortunate.

Two points worried him.

According to the methodically detailed but indiscreet papers that Lupescu had left behind, they would have a long wait before the KGB people made their move. Bonneaud's actions were, of course, completely unpredictable, so total relaxation meanwhile would be out of the question.

The second worrisome fact was that the sun was strong and would shortly beat down on them with uncomfortable fierceness. For an hour or so, this grassy depression would be a sun worshipper's paradise which might well change to a miniature torture chamber. Forsyth would have endured the discomforts stoically, but he looked at the girl's white tension and was filled with an unusual irresolution.

He set about the task of settling in as though making camp.

Once in the hollow, they would be completely hidden from below, though a watcher from the highest point of the meadow would spot them at once. The tall, poppy-strewn grasses on the rim of their saucer formed a knee-high screen, so that Forsyth had to raise himself cautiously to look down on the buildings. From a position on his knees, he could see the sun-baked roof of the prison. It had an eerie, deserted air, as if even the birds avoided it, but the smell of new-mown hay and the sight of a solemn column of marching quail on the driveway anchored it tenuously to reality.

He did not waste any time in speculating about how the Russians would get their colleague out. His position now was simply a lookout post and not a sniper's hideout.

His eye measured the distance between the hollow and the villa. He was satisfied that he could get there quickly, and short of bad luck or bad timing, remain unseen.

There was no need to hurry his preparations.

The anorak dangled from Nicola Beaufort's hand. She smiled at him shyly as he took it from her. Quickly, he filled it with the sweet-smelling meadow grasses, then zipped it up to form a pillow. She lay down obediently, cushioned among the strident beauty of the poppies like a tall, pale Ophelia.

Forsyth looked at her exhausted face and felt the new, disturbing tug of anxiety.

"You'll be baked in that pullover," he said brusquely. "This is no time to be modest. Take it off." He reached forward and pulled the white polo-necked sweater over her head. She did not resist.

As she lay back again, she gave a tiny sigh of pleasure. "Better!" she murmured.

Quickly and automatically, he looked around, and wondered that the possibility that the girl might be seen in her brassiere should worry him.

He dropped on his knees beside her and sat back on his

heels. She watched him gravely, the tilted amber eyes wary and veiled. He felt that she was mutely denying the emotion-charged interval in the car. The rejection pained him as if she had struck him a physical blow.

"Don't you think," she said evenly, "that you should follow suit—take off your jacket and tie?"

While his hands were busy, he said, "You have had a bad shock. You need to rest. Try to sleep now before the sun gets too high. Later, I'll see if it is possible to rig up some shelter, but meantime I have to go back to the villa. I have to make a phone call. Then I must get the wheelchair and our cases out of the car. Can I bring you back a thin blouse or anything else from your case?" He lifted the woollen sweater. "I'll pack that for you."

Shock, exhaustion and the sudden release of tension were beginning to carry her beyond reality. Forsyth saw the unfocused gaze and sighed.

When he stood up, he took off his shirt, folded it and placed it neatly on top of his jacket. A disheveled Dr. Lupescu would attract attention. With the addition of a pointed beard, he thought, he would not have looked too unlike the Rumanian, at least at a casual glance.

In the girl's drowsy gaze, he seemed immensely tall and strong against the skyline. The broad shoulders and tapering waist carried not one ounce of superfluous fat. The muscles in back and forearms rippled as he moved the plastic bags into a patch of shade. The long grooves in his cheeks seemed to have deepened in the last few days and the blue shadow of his beard gave him a sinister, piratical look.

She moaned like a hurt animal, turned convulsively and buried her face in the softness of the anorak. For a moment, Forsyth looked down at her, perplexed and troubled, but then he walked quickly through the meadow toward the villa.

It seemed to him that the sickly smell of corruption was

now stronger in the hall. He draped the girl's sweater across his knees, seated himself at the hall table and gritted his teeth against the savage itching of his skin under the adhesive bandage.

His call to the Jordanes's villa went through promptly. The servant was courteous and unsurprised. "Madame Jordanes asked me to let her know the moment you called, Monsieur East. She will be with you shortly."

Forsyth grinned with pleasure at the sound of Chi-Chi's cool, amused tones. *I was born knowing these women,* he thought indulgently.

"Oh! Monsieur . . . East." He smiled with appreciation of the telling pause. "I hope everything has gone well for you. Perhaps I have been able to be of a little assistance."

Briefly she described Bonneaud's encounters with her and with Alida Ramirez. Her laughter rang out as she outlined her plan for Bonneaud.

Forsyth's smile broadened.

"Madame Jordanes, I love you!"

He had the professional operator's genuine appreciation of intelligent help. It looked as if, with luck and Alida Ramirez's judicious use of the tetrahydrocannibinol, there was now an excellent chance that Bonneaud would go straight to the Bucharest airport and not have time to come near the villa or the prison. All he, Forsyth, could do now, he decided, was to hope for that extra slice of luck.

Some of the tension went out of his big frame. He scratched absently at his chest and thought about Alida Ramirez's deadly cocktail. His lips tightened as he considered how much depended on her judgment.

"I'm not too familiar with the properties and effects of THC," he said slowly. "Isn't there a risk that it may cause dangerous hallucinations?"

"Yes." She sounded impatient. "Alida and I are both aware that it is at least ten times stronger than the normal cannabis. We don't have a real drug problem in Rumania yet, but our geographical position certainly ensures that we don't live in Cloud Cuckoo-land as far as drugs are concerned." She laughed harshly. "Alida and I know the facts of life. You can be sure that, at this moment, Bonneaud is deliciously content, probably in a light sleep. He certainly doesn't need a canvas jacket. Relax, Monsieur East! You can trust us."

"I'm sure I can." At the other end of the phone, Chi-Chi smiled happily at the unfeigned admiration in his voice. "I'm going to spend sleepless nights wondering how to repay you. Unfortunately, I have a further problem. It concerns your Lamborghini. I now find that it is impossible for me to leave it at Otopeni."

"Where is it now?" she asked crisply.

"In the Lupescu garden. Inevitably, the local police will be here—not too soon, I hope—but certainly within days. The presence of the *late* owners of the villa and of your car would be, at the very least, a considerable embarrassment to you. I haven't time to drive it a safe distance away and walk back. Frankly, I'm at a loss at the moment."

The moments ticked away.

"But I'm not, Mr. East," she said cheerfully. "Can Bonneaud be tied up with the Lupescus?"

"Certainly. The Rumanian police are pretty smart and fiercely resentful of any international intrigue on their territory. They know all about the SMR and its top brass. They'll dig fast and deep and come up pretty speedily with the right answers."

"Good! Forget about the car. This will cook Bonneaud's goose completely." Her laughter rippled over the wires. "Don't you think he was a foolish man to steal my car, Mr. East?" The voice was demure.

Forsyth grinned wickedly.

Her voice purred in his ear. "I must be very careful that I report its loss at exactly the right time. When do you expect to leave our country, Mr. East?"

Forsyth gave a sigh of pure pleasure. There were certain advantages in dealing with an experienced woman.

When he replaced the receiver, the characteristic humorous quirk to his mouth was much in evidence. He yawned, stretched and got rather painfully to his feet, retrieving the girl's sweater from the floor where it had fallen. Nobody, he decided, would be coming immediately to prepare a meal for Rothman. If Bonneaud had already been in touch with an associate, probably Rothman would not be getting any more meals from them.

At the thought of Rothman, Forsyth's sensitive hands turned to fists. The blue eyes were wintery. He kicked the chair deftly over on its side, draped Nicola Beaufort's sweater over the newel post and went up the stairs, taking them two at a time.

As he showered and shaved, he went on planning, but the thought of the girl kept intruding. He frowned at himself in the mirror, but he was aware that somewhere under the layers of cold calculation and ruthlessness was a tiny, springing well of happiness. He hissed contentedly through his teeth like an ostler grooming a horse. Grinning, he used Lupescu's after-shave lotion liberally and tucked a tube of Ambre Solaire into a trouser pocket. He soaked a sponge in eau de cologne and dropped it into a floral plastic toilet bag. He had a tremendous feeling of well-being and alertness, in no way lessened by the slight discomfort of the sodden girdle of adhesive bandage.

He went lightly down the stairs, retrieved the sweater from the post and moved into the kitchen, letting the door swing gently behind him.

Caution made him close the outer kitchen door before he went across to the car.

When he snapped open the locks of Nicola Beaufort's case, he stood very still for a moment with his hands resting lightly on the silken pile of her clothes. A faint wave of Joy perfume came from the case and it did not strike him as strange that he no longer thought of the girl who had given him the brown towels.

When he had found a short-sleeved, white silk blouse, he put the sweater into the case and snapped the locks shut. He put the case on the ground near the car and draped the blouse over it.

From his own valise, he took the two small boxes packed by Brett in Neville's flat, and looked doubtfully down at his trouser pockets which already held his gun and the Ambre Solaire. After a moment's hesitation, he put the boxes and the tube of sun cream into the floral plastic sponge bag.

A little belatedly, it occurred to him that he might have unearthed the girl's own toilet bag. He shrugged and set about unstrapping the wheelchair.

The sun beat pleasantly down on his naked back and shoulders. He felt guilty about walking over the petunias which seemed to be everywhere. The garden was incredibly peaceful, though alive with sound. Frantic blackbirds went *chuckchuckchuckchuckchuckchuck.* Fat wrens sang cozily, while, above them, the doves wheeled and tore at the wind with their wild, flushed wings. Forsyth was full of nostalgia for the unreturning summers of childhood. Fleetingly, he thought of Stanmore Manor and of how good it would be to be back in the gentle English countryside.

He shifted the gun in his pocket as if to remind himself of how much he had still to accomplish.

If I'm not careful, I'll probably end by shooting my own leg, he thought wryly.

But it was hard to dispel the elusive feeling of happiness and expectancy. Some instinct told him that he was on the verge of a new experience. At another time, he would have laughed at himself as an imaginative fool, but the antennae were out and he trusted them.

At the back of the trunk, he found a large green golf

umbrella. The sight of it brought a grunt of pleasure from him. He put it on the ground beside the toilet bag. It looked as if he had found the answer to the sun problem.

As he pushed the wheelchair toward the back door of the villa, the rumble of the wheels mingled with the deep, meditative voices of frogs. A scarlet-enameled ladybird dropped delicately on the back of Forsyth's hand. He smiled at the lucky omen.

When he had opened the back door, he moved silently into the kitchen to prop open the swinging door into the hall.

Halfway across, he froze.

Someone had already done so. A kitchen chair had been placed against the door.

The hall was empty.

In one fluid movement, Forsyth glided behind the door and reached for his gun.

The phone rang harshly, shredding the stillness.

Through the crack in the door, he saw Fouquet, whom he did not know, emerge from the room opposite the surgery, upend the chair and sit at the narrow table facing the blood-dotted wall.

Forsyth's finger on the trigger eased. Breathing shallowly, he listened to Fouquet's aggrieved recital of complaints and difficulties.

So, Bonneaud is awake! Forsyth realized. *At least, he seems to suspect nothing.*

Fouquet's harsh French spat out the tale of the Lupescus' treachery and deaths, of the KGB plot and of Rothman's condition.

Forsyth strained to hear, willing the unseen Bonneaud, in some way, to reveal his plans.

The sun shining through the window at his back was scorching his shoulder blades. He moved them gently.

"Right" said Fouquet subserviently. "I've got it. These

are the orders—one, I kill Rothman now; two, I don't under any circumstances kill Forsyth; and three, I meet you in Paris a week from today."

Through the crack, Forsyth could see the sullen expression on Fouquet's face as he swung around on the chair to face the kitchen door and put out his hand to replace the receiver.

As Forsyth moved his head back from the crack and his finger tightened on his gun preparatory to diving around the edge of the door, he did not see the expression on Fouquet's face change, nor the way in which his hand froze on the receiver.

Stretched across the shiny tiles of the kitchen floor from the edge of the door was the grotesquely elongated shadow of a man. Fear glittered in Fouquet's eyes. Like quicksilver, he was out of the chair and at the foot of the stairway, before the crash of the chair reached Forsyth's ears.

As Forsyth erupted from the kitchen, he was keyed up with elation and a deadly determination to stop Fouquet. The situation, he thought exultantly, was opening up like a fissure in the ground. It was now vital that this man should die. He must not reach Rothman. He *had* to die.

At once the world began to explode in agony.

Forsyth had taken one flying leap beyond the kitchen when a shaft of lightning seemed to strike the hand holding the gun. A heavy bronze statuette clattered along the floor and his gun slithered after it.

Through the spars of the bannisters above his head, Forsyth saw Fouquet's tense face. Liquid fire ran up the Englishman's hand to his shoulder. He realized, bleakly, that his gun hand was useless.

He was at the foot of the stairway before the gun had stopped spinning and sliding. Above him, there was the slam of a door. He took the steps three at a time.

The man, he reasoned, *will be in the first bedroom.*

Again and again, his shoulder crashed against the locked door. The panels shivered, but held.

His eyes were brilliant with the pain from his ribs. He breathed in shallow, tortured gasps, moved swiftly back across the top hall, flew at the door, bringing the sole of his foot up to shatter the lock.

The door crashed open. He took in the closed window. The room was empty. Behind him, on the landing, there was the quick, furtive scuff of feet.

He wheeled and hurled himself on Fouquet, who had reached the top of the stairway. Feeling had come back into the Englishman's right hand. It shot forward, grasped Fouquet by the hair and dragged him backward. A keening sound came from the Frenchman's lips. He twisted like an eel in Forsyth's grasp and jerked a knee convulsively in the direction of the other man's groin. The knee slid harmlessly upward to the soft part of the Englishman's belly, losing impetus on the way.

The two men grappled, locked in grunting, straining battle. They smashed against the walls and doors of the hallway, clinging like leeches to each other. Again and again, Forsyth's fist slammed against Fouquet's face, but could not find a vital spot.

The Frenchman's quick brain had taken in the significance of the taped ribs. Fiercely, he concentrated on getting his arms round Forsyth. He squeezed slowly and mercilessly, holding on with the strength of desperation. He knew that he must and that he would be dead if he tried to reach the gun in his pocket.

Pain whistled through Forsyth's teeth. He was dimly conscious that his eyes were burning and bulging from his head in agony.

Together, like a horrible version of Siamese twins, they stumbled toward the top of the stairway. Forsyth knew that he was almost finished. Beneath him, Fouquet's face was a pale, trimphant blur.

Desperately, Forsyth opened his fist, heaved shoulders and arms upward and backward like a drowning man surfacing for the last time. He brought the side of his hand down like a sledgehammer on the side of the Frenchman's neck into the carotid artery. The second blow on the top of the spine killed him. Fouquet's body tumbled over and over as it thudded to the bottom of the stairway.

Forsyth shakily put a hand out to grasp the top of the bannisters. The world was spinning round him in slow, widening circles. The sound of his breathing was a harsh, rasping echo. He looked drunkenly down at the sprawled figure, then slid suddenly to the floor of the upper hallway.

He came to with the taste of dust in his mouth and the smooth coolness of wood beneath his face. Like an old man, he flexed arms and legs and got painfully to his feet.

As he splashed cold water over his face, the bathroom mirror gave back the image of a dead man. *I look like Lazarus,* he thought with bitter humor.

Methodically, he closed the door of the bedroom opposite and went carefully down the stairs, clinging like a lifeline to the rail.

There was nothing in Fouquet's pockets, other than his gun, which Forsyth stuck into the waistband of his own trousers. He retrieved his own gun which he again tucked into his waistband on the other side.

Deadwood Dick! he thought, picturing Neville's sarcastic face.

He was slightly relieved that there was no bunch of keys. At least, he did not have to do anything about Rothman yet.

By the time he had pulled Fouquet's body into the surgery, he was bathed in cold perspiration. He rested, then went out to get the wheelchair, which he put in the small room across from the surgery. It took two trips to bring in their cases. He thought for a moment and then put the

Lupescu luggage in the surgery, locking the door behind him.

He tossed the surgery key into the trees before he gathered up Nicola Beaufort's blouse, the toilet bag and golf umbrella and walked leadenly across the meadow to where she slept in the clear air.

In London, Brett clutched at his diaphragm absentmindedly and looked with satisfaction at the date on the desk calendar. With luck, Neville should be seeing the prime minister the next day.

He touched a bell and asked that a messenger be sent for a supply of milk. The six bottles were to be put in the refrigerator. He checked his supply of tea biscuits and of Mucaine, like a man preparing to withstand a lengthy siege.

In Sussex, Amy Neville turned from her blind study of the parkland to say stiffly to her husband, "Nicola left the Beauty Farm more than two weeks ago, though heaven alone knows why she went. There's nothing wrong with her health or figure. I feel guilty that I wasn't here in case she came home. I wish I knew for certain whether or not she did come home."

"She did." The thought of the missing gun was a private agony that he would not allow to surface.

"Then where is she now? None of her friends seem to know." Her eyes accused him. "Since she walked out of Hurst Grange, nobody knows a thing about her."

He bent and kissed her gently. "Be patient, Amy. She'll be home by tomorrow or the next day at the latest. I promise you. It's late. Let's go in to lunch." He began to talk of the Matisse exhibition at Burlington House.

At Mount Furnica, Chi-Chi Jordanes pirouetted gracefully round the mirrored bathroom, dark head held high and slim fingers lightly holding the floating billows of skirt. Her spine arched as she at last flew upward in a fluttering *pas de bas.*

Panting slightly, she blew an airy kiss in the direction of the sunken bath. The black silk jersey dress—without the pearls, naturally—would do very well for the funeral the next day. She would wear a double veil to hide her triumphant face.

She peered at her reflection and thought a little wistfully of the man East. But she was a realist. Already he had another woman's stamp on him.

She drifted toward her bedroom to remove her nail varnish and to wait for the hours to pass before she would again phone Alida Ramirez.

In Cimpina, Yuri Danilenko and Sergio Eliasberg finished an early lunch.

The manager of the hotel passed their table and paused to ask solicitously, "Have you completely recovered, Monsieur Eliasberg?"

There was the stink of Russian authority about these men that he did not like. He would be glad when they checked out that afternoon. The smile on his face grew more expansive at the thought.

"Perfectly." It was the older man who answered for the other. "We will be leaving in an hour. We have been very comfortable. Thank you."

He patted his lips with his napkin and the manager noticed his excellent teeth. They were the only distinctive feature in a heavy, anonymous face. *The faceless men!* he thought with a frisson of fear. The unconquerable Rumanian pride stiffened his spine. *Smug swine!* he accused them silently and moved on, wishing that there was some way in which he could ruffle the pair's monumental calm.

In Doftana, Tony Rothman was hard at work, marshaling his scanty store of facts and endeavoring to interpret them.

At breakfast time, Fouquet had fed him badly and inadequately with a piece of stale bread and some tepid black coffee. The supply of pain-killing tablets had long since been exhausted and Dr. Lupescu had not appeared to renew them. Conviction grew in Rothman that the doctor would not be back and that Fouquet was in sole charge.

His feet throbbed dully, but apart from the fact that he had a headache from the fetid air in the cell and that his body had an unaccountable tendency to slump to the left, he considered that he was not in bad shape. Nevertheless— and his lips went back in a vulpine grin at the thought— Moscow would rap the fingers of the members of the SMR for their interference. For his jailers *had* to be members of the French communist society. "Fools!" Rothman said aloud to the empty cell.

"I'll be back in an hour. I'm off to prepare a meal," Fouquet had explained.

But it was well past the hour now. Rothman felt his stomach knot hungrily. He had lost track of the days, bemused by the changes of locale and by the periods of induced unconsciousness. His earlier sanguinity had been replaced, first, by a stoical acceptance of his situation and now by a feeling of growing doubt and apprehension.

Could he and the Russians have miscalculated?

From the beginning of the exercise, he had had almost unbelievable luck. It had jolted him when Neville had sent him on exactly the same mission as the KGB but Danilenko had explained to him that this was the biggest piece of luck of all and how he must make use of it.

"World Peace Treaty!" Rothman jeered at the unresponding walls. "The only true peace will come through the spread of communism!" The light in the baby-blue eyes was less that of fanaticism than of unbridled ambition.

His thoughts went back to the SMR. If they were cosseting him in the hope that he would lead them to the crown, they hadn't a chance.

He went coldly over the events preceding his capture. Danilenko did not know that he had located the crown, but he would certainly approve of the steps that he, Rothman, had taken since he had traced it to Sinaia. It was with such groups as the French communists in mind that he had attempted to create a smokescreeen by going from Sinaia to Brasov and then returning to Constanza as if he had failed.

When he became conscious that he was being watched, he was not worried. He had barely resisted when he had been grabbed by the Frenchmen. That suited very nicely, since Danilenko and Eliasberg were watching every move. They would get him out at the right moment. Meanwhile, it would throw fresh dust in the eyes of that decadent pig Neville. It would have been a pleasure to have watched his face when the truth finally dawned on him. British Intelligence had a long way to go before they would outsmart the Russians. At the peace conference, they would be shown up for the inefficient, conniving bastards that they were.

Probably Neville would send out his bright boy Forsyth. British Intelligence made a fetish of rescuing stray operators.

In their friendly bouts in the Eton Avenue gym, it had been hard, Rothman reflected, not to put in that extra punch that would have spoiled Forsyth's amused smile. Now it looked as if he would never get the chance.

"Good-bye, Piccadilly! Farewell, Leicester Square!" he bellowed happily.

It was a bad moment when I thought that the French boys had picked up the planted clue in Mamaia, he thought. *But I'll bet that Forsyth has it by now. He's a very bright boy. I wouldn't be surprised if he actually has the crown at this moment—I hope so—and is dutifully preparing to carry it back to just where we want it—to the Eton Avenue house.*

He lay and thought about that.

Danilenko will be delighted, he deduced. *It will save him a lot of trouble. If that is how it has worked out, Eliasberg can go back with us to Moscow.*

For a moment, doubt clouded the bright eyes. But Danilenko must get him, Rothman, out soon. What was he waiting for? Was he giving Forsyth time to get the crown? That must be it.

At the delicious irony of Forsyth's carrying the crown like a modern Trojan horse right into the camp of their enemy, Tony Rothman's laughter boomed out and echoed round and round the cell.

But Forsyth hasn't got me! Without me, having the Crown of Saint Stephen is as good as carrying a hydrogen bomb around. On the day of the opening of the conference, it would blow up in Britain's smug face.

Rothman's faith in Danilenko came flooding back. Whatever the reasons for the delay, he would come.

Forsyth, the pawn, might have taken the KGB's bishop, but he would never get their king!

Rothman laughed and laughed, the sound teetering precariously on the edge of hysteria.

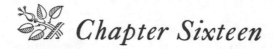 *Chapter Sixteen*

NICOLA BEAUFORT had fallen asleep, co-cooned in an enveloping awareness of Charles Forsyth's protective strength. Now some atavistic instinct brought her instantly awake as he rocked gently on his feet like a man balancing on a heaving deck. Almost at once she was on her feet with the fluid grace with which she had recovered from his blow at Heathrow.

His face was ashen and he seemed to be having difficulty with his breathing, but he managed to give her a reassuring smile that wrenched her heart. When she saw with what care he was carrying the silk blouse, her eyes filled with tears.

"I had a run-in with one of Bonneaud's men," he explained briefly. "It looks as if the Société des Mains Rouges won't be troubling us anymore." He sat down heavily on the ground at her feet as though the long legs would no longer support him. "I must be getting old," he smiled, "or maybe hungry. Time for our picnic, perhaps."

She shrugged her way into the blouse, which felt cool and soothing against her hot skin. Without speaking, she pushed the anorak under his head, and considered the golf umbrella for a moment with her delicate brows knitted thoughtfully.

Her eyes went to the guns at his waist.

"You look like the sheriff of Deadend Gulch." Her

glance was humorous. "If you fall asleep wearing that armory, you may wake up minus a big toe."

He smiled and put the guns at his side.

"Do you have a knife?" she asked.

When he had taken one from his pocket, she dug rapidly, attacking the ground close to his waist with short, vicious strokes, finally scrabbling with her hand until she had made a hole deep enough to take the stem of the umbrella. He watched her with detached disinterest as she stamped the soil vigorously into place around the handle.

Her resilience never ceased to amaze him. For a strange moment, he had the feeling that he was resting on her strength, as if by some weird osmosis they were able to draw courage from each other when necessary.

It was pleasantly cool under the opened umbrella. The green cover printed damask shadows on her cheeks and softened the glow of her bright head. He felt the great amber eyes searching his face with the same expression of loving care that he had first seen in them in the Villa Florica.

Of their own volition, his arms went out, enfolding her strongly and drawing her down until her head rested on his chest. A great peace wrapped them round. In that moment, they knew each other and were moved by the same piercing sense of joy.

Through the silk of her blouse, the soft mounds of her breasts seemed to fuse with the naked flesh of his chest. He was shaken by a passion greater than he had ever known, but it was desire lit by compassion. He drew her upward, then framed the radiant face between his hands, studying each feature like an artist who must know the bones beneath the skin.

"My love . . . my dear love . . ."

Their kiss was like a marriage—a seeking and a knowing in the great blinding moment of its consummation.

Reckless and uncaring, he gave a great triumphant shout and gentled her trembling until she smiled and lay back, relaxed and happy. His lips discovered her, finding the soft hollows where the collar bone met the slender throat, exploring the pulse at its firm base, tracing the sweet curve of ear and nostril and brow.

The Braille of love amused and delighted her. She teased him gently, finding instinctively the wry humor at the heart of the emotion.

"Charles," she murmured.

He looked inquiringly into the green-flecked eyes.

"Just . . . Charles." She was content to speak his name, openly and possessively, as if sealing a pact.

His mouth was full of strange words of love that he struggled to utter. As she lay peacefully in the hollow of his arm, he said into the soft masses of her hair, "Someday I will take you to the Olt Valley. It's a place for lovers." His voice laughed at himself. "That's the region of the love spell, by which Rumanian lovers wish each other all that is most beautiful in nature."

"Tell me," she commanded dreamily. "Wish me the love spell."

He recited softly:

> *"To wear on your brow*
> *The morning star of the mountain;*
> *On your lips two honeycombs,*
> *In your eyes two blackberries,*
> *On your eyebrows an ear of wheat;*
> *In your bosom, the Sun,*
> *At your back, the Moon,*
> *In your lap little stars."*

"In my lap little stars . . ."

Under his lips her cheeks were wet with tears. His urgent mouth could not stop their flowing. She twisted convulsively away from him, her body wracked with sobs.

Perplexed, he heard the heartbroken sound rise as if it would break in a wave of hysteria. He pulled her close, soothing her, but she would not look at him.

"You don't know!" she sobbed. "You don't know!"

"What don't I know, darling?" His arms tightened and his expression changed. "Is it Tony Rothman?"

By her stillness, he knew that he had been right. The words seemed to stick in his throat, but he brought them out stiffly. "You're in love with him?" It was less a question than a statement.

"No!" She twisted like an eel in his grasp. "I *hate* him! I wanted to kill him! I meant to kill him. I came here to kill him, but now . . ." Her voice died away uncertainly. "Now, I think, all I want is to get home and forget him." She pushed her hands childishly over her tear-stained face.

He stretched across her to find the plastic toilet bag and, as if she were a little girl, he wiped her hands and face with the sponge soaked in Chantal Lupescu's eau de cologne. His tone was purposely brisk and matter-of-fact. "Now, calm down and tell me what possessed a nice young girl like you to come gunning for Tony Rothman." His voice held a hint of teasing, but the blue eyes were cold and watchful.

She struggled for control and he steeled himself against the shame in her eyes. Sitting bolt upright, she looked straight ahead at the fringe of poppy-strewn grasses that edged their hollow.

"He betrayed me," she said flatly, like some heroine in an old-fashioned melodrama. He looked at her incredulously and she caught the astonishment.

"Not quite as you think," she said tightly. She turned to face him directly and he saw that her eyes were full of remembered pain and horror. "Because of Rothman, up to a couple of weeks ago, I spent several spells in a strait-jacket."

The muscles of Forsyth's throat tightened with shock.

"My father had warned me years ago that people might try to get at him through my mother or through me. When I thought about it at all, I suppose I thought that we might be kidnaped or even killed. I did not imagine the Tony Rothman approach."

Above their heads a flock of birds wheeled and darted, weaving joyous airy patterns.

"What did he do?" he asked evenly.

"We met at a party at the house of one of my friends. He was very attentive—too attentive, I thought. After that, he kept turning up wherever I was. I suppose I should have been flattered, but only a fool is unaware when a man's attentions don't seem to have an authentic ring. I was suspicious and questioned the friend at whose house we had first met. She was astonished. 'But he told me he had come with you!' she said. That confirmed my suspicions."

"Why didn't you go to your father?"

She gave him a bleak look. "I know now that that was the sensible thing to do, but I was angry and wanted to catch Rothman out in some way. I suppose I was insulted that he was clearly only interested in using me for his own purposes and I was certainly curious."

Forsyth had a moment of enlightenment. "You were to provide Rothman with bargaining power if General Neville caught him out as a double agent!" He glanced at her quickly.

"I know," she said quietly, "I guessed that. Foolishly, I accepted an invitation to dinner—a foursome, in a public restaurant. I thought that was safe enough. It wasn't." Her voice was a strangled whisper.

He said nothing, letting her take her time.

"Rothman made a great fuss about the dessert. It was to be special—a delicious crepe concoction filled with soft maple fudge, walnuts and truffles. There was a lot of laughter and badinage when he insisted on taking over from the waiter, lighting the warmed brandy, pouring it flaming over the crepes and quickly adding the pièce de résistance—a couple of squares of maple sugar."

"Soaked in LSD?" Forsyth brought the question out evenly, but the eyes were terrible.

"Yes. The ghastly thing was that I hated it. I forced myself to swallow it. I woke up in his bed." Her voice died away.

Forsyth's hands balled into fists.

"That wasn't the worst bit. He was there—trying to force himself to make love to me. He couldn't—" Hysteria was rising in her voice.

He hushed her automatically. "Couldn't—?"

"He looked—disgusted."

Forsyth had a swift recollection of Jan Balanescu's account of Rothman's meeting with "a pretty man" at Ovid's statue in Constanza. The savage pain in his chest grew and grew.

"I blew my mind—literally—I blew my mind. When I came to, I had just enough sense and control to phone my friend. Her fiancé, Dr. Lew, got me into a private room in a beauty farm and treated me there. His aunt owns the place, so I suppose I was lucky not to land in a loony bin. I understand that I was unlucky, however, in my reaction to the drug. I had a bad trip on the LSD and nobody knows if, and when, it may happen again." Her expression was stony.

His arms went round her. "We'll face that problem together, if need be. You'll be all right, my love." Above her head, his expression was frightening. He said softly, "Leave Rothman to me. But, first of all, he goes back to London. We'll both see to that."

His hands and mouth were deft with their new wisdom, reaching beyond her pain to soothe and heal. She sighed like a weary child who had at last come home.

To amuse her, he sang softly and drolly the words of an old Irish ballad, each verse concluding with the reminder that it would not be long till their wedding day. She laughed at his efforts and went gaily to work, setting out their meal and the wine as though they were simply lovers, bemused with each other and the airy freshness of the flower-strewn meadow.

They talked endlessly, tirelessly, as if they could never have enough of knowing about each other. She watched his face as he spoke of his father. Through his eyes, she saw the gold and gray perfection of Stanmore Manor, with the flaming scarlet and yellow of the Virginia creeper striking the only peacock note in that opulent, languid beauty. With the hot Rumanian sun straining at their green shelter, he made her see the gentle gold of autumn along the River Losk, with the old trees raining down golden leaves and the gold carp moving lazily in the fish ponds. Confidently, he saw all their tomorrows in her luminous eyes.

But as the fingers of light slanted across the meadow, he moved away from her.

"Is it time?" she asked quietly.

"It soon will be." He put on the glasses and the wide-angle lens showed him the whole stretch of Doftana.

She did not tell him that in them he looked forbidding and unfamiliar.

"What are you going to do? How will you get him out?" She was very calm now, but afraid for him.

"We aren't going to do anything meanwhile, except sit and watch. I've no intention of trying to get Rothman out. The Russians are going to save us that trouble." He reached for his shirt and collar. "Get yourself dressed up as Florence Nightingale *and keep out of Rothman's sight.* That's very important—crucial, in fact."

His eyes kept up their study of the stretch of drive between the highway and the prison. He checked the two cardboard boxes and put them in his pockets.

"What are those?"

"Once I get my hands on Rothman, I must keep him

sedated until we get to London." He hesitated. "If anything should happen to me, try to get him there. But nothing will," he added hastily as he saw fear flare in her eyes.

He showed her the bottles marked *Insulin* and watched the shock grow in her face as she read the underlyiing label. He touched the second box.

"This is a fairly new drug, called Ketamine. The dose is related to body weight, but we don't have to worry about that. It has been premeasured. There will be an adequate supply in each syringe for a man of Rothman's bulk. It acts within three minutes and the effects last for two hours. We daren't use anything stronger."

She was not listening. "What if we have to go through the security check and they find the crown?"

"They won't." He was quite confident. "It was sheer luck that neither of us were caught with the guns at Heathrow on the journey out. They don't always have security checks there, but, so far, Rumania has had no reason to set them up. We won't have any trouble."

He went back to his scrutiny of the building.

When she joined him later, it was as if she had put on a new personality with the uniform. She looked cool, professional and efficient. He eyed her critically and could find no flaw.

After a moment, he took the rubber sponge from the plastic bag and hacked at it with his knife until he had an oval-shaped piece.

"Not very hygienic, I'm afraid, but try it. If you have a gumboil, nobody will expect you to speak. Mutter if you have to."

She put it matter-of-factly into her pocket and sat down beside him to wait. Silently, he handed her a gun which she put into her handbag, as if it were the most ordinary thing in the world.

They sat quietly, shoulders touching, each thinking of the other.

Danilenko said angrily into the telephone, "Nothing in this damned country seems to work. Our official car has broken down and it's a holiday—a holiday, I ask you!—so nobody can repair it!"

At his seat by the window, Eliasberg smiled. The old fox was good!

At the other end of the phone, the official sputtered, "But, sir, can I help? May I send a car? It will be no trouble."

Danilenko allowed himself to be mollified. "Thank you, but that will not be necessary. The hotel here has been able to arrange it. Our driver is still at the garage, so my sub-inspector will drive. But thank you." His voice became pleasanter and more friendly. "We are both, it seems, the victims of officialdom. I must make my inspection; you must lose your holiday. We are comrades in distress." His great laugh boomed over the wires, so that the official quickly held the receiver away from his ear. "At least, we can get the business over fairly quickly." His voice deepened and took on the harsh note of authority that the Rumanian official knew only too well. "But the inspection must be thorough. You understand that? Top to bottom, cupboards, offices, state of the roof, the walls . . . so I hope you have the plans ready. And no fumbling for keys. I warn you, we will be thorough, but speedy. My sub-inspector is a good man. We will not take up too much of your holiday. Now, get on to your assistant and we will meet both of you at the entrance to Doftana in, say, half an hour." The receiver went down with a final, authoritative click.

Danilenko and Eliasberg exchanged satisfied grins.

"He swallowed it?"

"Naturally! The documents will confirm it." He checked the papers in his pocket. "Impossible to fault them! In Europe it seems, money can achieve any kind of documentation. Decadent swine!"

A quiver of uneasiness crossed Eliasberg's stolid face. "I don't like the fact that we haven't heard from Lupescu. Don't you think we should take a chance and phone him?"

"Certainly not. More operations have been ruined by members trying to improve on the Department's plans than I can tell you. We stick to our orders. Lupescu has been a sleeper too long in the Société des Mains Rouges to take any chances or to slip up at this stage. He and Chantal will be ready when the ambulance arrives. Depend upon it." He hesitated with his hand on his valise. His eyes were cold. "You are quite clear about what you must do?"

"Perfectly. When Rothman has told us where the crown is and the ambulance has left for Otopeni Airport, I take the car, go for the crown and get it to London as speedily as possible. I give it to the man Brett, and the rest is up to him. He knows how to time the exposure. After I have given Brett the crown, I get back to Moscow as quickly as possible with the photographs of Brett accepting the crown." He smiled at the thought. "The anonymous donor will, of course, be an Englishman—a man of straw. It will be immaterial whether he is traced or not."

"Good! Now, let's go! You will, of course, be careful not to kill any SMR agents, if that can be avoided." His tone was ironical. "It must be remembered that we have common fraternal aims. Our French comrades are, however, due a lesson in method."

Danilenko enjoyed the short drive out to Doftana. As the car turned into the drive leading to the prison building, his eyes went keenly over the steep rise of the meadow and he noted with satisfaction the intangible air of remoteness and solitude.

A car was already stationary at the entrance. Danilenko and Eliasberg got briskly out to join the two men who stood stiffly at attention, like members of a military welcoming party. Danilenko went forward with outstretched hand. He exuded a brisk friendliness. "When I look at this place, I think you are a fortunate man." He clapped a hand on the curator's shoulder. "Beautiful surroundings and no troublesome inmates! If the minister decides to call, arrange that it rains that day and that half the school population is here. Otherwise he will think that your job is a sinecure."

He extended the documents. "Better keep these for your files. There are bound to be some places needing attention, but the builders did their jobs well. I'll be surprised if you have to be troubled with many serious repairs."

He looked around the entrance hall appreciatively. "A fine place! Too good for prisoners, eh? Where do you suggest we start?"

The curator had relaxed. This sounded a reasonable fellow. With luck, the inspection would be only a token affair. He would be home in time for his favorite television program.

"Top or bottom?" he asked. "I imagine the basement cells will be more or less in the same condition. They are inspected and aired at intervals, but it is possible that there could be some deterioration there."

"Right! What do you say if we make a spot check of a couple of cells? That should be sufficient there."

Danilenko chatted amiably as the four men made their way to the chill depths of the building.

None of them had noticed the glint where the sunlight had caught the edge of Forsyth's special glasses.

The deputy curator had turned on the electricity at the main switch, but the light in the basement corridor still left pools of shadow that were vaguely menacing. Their footsteps had a hollow ring on the stone floor.

Danilenko said genially, "Let's have a look, first of all, at the last cell on this side. If it is sweet and dry, we won't need to linger."

He and Eliasberg stood politely aside as the deputy

thrust a key into the lock. His eyes went coldly to Eliasberg and somehow the two Rumanians found themselves
the first to step into the shocking unexpectedness of the
brilliantly lit cell.

Their eyes went in stunned amazement to the man in the
bed.

The curator's mouth opened, but his eye caught the
growing terror in his colleague's face and, at the same
moment, he felt the vicious stab of the gun in his own
back. He froze.

As the cell door had swung open, Rothman had been
amusing himself with a religious parody in which he sang
that there was a happy land, far, far away in which they
got bread and cheese three times a day. The blue, dishonest
eyes went beyond the Rumanian officials in pleased recognition to Danilenko.

His breath came out in a tiny sigh of relief, but he said
nothing, waiting for his cue.

"Against that wall! Hands above your heads! Palms flat
on the wall! Feet well apart!" Danilenko barked. "Remain
perfectly still or I'll blow your heads off."

Eliasberg went quickly forward to the bed. He worked
deftly to release Rothman's legs, but his lips tightened as he
saw the bandaged feet.

Rothman swung his legs over the side of the bed and
tried to stand, but his face whitened and he sat back
abruptly.

Eliasberg took the bunch of keys from the deputy-
curator, went next door to the emergency theater and the
trundling rattle of a cart could be heard. He returned and
half carried Rothman to the cart.

The two Rumanians held their positions like men carved
in stone, but the deputy's heavy breathing seemed to fill the
room.

There was the loud rattle of the departing cart.

The minutes ticked away.

The rattle of the returning cart got louder and louder. There was the clang of a cell door.

Eliasberg said quietly, "He's in the car. No difficulty." He went forward to the curator and took the false documents from the man's pocket, laughing as the Rumanian jumped like a fish.

Danilenko nodded silently to him. Almost simultaneously, the Russians shot the two men in the back of the head.

Methodically, they turned off the heater and switched off the light before they turned the key in the cell door.

Before they left the building, Eliasberg turned off the electricity at the main switch. When he had locked the front door, only the car outside gave any indication that the Rumanians had been there. He got behind the wheel and drove the vehicle to the rear of the building where he left it.

When he took his place in their car Danilenko gave him a pleased smile and, from the rear seat, Rothman said in faultless Russian, "Name your brand of champagne! You've earned it."

They drove swiftly toward the villa.

It was four fifteen.

Through the lensor spectacles, Forsyth was able to get practically a bird's-eye view of the area. He watched the first car turn off the road, drive up to the entrance to the prison museum and two men, obviously officials, get out.

"They seem nervous," the girl said softly at his side, watching their uneasy pacing through the binoculars. "Do you think they are helping the Russians?"

"I don't know. I hope not, but it won't be long until we find out." If they were colleagues of the KGB men, his plan was useless. He could not afford to wait to find out. Nicola must do that. "You are quite clear about what you have to do?" She nodded tensely. "Bring the binoculars, but leave everything else. I'll take your slacks. We don't want to leave anything behind that suggests that a woman was here."

He put his arms around her and held her tight for a moment, feeling with a spasm of dull anger the rapid beating of her heart. "As soon as the Russians appear, I'll take off. When they come out again, you follow me like the wind. If they have only Rothman with them, say nothing at all in the kitchen. If they have the Rumanians with them, show me two fingers. *But not a word!*"

"I'm quite clear about what you want me to do. I won't let you down."

"I'm sure you won't." He tilted her face and kissed her gently. "You think you can handle the hypodermic part?"

She moved impatiently. "Stop worrying! Of course, I can." She twisted in his arms. "Look!"

Forsyth watched the Russians' car approach the old prison. He waited until the four men had gone inside, then, with a final encouraging look at Nicola Beaufort, ran toward the villa.

In the kitchen, he adjusted the shutters to dim the room, then propped the swinging door open. He deposited Nicola Beaufort's clothes on the counter top.

He went quickly through the hall and opened the front door, as an eager Dr. Lupescu might have been expected to do. The bright afternoon sunlight could not penetrate the hall, which remained shadowy.

He switched on the lights in the shuttered room opposite the surgery and saw with satisfaction that the table was against the opposite wall. Rothman would have his back to the door as he signed the documents. Gritting his teeth against the pain in his ribs, he pulled the wheelchair forward until it blocked the doorway to the room.

Leaving the light burning, he went back to stand behind the kitchen door, lighting one of Dr. Lupescu's cigarettes as he went. The slight draft from the back door carried the strong smell of the tobacco into the hall.

He checked his gun and verified that he had the correct syringe. Then he settled down to wait.

When his straining ears heard the sound of the approaching car, he glanced at the luminous dial of his watch. It was four sixteen.

There was a scuffle at the front door.

Through the crack of the kitchen door, Forsyth could see Eliasberg supporting Rothman.

The Russian bellowed imperiously, "Lupescu!"

When he saw the wheelchair, he pulled it into the hall with one hand and, sweating profusely, helped Rothman into it. He pulled the chair back into the lighted room.

He said cheerfully, "I'll strap you in—don't want you sliding out when the ambulance men lift the chair and we certainly don't want them wondering about your feet."

There was the low rumble of Rothman's voice, but the words were lost.

Forsyth felt the girl's soft, quickened breath on his cheek. Her timing was excellent.

He tensed. He drew hard on the cigarette and, as Danilenko came through the front door, Forsyth blew a smoke ring which drifted lazily into the hall. The girl took the cigarette from him, dropped it to the floor and crushed it with her foot. She waited until she saw Forsyth's tiny gesture with the gun, then she walked swiftly across the kitchen to the cluttered sink. She kept her back to the room.

Danilenko's eyes went in annoyance from the smoke ring to the open door. He had a glimpse of a woman's figure in a nurse's uniform. His lips tightened in anger.

"Chantal!" he barked and strode into the kitchen.

He felt the prick of the needle in his right buttock and Forsyth's gun jabbing viciously into his side at the same moment. He stood absolutely still, brave in what he accepted was the moment of death.

Forsyth's voice breathed in his ear, "Out through the back door without a sound and I do not kill you!" He withdrew the needle.

They moved quickly and silently, as if joined by an invisible chain.

Nicola Beaufort drifted quietly over to take Forsyth's place behind the door. For a moment, she trembled violently, then was calm.

Forsyth signaled to Danilenko to walk on the grass.

He opened the car door and motioned the Russian into the back seat. The man got in sluggishly. He looked at Forsyth with recognition flaring in his eyes. Suddenly he jerked convulsively, and his whole body slumped. His breath whistled strangely in the paralyzed throat.

"Sometimes death is better," Forsyth said softly to the inert, hating figure.

The girl appeared around the side of the villa. There were two hectic spots high on her cheeks, but she prodded Eliasberg forward smartly with her gun and she had remembered to hold on to the syringe.

Forsyth put Eliasberg in the front seat, waited until the paralyzing drug had taken effect, then dropped both syringes in the car at the feet of the men. The police would assume that the drug had been self-administered or that they had drugged each other.

Nicola Beaufort got behind the wheel, drove the car quickly to the entrance to the museum and got out. Before she turned to run back to the villa, her eyes met those of the helpless Danilenko. Under the nurse's headdress, he saw the aristocratic face of the girl he had noticed in the gift shop in Bucharest. *And he had dismissed her as soft!*

Meanwhile, Forsyth had slipped like a shadow into the lighted front room. The chair was pulled up to the table and Rothman was reading a document. A pen lay on the table.

Rothman scarcely noticed the needle going into the thick pad of shoulder muscle. Behind him, Forsyth muttered in Russian, "A little sedative, my friend, for the journey. Read the papers. There will be plenty of time to sign them in Moscow. Now that we know that the crown is in Sinaia, there is plenty of time for everything."

Rothman's blond eyebrows met in a puzzled frown. He could not recall telling where the crown was, but things had happened so fast since the Russians had appeared that probably he had given them the information. That was good, for he felt so hazy that now he might have given them the wrong information. Yes—it was good. The consoling pat on his shoulder was a reward and a promise. His head drooped. Presently he slept, snoring gently. The papers fluttered to the floor.

Behind him, Forsyth waited.

It was four twenty-six.

He bent and retrieved the papers and stood for a moment looking down at them. For once, he had a wild flight of fancy. It seemed to him that they were heavy in his hand, as if he held the peace of the world there. His expression as he looked at the golden stubble on Rothman's head was unreadable.

The soft whisper of the girl's feet on the tiles roused him. He went out to meet her, anxious to postpone the moment when she must look at Rothman. She was breathing quickly and her eyes were wild, almost frantic. He gathered her close to him, soothing her with his kisses and muttered endearments.

"Hush!" he whispered. "We must be very quiet. Rothman is asleep, but at the moment, it is a light sleep. We mustn't disturb him."

Her lips were trembling. "That man!" she whispered and

he knew that she meant Danilenko. "His eyes were terrible. What will happen to them?"

"They will be charged with the murder of the two Rumanian officials." He chuckled. "That's one item that I must attend to before we leave." He hesitated, wondering what to say to her about Rothman. "You must prepare yourself for a shock," he said finally. "Rothman looks rather odd. He has had his head shaved within the last few days and it doesn't improve his appearance."

Her face was stiff. He put a hand on her shoulder and shook it gently. "A good nurse can usually rustle up some brandy in an emergency." he smiled. "See what you can find for us in the kitchen. Lupescu looked just the type to keep his wine in the kitchen. I'll put out the bags, your slacks and the rest of our paraphernalia in readiness at the door."

He went back into the small room.

Finally, he wheeled the unconscious Rothman into the hall close to the front door, making it as easy as possible for the ambulance attendants to get the chair out.

In the cluttered kitchen, he saw that she had brandy already in the glasses. He toasted her silently and they drank solemnly, seeing hope and confidence grow in each other's eyes.

"Remember," he warned her, "to keep behind Rothman, if at all possible. I don't want him to see us or to hear us speak, if I can possibly avoid it. I haven't worked with Ketamine before, so I can't be sure how effective it is. If I can avoid it, I won't use the "insulin." In Rothman's precarious condition, the result would be unpredictable. I'll give him another injection at the airport."

Under his gaze, her eyes slid away. Forsyth's big frame grew still. He felt rather than saw her hands tighten on the strap of the gray shoulder bag.

The love that was between them lent him wisdom. He

knew as surely as if she had cried out that a struggle was taking place within her. The great amber eyes were huge with effort. He saw how cruelly her grasp tightened on the bag. If it had held some evil, living thing, she could not have clutched it and held it shut with greater, more fierce determination.

He waited, forcing calmness and reassurance into his expression.

What, in the name of God, does she need from me at this moment? he asked himself desperately.

Trust—that's it! Trust!

His eyes reassured her.

As before, Nicola had felt the first, faint stirrings of the alien impulse and knew, despairingly, what would happen. She would watch herself doing the evil thing, striking out blindly, while her other self felt no shock, no repugnance, no compassion. Like a spectator at some horrible play, she would wait indifferently until the girl with the bright, coppery hair and the wild, amber eyes took the box of green-feathered darts and plunged the poison into the helpless Rothman. Later, she would feel revulsion, but not now.

But it was *not* as before!

When, before, had she felt this initial despair? When, before, had she been able to hesitate, to know what she was about to do and to realize that it was wrong?

She felt the perspiration beading her upper lip and knew, as she looked into Forsyth's eyes, that, for the first time, it might be possible to resist, to exercise her will-power.

Convulsively, her hands closed on the bag, as she fought for control. From somewhere deep inside a voice was telling her that she would not go to pieces. She would not take out the darts.

She tilted her head, as if listening to the voice of love.

She would not! She would *not!*

Her hands ached with the effort of keeping the box safe inside the gray bag.

"I want—" She struggled to say it. "I want you to get rid of the box of darts."

Now her hands could go steadily to the clasp and take the box out and hand it to him calmly. It was as if, with the uniform, she had assumed a nurse's impersonal strength. She smiled at Forsyth, feeling a new emotion and knew that it was joy.

He gave her a bright, almost amused glance, taking care not to let her guess at his proud delight.

"I'd like to use them on Rothman," he said lightly, shielding his knowledge of her intention, "so perhaps I should get rid of this before I am tempted seriously. Nobody could blame me for wanting to scrub him out, but actually doing it is another matter."

It was difficult for Nicola to keep the elation out of her voice as she told him, "I wanted that too, but oh! Charles, I'm so happy that I can put these thoughts of revenge aside. It makes me feel more . . ." she strugggled for the word, "more human."

"He deserves worse than a quick death," he said soberly. "Unfortunately, my job is to see that he gets worse. Revenge doesn't come into it. Nicola, I simply must take Rothman back. If I don't do that, we are all in the soup. You're my girl now and you can help me to do my job. Nicola, my love, I *need* you."

Her head came up and she smiled with great sweetness. "I'll help you, darling. You can trust me." She knew that it was true.

Together they went into the garden and burned the box, watching the blue and scarlet flames until they had died away.

Nicola felt a great relief. The box itself was unimportant. Somehow, she was quite certain that a battle had been won; that the darts could have remained within her reach and she would not have used them. Clearly she had thrown off at least some of her shackles. She raised a radiant face to him and saw that he knew and shared her sense of achievement.

When they went back into the hall to stand behind the wheelchair, it was exactly five o'clock. She gave his hand an encouraging squeeze, as though she, and not Forsyth, was the strong one.

There was a screeching of tires at the front door. Carrying Lupescu's authorization, he went out to meet the ambulance men.

When they were ready to leave, Forsyth went back into the house to make a telephone call.

The policeman at Ploesti listened intently. The officer was quick and intelligent. "You suspect that these men were Russians and that they have either injured or killed two Rumanians? You saw four men enter, but only two leave? Good! I have that. You think that the two men drugged each other? Good! We will attend to the matter. Please wait until we come."

Forsyth was smiling as he joined her inside the ambulance. Her hand came out to grasp his warmly.

Rothman, too, seemed to smile in his sleep as the ambulance sped toward Bucharest.

Bonneaud was whistling gently as he parked his car at Otopeni Airport. The attendant came forward to speak to him, but the man's words were lost in the roar of a departing plane. Involuntarily, Bonneaud looked skyward, saw the white smoke and the flicker of flames from the exhausts and wondered idly where the plane was bound for.

"The plane for Copenhagen," the attendant said helpfully.

Bonneaud glanced at the clock on the dashboard of the

car. "Nonsense!" he said irritably. "That leaves almost a couple of hours after the London plane."

He ignored the man and strode toward the air-terminal buildings, noting automatically the unfinished construction work on the left.

The hall was a milling mass of people. He edged his way between the groups, feeling comfortably anonymous and secure in the crowd. All the time, his eyes went restlessly round, looking for the Russians or for Forsyth. Characteristically, he did not give Fouquet a thought. He had had his orders.

His best plan, he decided, was to get into the departure lounge as quickly as possible. There, the men would be easily spotted and besides, he could pick a safe spot from which he could watch. He plucked thoughtfully at his lip. At the check-in counter, he could not avoid being very conspicuous. For a moment, he considered the matter. Then he beckoned to one of the porters.

The man, a dim-witted fellow who had started in the job only the previous week, came shambling over. The heavy peasant face was greedy and expectant.

"I have to check-in my car with the Hertz people. Will you be good enough to collect my ticket for London at the counter over there? Then check my flight? Bonneaud's the name. I have only cabin luggage."

He handed the porter the necessary money and strode confidently toward the car rental desk, drawing out the car documents and ignition key as he went. Subconsciously, he noted that the lights were now blazing throughout the hall.

At the check-in counter, the girl flipped the air ticket carelessly across to the porter. "Tell him he has missed his flight. That plane has gone. There won't be another London plane until tomorrow. Ask the gentleman to see me about changing his ticket."

She went back to a passionate study of her nails.

The porter shrugged, thought for a moment, then shuffled over to Bonneaud. He handed the Frenchman his change and the ticket, accepted the generous tip and moved slowly away.

Bonneaud went briskly forward to passport control.

Behind the glass barrier, the official raised his head, looked keenly at Bonneaud and scrutinized his passport photograph. He stretched a hand out. "Boarding pass, please!" he demanded.

Bonneaud looked at the papers in his hand with growing annoyance. That fool of a porter had not picked up the boarding pass.

The official took the air ticket. "London flight? You've missed that." He looked at him curiously. "That plane left a long time ago."

Bonneaud stared at him. "But that's impossible!" He glanced at his wristwatch. "Impossible," he repeated with more confidence.

The official looked pointedly up at the clock on the wall.

Bonneaud's horrified gaze went from the wall clock to his watch and back again. For the first time, he noticed the rectangles of blackness beyond the windows.

It simply could not be true! He dared not admit to himself that he had lost, not simply an air flight, but a king's ransom. How could he possibly have misjudged his time with Alida Ramirez? There must be, there simply had to be, some mistake.

Automatically, he took an uncertain step nearer to the departure lounge.

Behind him, a voice said evenly, "You are Monsieur Bonneaud?"

At the sight of the police uniforms, Bonneaud's heart raced. He struggled to keep his voice calm, reminding himself that there could not possibly be any charges against him.

"I must ask you to come this way, sir. There is a difficulty which you may be able to help us to clear up."

Fuming and afraid, Bonneaud preceded the two men into a small room off the departure lounge. Part of his mind was busy with the stunning thought that, for some insane reason, Alida Ramirez had deliberately altered the clocks so that he would miss the London plane. It was inconceivable that she had also planned that he should lose the crown.

So he scarcely heard the official's stilted explanation.

As the significance of the words penetrated, he sputtered, "Stolen a diamond bracelet! You must be insane! Do I look like a petty thief? Madame Ramirez must be mad to have made such an accusation."

But there was a sick feeling in his chest as the policeman searched his valise. He was not surprised at the sight of the bracelet dangling, winking and evil, from the official's fingers.

His expression was stony as the cold voice continued. "There is a further charge. A Madame Jordanes claims that you have stolen a Lamborghini Espada belonging to her. The car has been located at Doftana, outside a villa belonging to a Dr. Lupescu, a man with whom you appear to have had some connection." The voice grew icy. "I have to inform you that the bodies of three people have been discovered inside the Lupescu villa. I regret that it will be necessary to detain you for further questioning."

For a blinding moment, his hatred for Chi-Chi held him motionless, then, like a cornered rat, Bonneaud leaped and erupted through the doorway. Behind him, there was a startled roar and the quick thud of feet.

There was a soft *phut!* and a bullet starred the wall ahead of him. Someone screamed thinly.

He tacked and veered, making for the front of the lounge and an exit to the tarmac. He had a confused impression of a blur of startled faces and a growing crescendo of alarmed voices.

He leaped a barrier into the blackness of the night and turned sharp left, trying to evaluate his chances in the clutter of the unfinished buildings or in the planes parked outside a hangar. In the mixture of noises of the airport, it was impossible to judge where the policemen were.

A plane sat in a pool of light close to the main building. The maintenance crew was disappearing into the darkness. A uniformed steward was strolling toward the steps which were in readiness against the plane.

Bonneaud's gun went into the man's side. He gave a startled gasp and stopped abruptly. Silently, he waved him toward the plane. The steward went at a stumbling run.

From the cockpit came the confused rumble of voices. The captain and the cockpit team were already aboard, but the rest of the plane was empty. Bonneaud drew a breath of relief. He motioned the man toward the rear.

"Cap, tie, jacket!" he commanded.

Terrified, the steward obeyed. He looked ill with fear. His eyes rolled toward the sound of the voices, as if he were trying to summon up courage to yell. With trembling fingers, he put on Bonneaud's tie and jacket. Uncomprehendingly, he watched the Frenchman tuck his flight ticket to London into the breast pocket.

Bonneaud thought fast. It would be dangerous to have the man on the plane. He took a quick look at the man's passport. He was a Belgian, Frans Desmet, forty years of age. Bonneaud pocketed the passport, carefully putting it in a pocket different from the one holding his own.

He signed to the steward to precede him.

At the top of the steps, the steward turned to look at him beseechingly, as if he felt that a new danger was imminent. Bonneaud smashed the butt of his gun across the terrified face and almost at once crashed it against the side of the skull. He caught the toppling body, heaved and sent it tumbling to the foot of the steps. He ran lightly down, saw the strange angle of the neck and dragged the body out of the revealing light into the unfinished building. He looked consideringly around, saw the steel beam and draped the body across it. It looked as if the man had fallen, smashed his face and broken his neck.

He settled his newly acquired cap at a jaunty angle and went back to stand at the top of the steps. At least he had bought a little time.

"Seen a man come this way?"

He looked down at the sweating faces of the two policemen.

He leaned chummily on the rail. "Yes . . . I did . . . a fellow in a deuce of a hurry . . . ran that way . . . round behind the building." He pointed to a distant hangar.

The policemen thudded away.

Two stewardesses, chatting animatedly, stepped out of the darkness. The passengers streamed behind them.

Bonneaud grinned at the girls as they climbed toward him.

"Hi!" he said amiably. "What's up with Desmet? He's been taken off the flight." One of the girls clicked her teeth with vexation. "I warned him repeatedly. Probably caught with contraband cigarettes. Silly fool! The captain will be mad, for he has already signed the crew manifest." She eyed Bonneaud curiously.

"I'm the poor bloody substitute." He leaned forward and whispered in her ear, his eyes dancing mischievously. "My first flight! Does it show?"

"The captain will eat you for supper," she laughed. Both girls had open, friendly faces. "Don't worry. We'll cover for you. The plane will be only half full."

The other girl said resentfully, "Old Sourpuss, the captain, won't come out of the cockpit until we get to Brussels." She looked at Bonneaud doubtfully. "Do us a favor?" We like Frans Desmet. If the captain knows about this, he'll refuse to have him aboard—ever. If you keep out of his sight, he needn't know about Frans."

"But how do I manage at Brussels?" Bonneaud's confidence was surging back.

The girls exchanged looks. Obviously it had been done before. "Go off with the passengers. Take off your cap. Fold your jacket over your arm. Look like a passenger. If anybody challenges you, say that you are assisting a sick passenger. But nobody will."

The first girl said warningly, "Your only real risk will be when you show your passport."

Bonneaud smiled at her brilliantly. His hand went comfortingly to his own passport in his side pocket.

The girl went forward and switched on the sign—*Fasten seatbelts. No smoking.* The engines roared.

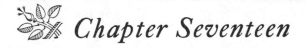

Chapter Seventeen

THE GIRL turned on him a face blind with happiness. It shone from her like a great light. Forsyth's hands tightened on his seat belt. From below, the magic carpet of Heathrow's lights sailed upward to meet them.

"It's over!" she said happily. "Can you believe that, in just a week, it is over?"

"Not over," he smiled, deliberately misunderstanding her. "For us, it is only beginning." The smile became a grin. "If slacks hadn't suited you, there would never have been a beginning. My wife will be living mostly in the country."

She sighed contentedly and rested her head against his shoulder.

"Hi!" he said in mock alarm. "Nurses don't smooch in public." His face sobered. "Only a little while now, darling, and this terrible experience will be over. Brett will have an ambulance laid on and, unless that old fox has lost his cunning, we should be speeded through. That last injection should keep our patient happy till I hand him over to your father. His cup will be full if I tell him you are safe at home." There was a note of interrogation in his voice.

"I'll do whatever you think best." He knew that she was thinking of all the times ahead, when the story of the crown would be like a child's fairy tale and the deaths and violence had faded like a child's nightmares.

"That's my girl!" His face was gray with fatigue, but he was filled with such happiness and sense of achievement that it was difficult to keep a silly grin off his face. He forced his tired brain to concentrate on the final plans. Somewhere in the hold below them, the Crown of Saint Stephen traveled safely and secretly in the chair. Stretched out on three seats in front of them, Rothman was sleeping peacefully in his nest of blankets.

Before morning, Forsyth thought grimly, those dreams would change to nightmares.

"You will come in the ambulance with us," he went on. "But once we are clear of Heathrow, you get into a taxi and go home. I'll have a busy night ahead of me, getting rid of two important items." Their eyes laughed at each other. "Your father won't let me off the hook simply because I'm going to marry his daughter."

"Will you tell him tonight?"

"No. I don't like the time or the place. Time enough for that when he trips over me tomorrow in his own home." He could feel part of his tiredness slipping away at the thought. "Matters have got to be attended to in their proper order."

She quirked an eyebrow at him and he looked with something approaching awe at the serene beauty of her face. His body strained against the seat belt as he bent to kiss her.

"First, I resign," he said and heard her breath go out in a great sigh of relief. "Tomorrow you and I start our lives together like normal people. Someone else can do the dirty work. I'm tired of killing and violence and treachery. Madame, will you marry me with indecent haste? I want to take you back to Stanmore. Will you come?"

The wheels of the plane thudded down, drowning her laughing answer.

Rothman came groggily awake and stared vacantly around the bedroom. There was a sour taste in his mouth and his throat was dry, but he felt rested and comfortable. Automatically he flexed his legs, feeling for the restraining dog collars, and then smiled as he remembered Danilenko's reassuring hands on his shoulders.

He closed his eyes, savoring the moment of fulfillment and anticipating the rewards ahead. He had brought it off! His happiness was like something physical in his breast.

He could remember nothing of the flight to Moscow. The KGB had cushioned him against all discomforts and he was grateful. He looked drowsily at the tiled Russian stove. England didn't know anything about heating a room. Trust the Russians to know how! But theirs was a somewhat old-fashioned comfort. He looked with affectionate indulgence at the dreary walls, the grim picture of Lenin, the typical coarse sheets and Belorussian bed cover. Soon he would be exchanging this for a good apartment and a *dacha* in the country.

In his ear, a gentle voice, with a Georgian accent, said in Russian, "Are you awake? The doctor is here and would like to examine you."

She was like a hundred nurses he had seen in the Soviet Union—calm, gentle, competent, with the broad cheeks and the dark eyes that he admired. She had a sweet, rather timid smile, quite unlike the brash grins of Western girls. She put her arms around him and heaved him up on the pillows, using her peasant's strength effortlessly.

The heavy red curtains on the single window were also a Belorussian design, he noticed. They were tightly drawn and were the only cozy note in the otherwise austere room. In an enameled tray on the bedside table was an unfinished bowl of borscht soup. The spoon was similar to those he had bought in Gum's, in Red Square, for his own little Moscow flat. He had no recollection of eating the soup, but Danilenko's sedative had probably been responsible for that blank spot in his memory.

On a stand at the opposite side of the bed was a square box with dangling wires.

Looks like a lie detector, he thought with amusement. *As if there could be any question of deceiving the* KGB*! If they could only know what a relief it is to speak the truth here—to be done, finally and forever, with all the lying and deception that I had to do in Britain!*

His eyes went to the door which was opening quietly. He did not need to be told that the man in the white coat was a doctor. He had a broad, bull-like figure which exuded a quiet authority, but the twinkling eyes behind the steel-rimmed glasses were friendly. One hand played with the stethoscope danging from his neck.

He nodded genially to the nurse.

"I see your patient is awake. That is good . . . good." His brows met in an angry frown. "Someone must be punished for abusing you." His lips thinned. "It is well that you are a healthy young man. We will soon have you dancing to a balalaika with Natasha here." The girl blushed.

The doctor's hands were busy at Rothman's chest. He said jovially, "You are a favored young man. None of my other patients get the prescription I have been asked to give you." He laughed. "Beluga caviar and champagne! But you deserve it . . . you deserve it." He nodded to the nurse who went out quietly.

"Look!" he said when she came back with a tray. "I will not say no if you ask me to join you." He laughed delightedly. "It is an honor to drink with a Hero of the Soviet Union." He put a finger on his lips and winked. "I am not supposed to know that, but I am not a stupid man. I know what the two men outside are waiting for." He whispered to Rothman. "Let them wait until we have had our champagne."

The nurse was busy heaping the black pearls of the

caviar on thin fingers of toast. The plastic cork flew out of the champagne bottle, hitting the ceiling above his head. Rothman ate and drank and wished that the night might not pass too quickly.

He was not drunk, just pleasantly relaxed, when the doctor allowed the two men into the room.

"Do not tire my patient," he commanded testily. "There must be no strain for this young man. If you are going to question him closely or at length, you must come back another day. I will not permit him to be upset."

The two men exchanged exasperated looks. "He is well? You said he is well. Then the sooner we have his report, the better. He knows how important it is. He is one of our best operators. Eh, Comrade Rothman?"

Tony Rothman smiled broadly. "I like to think that I am." He looked at the doctor. "I have been on a most important mission for the Soviet Union. It is imperative that I report as soon as possible. I feel fine. I'll feel even better when I have got rid of all I have had to bottle up for years."

The doctor looked unconvinced. He glanced uneasily at the officials. "Very well," he said reluctantly. "But I must stay. Is there any objection to that?" His tone was fierce, defying the officials to put him out.

The elder of the two nodded a curt agreement. The other man left the room and came back with a tape recorder. He left again and returned with an instrument that looked like an electric typewriter. He began to plug in various wires.

Rothman settled himself comfortably against the pillows. This was a routine with which he was familiar. He knew the function of the second machine, which had been designed by an East German communist.

"As you record," the first official explained unnecessarily, "this second machine makes a typed record of your statement. At the end, you will sign the original and two copies." He gave Rothman a wintery smile. "Then you collect your Hero's medal!"

They all laughed at the joke, which was not quite a joke.

"Start with . . . 'My name is Anthony Rothman . . .' "

Rothman began to speak.

In the adjoining room, Neville, Brett and Forsyth exchanged delighted grins. They watched the whirring tapes on the instrument before them and listened to the cultured English voice pouring forth its account of treachery. The floodgates were open and it gushed out, as if Rothman were eager to equal the records of Burgess, Maclean and George Blake. Forsyth's smile grew stiff.

He said almost inaudibly, "I don't think I want to listen to this."

Neville quelled him with a look, as if he were the hired help without a right to an opinion.

The Crown of Saint Stephen stood on a shabby cushion in the middle of the table. As a heavy truck passed in an adjoining street, the house shook very slightly, sending the light dancing along the heavy rubies, amethysts and emeralds. For a moment, Forsyth had a picture of Nicola Beaufort's slender finger on the pearls outside the Jordanes's villa.

He thought that he must be lightheaded, for Father Damian's gentle face seemed to smile at him from across the room.

He *was* lightheaded, for Neville had to say to him sharply, "You don't look as if you feel like turning handsprings. You should. Can't you understand what you've achieved? The crown and the man . . . the greatest traitor since Blake." He closed a fist and held it up before Forsyth's weary eyes. "And we have him like that! Let Rothman squirm as he likes at the Old Bailey. He won't wriggle out of this." He laughed contentedly. "Naturally, the prime minister will wait until the peace conference is over. Churchill wasn't far wrong. England is still pretty good at games."

Forsyth thought that, as well as pride, there was a glint of moisture in the keen eyes.

The tapes had stopped turning. The room was full of a dreadful finality. From the background, Brett said suddenly, "I owe you special thanks, Charles. I asked you to bring back the crown and you did—without asking any questions. Thanks for both of those." He laughed drily. "Danilenko had approached me to accept the crown when it was traced and his plan was that I was to plant it here at headquarters. General Neville was all for letting the Russians find the crown and for me to accept it, while we concentrated on trapping Rothman. I confess I wasn't too happy with my role, so . . . thanks, Charles."

Forsyth roused himself to say amusedly, "Danilenko gave payment in advance, of course!"

"Naturally." Even Neville permitted himself a quirk of the lips at the thought.

"And, naturally, you will return the money?" It was schoolboy humor, but Forsyth was incapable then of anything more subtle.

"General Neville and I thought that it might be used to buy language teaching machines for our young officers in our Russian language classes in Dorset." Brett's voice was prim.

Neville grunted impatiently and got to his feet. "It's time to go in and have a little chat with Tony boy. I'm looking forward to it."

"Just a moment, please." Forsyth got stiffly upright. Neville's thanks had been warm and generous—unexpectedly so—but Forsyth had felt none of the satisfaction that he normally experienced at the end of a successful operation. Suddenly he felt alien in the military atmosphere. There should, he felt obscurely, be room somewhere for pity and mercy for the doomed man in the next room. He knew that there would be none from Neville or Brett.

Forsyth knew then that he was no longer of any use to the outfit.

"I wish to resign, sir . . . from tonight." His tone was formal and uncompromising.

Neville halted and went on as if he had not heard him, "Aren't you coming in to watch this show?"

"No." He did not want an audience round-eyed with admiration at his triumph over Rothman. He did not want the mean satisfaction of seeing how well his trick had worked—how shattered Rothman was when he found that he was at British headquarters and not in Moscow. Strangely he found himself saying, "I would like to sit quietly here for a little while." Then, with an attempt at levity, "I haven't had a good look at the crown. I promise not to make off with it."

"There are two guards at the door to make certain that you don't," Neville said drily. He and Brett went out.

Forsyth sat and looked at the crown and thought, not of Saint Stephen, but of an obscure priest, probably saying Mass at that moment high in the Carpathians. He was probably, too, the only man in twenty years who had looked at the relic with true love and understanding. Forsyth felt humbled, yet at peace.

Above his head, from a loudspeaker in the wall, Rothman's voice came in a strangled gasp. "Neville!" The horror and disbelief in the voice were shocking.

Forsyth got up and flipped the switch. He drew back the curtains and let the warm morning light stream into the room. The crown was ringed in fire, with spears of gold and ruby lancing the dust-laden air.

The long night was over.

Forsyth switched off the electric light and went out past the sentries and past the room where a traitor was tasting the bitterness of failure.

He closed the front door quietly behind him, deeply happy because it was for the last time. He had to savor the elation, make it last, so that, when he told Nicola, she would know that there would never be any looking back, no regrets.

He stood at the top of the short flight of steps and saw that the leaves were beginning to change color. At Stanmore, the woods would be magnificent. He had a moment of piercing joy when he thought that, when autumn came again, she would almost certainly be carrying his child. He ran down the steps as if she were waiting for him at the next corner.

Nicola woke at dawn in her father's house and lay quietly in the semidarkness, savoring the new-found calmness and contentment as if they were infinitely precious. Under the sheet, her body felt light and strong. From some deep well of happiness came the conviction that, with the shedding of fear, there had been laid aside also a heavy physical burden.

She threw off the bedclothes and padded to the window to watch the dawn come up beyond the dark curve of the chestnut trees. It would be a fine day. Against her forehead, the glass was cool and smooth.

It might have been the first sunrise since the world was made. Her eyes widened as the miracle began. Like someone studying a lesson, she watched the slow creaming of light along the ebony tips of the trees, the trembling translucency that deepened to butter-gold, to apricot, to the uncertain flush of shell-pink that became rose-shot-with-gold. The black shadows of the trees were pushed relentlessly behind, to fade to a pearly gray that was soon lost and swallowed up in the great blaze of triumphant light.

Her sigh of wonder left a tiny ring of mist on the glass as she turned back to the room to choose what she would wear for Charles and for her first meeting with his father.

Laughter welled in her. No bride adorning herself for her groom could have been more meticulous. As she scrutinized and discarded, she mocked herself gently.

She ran to the mirror. The sleep-rosy face; the wide, expectant eyes; the bronze fall of hair—all these were good. The sight gave her an absurd thrill of happiness. As she laid out the thin beige suit with the apple-green blouse, she felt urgent, eager to rush toward the new life that she knew lay just ahead for her.

Dreamily she soaped herself in her bath. She smiled at the foolish thought that she was grooming herself also to please the house, as if Stanmore Manor were a living, sentient being that waited to welcome her.

The upper corridor was very silent. She went quietly past the bedroom doors. On an impulse, she hesitated at the head of the wide oak staircase. Then, impishly, she swung up on the smooth balustrade and went swooping breathlessly downward, as she had loved to do as a child in her first home.

Arms and legs flailing wildly, she went in a tumbling heap into Charles Forsyth's waiting arms and was caught up and held in a warm, protective clasp. Their laughter mingled.

"Hey!" she protested. "You'll crush my blouse. I'll be quite unpresentable."

"Don't flirt with me. Save your wiles for my father." He kissed her eyebrows.

She saw that, even in a day, his face had lost much of its look of strain and grim watchfulness. With a finger, she traced the outline of his lips until they parted and the white teeth closed gently on her forefinger in a new, sweet intimacy. Through the thin material of her suit, she could feel the remembered strength of his arms. She pushed her head closer into the curve of his shoulder in the ancient, feminine gesture of possessiveness.

My man! she thought fiercely and trembled with joy.

Thoughtfully he massaged her ring finger. "For two hundred years," he said softly, "the Forsyth women have worn the same betrothal ring—a quaint but very lovely arrangement of amethysts and pearls. Tonight, you'll wear it." He paused. "It has a broad band with a tiny inscription in strange, old script—*Listen to the Song of Life.*"

"Listen to the Song of Life!" she repeated, savoring the words. "Oh! Charles, we will!"

They moved through the quiet of the hall into the freshness of the early morning. While they walked in the walled garden, they talked softly of the weeks ahead and their shadows fell behind them, merging into one.

"I have just one thing to show you," Forsyth said gently, "and then we need never speak of it again." He took a newspaper cutting from his pocket. "This was in the morning edition." He smiled reassuringly.

Nicola bent her bright head to read.

SHOOTING INCIDENT IN BRUSSELS

In the early hours of yesterday morning, a man was shot dead by a Belgian policeman in the transit lounge of Brussels Airport. Passengers were preparing to board a London plane when the incident occurred. There was no panic and the flight was not delayed.

The man was identified as Alan Bonneaud (36), well-known communist leader of the notorious Société des Mains Rouges. No official explanation of the tragedy has been issued, but it is believed that the Frenchman had traveled from Bucharest some hours earlier. The dead man is said to have been wanted for questioning in connection with three deaths in Rumania.

Forsyth took the cutting from her and screwed it into a ball. For a moment, his features took on the harsh lines that had first terrified her at Heathrow.

"Don't waste your pity. He played for high stakes and

lost. That's all. He isn't our concern anymore." His hand went out to clasp her waist as he guided her along the path, back to the front of the house where the car waited.

"No. He was a lost soul. Just as Tony Rothman is a lost soul," she said slowly. Amazement grew in her that already the events of the past weeks were blurring around the edges, like an old photograph that was out of focus. "But that doesn't mean that we have to be lost too." A great tremor seemed to run over her. "It was petty of me to want revenge. How can I explain how I felt? It was as if I had stepped outside myself. I could watch myself doing those dreadful things, feel myself wanting to do them, and yet I could not stop myself."

"Forget about it. Put it right out of your mind. It is over now, darling."

"Yes. I don't know why I am sure of that, but I *am* sure." She turned a calm, glowing face to him and moved closer. "If I did not know, really *know* that everything is going to be right for us, I could not go with you now to Stanmore."

With his arm about her shoulders, they moved toward the car. Like a secret incantation, the words danced in her brain—

Listen to the Song of Life!